Passi

Passion Flowers

CELIA PARKER

Black Lace novels are sexual fantasies.
In real life, make sure you practise safe sex.

First published in 1996 by
Black Lace
332 Ladbroke Grove
London W10 5AH

Copyright © Celia Parker 1996

The right of Celia Parker to be identified as the Author
of this Work has been asserted by her in accordance
with the Copyright, Designs and Patents Act 1988.

Typeset by CentraCet Limited, Cambridge
Printed and bound by Mackays of Chatham PLC

ISBN 0 352 33118 6

*All characters in this publication are fictitious and any
resemblance to real persons, living or dead, is purely
coincidental.*

This book is sold subject to the condition that it shall
not, by way of trade or otherwise, be lent, resold, hired
out or otherwise circulated without the publisher's prior
written consent in any form of binding or cover other
than that in which it is published and without a similar
condition including this condition being imposed on the
subsequent purchaser.

Chapter One

Katherine stood in the entrance way to the plane, her dark clothing a dramatic contrast to the brightness of the day. She was a tall, slim woman, her voluptuous figure ill-concealed beneath her plain, tailored suit. She drew her hand across her brow and pushed back a little wisp of dark hair which had escaped the confines of the sleek chignon at the base of her neck. It was a humid day and already perspiration was beginning to trickle down between her breasts. She was exhausted from the flight and felt crumpled and sticky. Had she been right to come? After all, she had let someone else make all the arrangements and she had never even heard of this place. A little frisson of fear skimmed over the surface of her skin and she shivered. She was beginning to wish she had stayed at home.

Katherine gave herself a little shake and continued to disembark. She was here now and she refused to turn and run just because she was a bit nervous. She had never done that before and she was not going to

1

start now. She would make the best of the situation and muddle through somehow. At least she didn't have to stand around waiting for her luggage. The brochure said someone would take care of her bags and drive her to the hotel. In the distance, she spotted a stretch limousine parked near one of the hangars. It was waiting for her just like the brochure had promised. With a sense of relief and rising anticipation, she headed for the car only vaguely aware of the breathtaking scenery around her.

A smiling young man introduced himself as Rolf, the hotel chauffeur. Then, after greeting Katherine by name, he ushered her into the roomy interior of the big black luxury car.

Katherine climbed on to the back seat and, with a sigh, sank back against the soft tan leather, relishing the cool, dim, air-conditioned interior. The car moved slowly off the aerodrome tarmac then gained speed when it reached the highway and settled into a smooth steady pace.

God, what I would give for a drink right now, Katherine sighed inwardly.

As if the chauffeur could read her thoughts, his voice crackled over the intercom, 'If you press the red button in front of you, miss, you will find liquor, glasses, ice cubes, anything you want.'

Katherine reached over, pressed the button and a little wooden panel slid open to reveal a fully equipped bar. She poured herself a gin and tonic, fell back against the seat once again, and let the drink and the steady hum of the big car work their magic on her.

She barely glanced at the landscape that was whizzing by outside the window; she was too tired to care what was out there right now. Besides, the gin was starting to have its desired effect and she was beginning to relax. It was heavenly being so far from the stress and tension of her frenetic life back home. She always felt under such enormous pressure to succeed and so ill-equipped to do so. She was never able to achieve that sense of personal power she knew she had to have if she wanted to be a success in a high pressure environment. These last few months had been unbearable. Her job demanded that she work long hard hours and, because of her escalating stress levels and inability to deal with them, her personal life was in shreds, her professional life as a lawyer was in serious jeopardy and her chances of getting the partnership she wanted so badly were almost nil. At least, that's what Phyllis Manion, her boss and senior partner, had told her at their last meeting. The older woman seemed to understand that she was at breaking point and that she didn't quite know what to do about it. Even the men at work, the strutting, self-important young male lawyers, were getting to her these days. Usually she was able to shrug off their sexual overtures and youthful arrogance but lately their antics had only added to her stress, so much, in fact, that she felt she was going to do something she would later regret. Even Phyllis was driving her crazy. There was something about the older woman which made Katherine uncomfortable and yet, at the same time attracted her. This made working with her very confusing and, at times, almost impossible.

It was Phyllis, however, who had taken Katherine aside and suggested she take a holiday so she could pull herself together. She had even suggested one of her own favourite spots: a very private place where you could leave your worries behind and sort out your life. She said it was a location where you could remain completely private and undisturbed or join in the communal activities. The choice was left completely up to you. Phyllis had even offered to make all the arrangements and Katherine had been too exhausted to protest.

Now, here she was feeling a little uneasy and unsure. It was an unusual situation. Everything had been done for her. There had been no contact between the travel agency and herself or even the staff at the hotel. She had been given only one piece of information: the name of the hotel manager, a woman named Martha Hind. She didn't know if she liked this arrangement but, at this point, she had to admit she felt somewhat intrigued. She needed rest and relaxation and some time to figure out what was making her feel so stressed. A few days of sea and sun might be just the ticket.

She took another sip of her gin and let the cool tart liquid roll around in her mouth. She savoured the taste for a few seconds then let it slide down her throat. After a while she could feel the tension draining out of her. Her thoughts turned to her sex life. Well, there was a joke, she thought grimly. Her relationship with her long-standing boyfriend, Paul, was pleasant but predictable and the sex was becoming humdrum; tedious at best. She sighed as she remembered all the evenings when she had faked it just to please Paul. She knew there was more to sex than that but she couldn't seem to find what it was she needed in the relationship with him. Even when she pleasured herself, which she found herself doing less and less lately, she still felt cheated when it was over. She knew she was missing out on something; something that made other women seem more vibrant, centred, and downright smug. A feeling of

4

resentment caught in her throat. She wanted to feel that way too. Why couldn't she? What was the matter with her? Sometimes she felt there was a secret, a riddle she had to solve before she could experience the full sexual enjoyment that was rightfully hers. She knew in her heart she was capable of a passionate sex life but she needed something exciting, something different to ignite the passions lying dormant inside her. She was convinced that what she had now was nowhere near the ecstasy that was possible.

Sometimes she felt the need to do something outrageous to try to break out of her rut; to do something that would help her connect with her true sexual feelings. There had even been times when she had come very close to doing wild crazy things; things that could have put her career and her reputation in serious jeopardy. She shivered slightly. Maybe on this holiday she would have the nerve to actually try some of them. Now would be the ideal time, she thought. She was far away from home and the setting was ideal. A place like this would afford her the anonymity she needed to experiment and try out certain things without worrying about being discovered by people who knew her both socially and professionally.

She caught herself short, wondering why on earth she was suddenly contemplating getting involved in unusual sexual activities. What was going on with her? The moment she had stepped off the plane, her sexual fantasies had reared up in her mind again; fantasies and desires she could never explore with Paul. Somehow, he inhibited her and the free expression of her needs. He was so straight-laced and conservative. It occurred to her that she may have been using his conservative mainstream sexuality as a means to keep her own feelings in check. However,

5

now that she was here, far away from Paul and her regular routine, she felt an exciting sense of freedom and a mounting urgency to let her hair down and make some of her wildest dreams come true.

She finished her drink and poured herself another. She felt wonderfully relaxed. She lay back against the seat and closed her eyes. She hadn't felt like this in a long time and she was going to enjoy every minute of it.

The moment her eyes were shut, images from the night before rose up in her mind's eye. Instantly, her whole body was suffused with heat and she squirmed deliciously in her seat.

She had left a boring dinner party early and had decided to walk home in the hope that maybe the cool night air would clear her head. As she made her way through the little park just across the street from her apartment building, she heard the sound of moaning coming from under one of the big maple trees. She found herself irresistibly drawn to the sounds and headed over towards the old tree. What she saw next made her stop dead in her tracks. There, beneath the tree, a shadowy silhouette was barely visible in the faint light of the moon. It looked like three people all wrapped around one another, moaning and gasping as they moved as one entity. She didn't dare show herself but she was dying to know what they were doing so she inched forward in an attempt to get a better look.

Suddenly, the moon emerged from behind a cloud and revealed the entire scene: it featured a woman and two men. One man was in front, the other behind. They were both wearing black leather jackets and jeans. Their flies were wide open and it appeared that they were both penetrating her; one from the front and the other from the back. The woman was naked from the waist up and her huge breasts were swollen and gleaming in the moonlight. Her dark nipples looked like sharp little spears. Her head was thrown back and her arms were draped around one man's neck – her legs wrapped around his waist as he plunged his penis into her over and over again. With each thrust she moaned and grunted, moving her body to meet his with matching passion. The man behind her was also servicing her, sliding his huge cock into her anus, matching their rhythm perfectly. They were totally transported, totally caught up in their passion, unaware of anything but their driving lust.

Katherine had remained transfixed, unable to breathe. She had felt the strongest urge to go over and join them. She wanted to be part of such lust and passion. She wanted to feel the kind of pleasure the unknown woman was so obviously feeling. Katherine's breasts had begun to ache and her nipples tightened and pushed against the soft flimsy material of her bra. Her juices oozed out of her and wet her panties. It was all so delicious and outrageous. She was watching three strangers fuck each other in a public park, giving themselves over to their wild primitive passion with total abandon. It seemed they didn't care who came by and caught them. Or maybe they even hoped someone would discover them, she remembered thinking. This would only add to their excitement. Her sex fluttered wildly at the idea. She knew that part of her own excitement came from the delicious possibility of being discovered like that and how it would add an extra thrill to such an experience.

Eventually, she had been able to break away and had walked home as quickly as she could. She had been so aroused by the incident that she had not been able to sleep a wink all night. She kept imagining she was that woman impaled on two cocks at once and how wonderful that must feel. She wanted to feel like that too. She wanted to make love like that, caught up in the passion of the moment. She wanted to be able to give herself without caring who might see her. Secretly, she even wished someone would find her like that because she knew her feelings could only be intensified by the electrifying possibility of discovery.

She had played with herself repeatedly during the night but the meagre pleasure she experienced was nothing compared to what she knew those three people in the park had felt.

And now here she was, riding along in a luxury limousine going God knows where, alone, and with no prospects of anything like that happening to her. She still felt aroused by last night's incident. The pictures of that wild sex were fresh in her mind. She could still see them moving and grinding into each other and her ears rang with the sounds of their pleasure.

Lazily, she trailed her hands up to the opening of her silk blouse and began massaging her breasts. Her nipples tightened and she squirmed deliciously in her seat. She slid her hand over her mound and tried to rub it but her skirt was too tight and she couldn't feel much. This small frustration only served to increase her agitation. She threw her head back against the seat and sighed deeply. Something was happening to her. She hadn't felt like this in ages. She finished off her gin, set the glass down in its leather holder, and continued caressing her breasts and thighs. Her breath was coming faster now and a deliciously familiar throbbing had begun between her legs. She wanted something to happen. She wanted –

With a shock, her eyes met Rolf's in the rear view mirror; he had been watching her the whole time, she realised in horror. In fact he was still watching her intently, an unreadable expression in his eyes. Her cheeks burned and she thought she would die of embarrassment.

Then, suddenly, she didn't care. She was sick and tired of always doing the right thing. Sick and tired of worrying about what others thought of her. To hell with that. This was one of those chances she had been dreaming about. This was one of those outrageous moments where she had the freedom and the anonymity to do exactly as she pleased. She was far away from home, and she was on her own. No one who mattered would ever know. She had to take a chance and go for it.

Boldly, she stared back at him and ran her tongue back and forth over her lips, darting it seductively in and out of her mouth. She continued fondling her breasts and running her hands up and down her thighs. She could see the lust rising in his eyes as she continued to play with herself. She felt like laughing out loud with the power and the pleasure of it all.

Slowly, she removed her jacket and began undoing the buttons of her blouse one by one. Soon it lay open, revealing her lacy bra and her generous breasts which swelled in luscious mounds above the half cups. Her hands lingered on her breasts for a moment, grazing her nipples through the silky material with her long red nails. She groaned with pleasure as she felt them peak beneath her fingers.

Once again she looked up and this time she could see the naked lust in Rolf's eyes. She knew what he wanted. She could tell. He wanted her. He wanted her right then and there. She wriggled in her seat and, as she continued to hold his gaze, she snaked her tongue in and out of her mouth in slow, circular motions and smiled at him, an open invitation in her eyes. She could hear him gasp at her brazen behaviour and this time she did laugh out loud.

Katherine felt bolder with every passing moment. As she held his gaze, she reached up and slowly unfastened the front clasp of her bra. Her heavy breasts sprang free, the big pink nipples erect now in full arousal. She arched her back so they jutted out towards him. Then she cupped them in her hands and raised them to his eager gaze, thumbing her nipples again and again until they were elongated even further. Loud groans escaped her lips as she continued to knead and play with her breasts in full view of the young chauffeur – he could hardly keep his eyes on the road. Then, slowly, she slid her index finger into her mouth and began sucking on it. Her other hand continued to tease and tweak the nipple on her left breast and her hips began thrusting forward in involuntary movements of pure pleasure.

This was too much for the chauffeur. Without warning, he pulled the car off the main road and parked in a nearly deserted country lane. In an instant, he was pulling at the door to the back seat.

Katherine was shocked at this unexpected turn of events. Her mind raced to assess the situation. For her it had been just a game; an experiment to see how far she could allow herself to go. She hadn't really considered Rolf at all. He had been just a face in the rear view mirror; someone she could play with and tease. She had definitely not thought things through. How naive and stupid she had been. What the hell had she been thinking, egging a man on like that? She didn't know who this guy was, and, more importantly, she didn't know where she was or how to get help if she needed it. If things really got out of hand, there would be no one to help her. She realised with a shiver that she was on her own and completely at his mercy.

Rolf got the door open and slid on to the seat beside her. Katherine looked down at the huge bulge in his pants and knew she had to take control of the situation immediately. If she didn't, she was in big trouble. Her intent had been to tease him, play with him but, in the process, she too had become incredibly excited. She had started something and now it was up to her to finish it. She had to take control and she had to do it now.

Rolf was gazing hungrily at her naked breasts. There was no mistaking what he had in mind. He reached out his hands toward her.

In that instant, Katherine's instincts rose up and took control. She pulled back with a start, turned halfway in her seat to face him, then pushed herself forward a little so that her left leg swung up over his lap. In an instant she was straddling him, her bare breasts just inches from his mouth. It was his turn to be shocked. He looked up at her, a mixture of surprise and lust in his dark eyes.

'You seem happy to be here,' she murmured as she reached her hand down to his lap and began rubbing the bulge in his pants. The minute she touched him she knew for sure he wasn't wearing a thing underneath the thin material of his chauffeur's uniform.

His sudden intake of breath told her she had done the right thing. He groaned aloud as she continued to rub and clutch at him. Then he strained his hips forward as she began to fumble with his zip.

She undid his flies and his huge member sprang free. She closed her cool hand around it and caught

11

her breath as it twitched and pulsed in her grasp. She began sliding her hand up and down its velvet smooth length, stopping now and then to graze her long red nails along the seamed underside.

When she heard his grunts of pleasure she smiled to herself and began moving her hand even faster. Her plan was working. She had taken command and now anything that happened would be orchestrated by her and her alone.

However, Rolf had his own ideas. He wanted more and this time when he reached for her breasts he wouldn't be denied. As he jerked his hips forward in a spasm of pleasure, he slid his big square hands over her breasts and began massaging them, palming the nipples and running his fingers around the edge of their delicate flesh.

This time Katherine arched towards him, her hands moving faster now along his inflamed penis. The touch of his fingers on her nipples was sending shock waves down between her legs and she began squirming on his lap.

She bent forward slightly, released his penis and whispered in his ear, 'Loosen your belt, Rolf.'

Rolf looked up at her in surprise but he proceeded to undo his belt and loosen the button on his trousers.

'Are you sure you know what you're doing, miss? Are you sure you want to go ahead with this?' he asked, his voice husky with passion.

'I know exactly what I want and I know exactly how to get it,' Katherine replied, hardly daring to believe what was transpiring between the two of them.

She slid off his lap and knelt in front of him on the limo floor. Thank God it was a stretch limo, she thought. There was no way she could carry this off in the back seat of a regular-sized car.

Rolf raised himself slightly off the seat so that Katherine's eager hands could slide his pants down over his hips. When they were around his ankles, she reached up to the top of his thighs and began running her nails up and down his legs, stopping every time she reached the top again to flick at his fully aroused penis.

Rolf's groans were turning her on more and more. She leaned forward and took the full length of him in her mouth. Slowly, she began licking and sucking on him until he was jerking and thrusting in her mouth.

Finally, he couldn't take any more and pulled her mouth away. He slid his hands under her armpits and half lifted her up on to the seat beside him. Dazed by this sudden reversal, Katherine could only stare wordlessly up at him through the haze of her own mounting excitement.

'Now it's your turn, miss,' he groaned.

Gently he pushed her back on the seat, knelt down in front of her and spread her legs as far as they would go. He let his eyes wander over her luscious body for a moment then looked deep into her eyes and licked his lips.

'You look good enough to eat.'

Katherine moaned as he buried his head in between her legs and began kissing and licking her swollen pussy lips. His hands reached up for her breasts and began teasing and tweaking her nipples. With a groan, she tangled her fingers in his thick black hair and rammed his face deeper into her moist crotch. He responded by opening his mouth even wider and sucking her whole pussy into his mouth. His tongue probed her crease, snaking in and out of her dark curls, then pushed deeper to explore her silky inner folds. As the tip of his tongue grazed her clitoris, her hips jerked in spasms of pleasure.

Her body ached to feel him inside her. She wanted to feel the full length and width of him filling her up, pinning her to the seat. She sighed and pulled his face away from her throbbing sex.

Rolf raised his head and, when he saw the look in her eyes, he moved quickly on to the seat beside her and pulled her on to his lap. He pressed a button in the armrest and the seat slowly slid out along a mechanical track until it was the length of an oversized twin bed. He eased her off his lap and pressed her down on the seat which was now big enough to accommodate the full length of their bodies. In a moment, he was on top of her, grinding his hardness against her. His lips closed over hers and he slid his tongue deep inside and began licking the tender lining of her mouth. As she moved her tongue in response his mouth closed around it and began sucking on it. Then he released her tongue and thrust his own so deep inside her mouth she gasped for breath. His hands were all over her now, kneading her breasts and tweaking her nipples between his fingers.

Katherine was completely caught up in this sexual whirlwind. Her whole body was on fire and aching for his touch. She caught her breath as his hands slid lazily up the insides of her thighs. She wriggled beneath him, raising her hips to meet his fingers then sighing softly as his hands slid between her legs. She raised her hips in response as she felt his hot hand on her naked flesh. Slowly, he began stroking and rubbing her. He tangled his fingers in her dark wet pubic curls, pulled gently on them then trailed his fingers back and forth over her mound. He lowered his lips

14

and clamped his mouth over her engorged nipples. Her hips jerked forward in a spasm of delight.

'Oh, God, yes,' she groaned, gyrating her hips lasciviously.

He closed his lips over hers again and her groans filled his mouth. She began to suck on his hard pointed tongue, giving it little nips as it slid in and out between her full sensuous lips.

She loved the feel of his hands on her, and the touch of his fingers as they slowly slid past her outer labia and snaked their way into her inner folds. Frantically, she began grinding her mons on his exploring fingers, urging him to go deeper. She was wet. She was ready. His fingers were deep inside her, exploring every nook and cranny of her most secret area. He stroked and caressed her, sliding his fingers, now wet with her dew, up and down the shaft of her clitoris. The sensations were driving her crazy.

She was bucking under him, yearning for more. Every nerve in her body was screaming for release. She cried out sharply as his fingers slid over the head of her clitoris and began rhythmically stroking her, softly at first, then more vigorously as he increased the tempo and pressure.

Finally, she could stand it no longer. 'Do it. Do it now!' she begged, thrusting her hips wildly towards him.

Rolf pulled back and looked down at her trembling body. Then, with one deft move, he took her legs, bent them slightly at the knees, and pushed them backward until each one was on either side of her head. Her moist throbbing sex was totally exposed. He moved closer, rubbed his rod over the head of her clitoris a couple of times then slid it down towards the entrance of her dark tunnel.

Katherine shuddered as she felt his huge member probing the opening to her vagina. She wriggled against him and tried to impale herself on his twitching shaft. What was he waiting for? she agonised inwardly. She wanted to feel him inside her now.

'Please, Rolf, please,' she begged, as she reached down and clutched at his penis.

Rolf groaned and slid into her like a long hot baton. He parted her wide, stretching her to the limit. She moaned as he filled her. She loved the feel of his long hard shaft pinning her, centring her. She raised her hips to meet him and together they began moving in the age-old rhythm. She matched him thrust for thrust as he ploughed and ravaged the deepest part of her. As her passion grew wilder, she began rocking and bucking in total abandon. Long moans escaped her lips as he pounded in and out of her, until she thought she could bear no more. The insistent ache in her clitoris was peaking and the walls of her vagina were beginning to contract. Slowly, her orgasm began to build. Her loins were heavy and aching for release. She began to ride the wave. It was taking her where she wanted to go. Her vaginal muscles contracted violently around his penis and he moaned as she milked him, bearing down on his throbbing hardness one last time before the waves of her searing orgasm crashed upon her. She shuddered as spasm after spasm surged through her.

Through her haze of sensual pleasure, she could hear the primitive animal sounds coming from Rolf as he grunted out his own climax.

Katherine lay sprawled on the seat. She was stunned at what she had just done. She also felt more alive than she had in years. She couldn't believe that she had actually had an orgasm during sex. And what an orgasm too, she thought, as she stroked her swollen breasts. She looked over at Rolf who had serviced her so well. He was lying face up on the seat beside her, his penis, that instrument of such amazing pleasure, flaccid now between his legs. Why had she never been able to have this kind of sex with Paul? It was always so dull with him, so predictable, so safe. Well, this certainly had been anything but that, she admitted to herself as she continued caressing her breasts. This had been wild and wonderful and bad. Yes, bad – that was the operative word. That was what had made it so exciting. Also, she was the one who had provoked the whole thing, so she had been in control of the entire experience. *She* had seduced *him*, a man she had never met, into having wild, anonymous sex – and in a foreign country, no less! Hey, you couldn't get much wilder than that, she mused. Or could you?

Suddenly, she became aware of a voracious sexual hunger within her. It was all-pervasive and almost overwhelming. She had never been aware of this before and she was shocked at the strength and power of it. She had not known it was there. It must have been growing inside her for a long time until it had become a raging demand.

She would have to do something about this, she decided. And there was no time like the present to get started. Years of hard work and boring sexual encounters had only dulled her senses and left her feeling starved. The great sex she had just experienced with Rolf had shown her how much she had been missing and how much more there was to be discovered.

She felt determined to change this desperate state of affairs at once. She couldn't let this go on one minute longer. It was no good to pretend. That approach had only made things worse. She knew now

17

she wouldn't rest until she had found every way possible to assuage this burning need. This holiday would be perfect, the ideal place to begin her explorations, she decided. And she would use her time well. That was one thing she was good at, she thought grimly, thinking of the long hard hours she had put in at work over the years. Well, this time she was going to use her time for herself and her pleasure.

This was going to be a very different holiday from the one she had originally envisioned. This was going to be a search for sexual pleasure and, despite her previous anxiety, she was going to open herself to anything and everything that would quench her new-found sexual hunger. It would be so wonderful if she could just relax and find some kind of fulfilment. Maybe, finally, she would find out why she always felt cheated after sex. Maybe, finally, she could make sense of the feeling that had haunted her for years, the feeling that there was a puzzle or a riddle that had to be solved before she could have the kind of pleasure that was rightfully hers.

'I think we should get going now, Rolf,' she whispered gently to her dozing lover.

The chauffeur opened his eyes. He smiled and let his eyes run down the length of her half-naked body. He said nothing about what had just happened and that was just fine with Katherine. She didn't want any complications. He had served a very important purpose and now she wanted to move on to the next phase of her vacation.

Silently, they rearranged their rumpled clothing. Then, without a word, Rolf got out of the back seat and took his place behind the wheel of the car. In a moment he had started the engine and driven back on the main road.

As they continued their journey, Katherine analysed her reactions. She was surprised at the way she felt. She was experiencing no self-recriminations, no guilty aftermath and, thankfully, no fumbling attempts at trying to construct some kind of a relationship out of what had just happened. She was amazed that she felt this way. She had never realised that her sexual appetite might want expression just for its own sake and that it was not always necessary to establish the context of an ongoing relationship to have what she wanted. She liked the sense of freedom this attitude gave her and, no matter what anxieties might rise up to frighten or deter her, she was determined to investigate it further as soon as possible.

She realised suddenly that, whatever happened to her during this holiday, her professional and personal life would never be the same again.

'We're almost there, miss.'

The chauffeur's voice broke into her thoughts, bringing her back to the present with a jolt. Much to her surprise, she found that her breasts were still tingling from the mauling he had given them and that the crotch of her panties was wet again. Quickly, she straightened up in the seat and tried to reorientate herself. She felt more stimulated and alive than she had in a long time.

But she must try and pull herself together. They were almost at the hotel and she didn't want to arrive looking flustered. Willing herself to calm down, she turned and looked out the window.

She gasped in delight as she caught her first glimpse of the place that would be her home for the next couple of weeks. The house was a magnificent stone mansion which stood majestically on a sheer cliff overlooking the sea. On the beach below, the ocean, sparkling like diamonds in the late afternoon sun, was rolling in against dark granite rocks, sending geysers of white frothy spray high into the air. She opened the window and breathed in the tangy sea air. Her head cleared immediately and she suddenly felt invigorated and ready for anything.

As the car continued its ascent up the steep serpentine driveway, Katherine shivered slightly with apprehension. What was waiting for her beyond those thick grey walls? she wondered. When the car pulled up in front of the door, she took a deep breath. This was it. After a quick check in her cosmetic mirror, she stepped out of the car and followed Rolf, who was carrying her bags up to the front door.

The chauffeur set her suitcases down on the front step and gave her a friendly smile. 'I hope you enjoyed yourself today, miss,' he said, with a knowing wink. 'I know I did. Well, I'll be leaving you here. The porter will take care of your bags. You're on your own now. The first little while is always the hardest. But I'm sure you'll get on to things in no time. I only hope this afternoon was the ice breaker you needed,' he added, running his tongue over his full lips as his eyes flickered over her body. 'Maybe we can get together again some time, perhaps in a slightly more exotic setting? That, of course, will be up to you, just like it was up to you today. Well, as I said, I leave you here. Good luck to you,' he added. Then, with a tip of his hat, he was gone.

Before Katherine could make sense of his puzzling words, the door opened and she turned to see a young maid dressed in a severe black and white uniform. The woman smiled and motioned to Katherine to come in.

With a feeling of excitement mixed with foreboding, Katherine threw back her shoulders and walked into the foyer.

Chapter Two

The place was beautiful. From where she stood in the cool marble foyer, she could see the elegantly furnished main lounge. Pastel Aubusson rugs graced the highly polished parquet floor, peach silk drapes framed the tall, leaded windows and, situated around the room, were chairs and sofas delicately upholstered in pastel silk. Exquisitely shaded lamps in matching colours and occasional tables of gleaming mahogany completed the decor. She couldn't place the period but she knew everything was genuinely antique. On several of the little side tables, big crystal vases overflowed with freshly-cut flowers. Everything bespoke peace, serenity and good taste.

The only jarring note was the picture hanging above the huge stone fireplace. It showed a woman with raven-black hair leaning against an old oak tree. She was wearing a sheer white gown which revealed her full pink-tipped breasts and, in her hand, she held a mysterious object. Katherine couldn't quite make it out but, whatever it was, the man in the picture wanted it very badly. He was dressed in a black period costume and was kneeling in front of her, his hand outstretched, an agonised look in his eyes. Although nothing explicit was happening, the intense sexual sub-text was obvious.

Katherine blushed as she felt herself respond to the naked eroticism of the painting. Her eyes travelled down to the man's crotch and then up to the woman's face. She gasped inwardly. There was no denying the huge bulge in his breeches and the knowing smile on the woman's face. A little shiver of sexual excitement danced over her skin and her nipples tightened.

'I'm Katherine MacNeil. I'm expected,' she announced breathlessly to the maid who had just finished giving instructions to the porter.

'Oh yes, miss, I know. Miss Martha told me you were coming. She asked me to show you up to your room the minute you arrived. She thought you might be tired after your long trip so she ordered supper to be served in your room and said she'll see you for your interview at ten o'clock tomorrow morning.'

'Interview?' Katherine asked in surprise.

'Oh, it's nothing serious, miss. It's just that Miss Martha likes to greet her guests personally and help them settle in.'

Katherine's stomach constricted with anxiety. What kind of a place was this? The surroundings were beautiful but the picture in the lounge gave her the impression that all might not be what it seemed in this beautiful old house.

Once again, her anxieties rose to the surface and she scolded herself for being so easily unnerved. She reminded herself of her earlier determined thought and that she was going to do everything in her power to relax and explore her new-found sexual needs. She

22

really did need a holiday and the sooner she got started the better. So there was a sexy painting hanging in the living room and there was an unexpected meeting with this Martha person the next morning. So what? She shook off her uneasy feelings and followed the maid upstairs.

When she walked in to her room, she stopped dead in her tracks. Instantly, her anxieties disappeared. It was the most beautiful room she had ever seen. It was like walking into another world, another time. A fire crackled in the enormous marble fireplace and, on a raised platform in the centre of the room, stood a magnificent four poster bed decked with ice-blue satin hangings and matching pillows and bedspread. The bed curtains were tied back with white satin ropes and beside the bed was a matching bell cord. The bed itself was made of walnut and the posts had been carved into big lush bunches of grapes and intertwined human figures.

The floor was covered with a thick white wall-to-wall carpet. In front of the fireplace, on a black fur throw rug, inviting in the firelight, was a *chaise longue* covered in rose coloured velvet and a big comfortable wing chair upholstered in white leather. Bookcases recessed in the walls on either side of the mantlepiece were filled with leather-bound books and, in another corner of the room, stood a dainty glass vanity case with all sorts of crystal decanters filled with different coloured liquids.

Delighted with her surroundings, Katherine crossed the room to the east wall where tall, narrow, leaded windows looked out over the spacious gardens and the stables beyond. To the right of the windows was an elegant little desk. Queen Anne perhaps, she thought, feeling a bit overwhelmed by the beauty and luxury of her surroundings.

On the other wall there was a massive walnut wardrobe with a full-length mirror where the maid was busy hanging up her clothes. To the right of that, there was another door.

'That's the bathroom, miss,' the maid explained, following her gaze. 'Take a look, why don't you, while I'm unpacking your things.'

Katherine shook off her shoes and felt her feet sink deliciously into the thick plush rug as she made her way to the door leading to the bathroom.

The bathroom was outfitted magnificently. The entire floor was carpeted with a thick black rug and in the middle of the room was a round pink and white marble tub. It had gold fixtures and a broad ledge around the sides held baskets of exotic soaps and more bottles of coloured liquids. Bath oil and perfumes, Katherine surmised, hardly daring to believe that all this was for her. Thick luxuriant towels of all sizes hung on gold racks which were placed strategically around the room. And, through a skylight placed directly above the tub, the late afternoon sun streamed down into the room bathing everything in a golden glow. In another section of the room, separated from the tub area by a three-quarter glass partition, there were the toilet, a bidet, a shower stall and sauna.

'This is too good to be true,' Katherine murmured happily, as she went back into the bedroom.

'I'm glad you like it, miss. Now, I'm sure you're tired and hungry after your long trip so I'm going to bring you a light supper. Then I'll run your bath for you so you can get to bed early and have a good sleep.'

As soon as the maid left the room, Katherine ran

across the room and threw herself on the huge bed. She felt like a kid let out of school for the holidays. She stretched her arms back as far as they could go and wriggled her toes. Then she laughed aloud as she felt herself slipping and sliding all over the satin bedspread. She felt divinely decadent.

Then, with a shock, she realised she was looking at her own reflection. There was a mirror positioned directly over the bed! She gasped when she saw herself. She was still wearing her dark business suit and, as she lay sprawled against the ice-blue satin, the contrast struck her as vaguely erotic.

She got up and walked over to the big full-length mirror. She trailed her hands over her breasts down to her mound and began rubbing herself. A delicious wave of sexual energy surged through her. Slowly, she began to remove her clothes. Her fingers trembled as she fumbled with the buttons on her blouse. She stared at her reflection. She barely recognised herself. Her cheeks were flushed and her long black hair, usually so neat and trim, was wildly dishevelled. That experience with Rolf this afternoon had really affected her and it showed, she thought, with a delicious shiver. She was still aroused from the working over he had given her and she was hungry for more. She ran her fingers over the smooth material of her bra. It was brand new, a red silk and lace nothing that barely contained her heavy breasts. Beneath her finger tips, she could feel her nipples peaking against the fabric.

Suddenly, her whole body began to tremble and she was flooded with an overwhelming need. She wanted to be naked. She wanted to be touched. In a quick – almost violent – movement, she ripped off her skirt. She gasped when she saw her reflection. It was almost as if she was seeing herself for the first time.

25

She was wearing red lace panties to match her bra, a red suspender belt which held up her sheer black stockings, and black patent-leather high heels. If the people at work could only see me now, she thought excitedly. If only they knew what I really looked like underneath my tailored business suits.

And yet, her new underwear had done nothing to revitalise her flagging relationship with Paul. And it certainly didn't satisfy any of the unarticulated needs and longings that tortured her constantly. She had worn the sexy red underwear almost like a guilty secret. So, how could she blame Paul alone for their unexciting sex life?

Well, her life was about to change; she would see to that. Given the discoveries she had just made about herself, there was no way she could tolerate her life continuing along the same rut it had been in for years.

She returned to her image in the mirror. She stretched sensuously and rolled her pelvis, arching her back so her breasts swelled even further over the top of the lacy cups. Her hand trailed down her body and fluttered over her mound.

'Oh, that feels good,' she said, surprised at her instant reaction. She feathered her fingers over her sensitive nipples and sighed aloud as little bursts of energy rippled directly to her clitoris.

Well, this place was definitely having an interesting effect on her. She never reacted this way when she touched herself at home. Of course, Rolf hadn't been in the picture then, she reminded herself with a contented smile. She walked back to the bed and lay down. This time she could feel the cool satin bedspread on her naked flesh. She looked up at her reflection again. She was lying sprawled on the bed, her hair loose now, spread out on the white satin pillow, her alabaster skin contrasting dramatically with her blood-red lingerie and the ice-blue satin beneath her. She liked the feel of the satin on her skin. She liked the way it caressed her. It excited her. She started to slide back and forth, feeling the cool caress of it on her hot skin, watching herself in the mirror as she writhed sensuously, her arms reaching far above her head, her breasts thrusting upward. She looked deliciously wanton.

She had never allowed herself to feel this way and she was both excited and bewildered. She was still aroused from this afternoon and her body ached for more pleasure. She had denied herself for so long she felt she would never be satisfied. She trailed her hands over her breasts and toyed with her nipples. She moaned loudly as she teased and tweaked them into hard little peaks. The sensation of her fingers touching them through the smooth silky material of her bra only added to her excitement. She closed her eyes and began rubbing her mound – which was barely concealed by the little red triangle of her panties. With a sigh, she slid her hand inside the waistband and let her fingers graze on her dark silky bush. Before long, her hips began gyrating as her pleasure mounted. She groaned and thrust her breasts upward, using her free hand to flick and tease her aching nipples. She watched herself in the mirror as she toyed with her nipples and slid her fingers inside her pussy, moist now with her dew.

Watching what she was doing and feeling it at the same time was an incredible experience. It was like she was three people: the one being pleasured, the one doing it to her and the one watching. And each one was getting their own kind of kick out of it. No wonder it made her so hot; it was deliciously erotic

27

and she wanted to prolong it as much as possible. She continued to watch as she pleasured herself. The more she went on, the hotter she got until long loud groans were escaping from the back of her throat.

Suddenly, there was a knock at the door. Katherine sat up with a jolt as the maid walked in and set her supper tray down on the table near the wing chair. Embarrassed, Katherine got off the bed and ran to get her robe in the bathroom.

The maid seemed completely unaffected by the scene she had just witnessed and proceeded to go about her business with a knowing little smile.

'Enjoy your supper, miss, while I run your bath. Oh, by the way, my name is Annie.'

'Thank you, Annie. You can call me Katherine,' she replied, trying desperately to hide how mortified she felt at being found in such a state.

God, how could she have let herself go like that? Especially when she had known the maid would be coming back at any moment. She walked over to the fireplace and sat down in the white leather chair. When she saw the food, she realised she was famished and set about making quick work of the delicious supper. Everything was perfect: the chicken was tender and done to perfection, the salad dressing was light, with a hint of fresh garden herbs, and the bread was hot and crusty. She washed it all down with a wonderful wine that was robust and full bodied; just the way she liked it.

When she finished, she lay back in the chair, overwhelmed by all the new sensations. She could hear the bath water running in the background and was delighted when the heady fragrance of roses began emanating from the bathroom. She realised now how tired she was and how she longed for a nice hot bath.

As she continued to inhale the scent of roses, she could feel herself beginning to unwind for the first time that day.

'Ready, miss? You can bring your wine with you if you like,' Annie announced.

Replete with good food and excellent wine, Katherine picked up her glass and eagerly followed Annie into the bathroom.

'Oh, how lovely,' she murmured.

The room was darker now except for the soft glow of the scented candles which Annie had placed around the room. The exquisite perfume of the bath oil – together with the wine she had just finished – seemed to go straight to her head and suddenly she felt a bit woozy.

'Let me help you out of those clothes, Miss Katherine,' Annie whispered softly.

Before Katherine could say a word, Annie undid the clasp of Katherine's bra and her heavy breasts tumbled free. Then the maid quickly removed her stockings from the suspender belt and unfastened the clasp to let it slide noiselessly to the floor.

Katherine was slightly embarrassed as the maid continued to undress her. She gasped slightly when Annie slid her panties down over her hips and asked her to step out of them. This kind of thing was totally foreign to her. Allowing someone to undress her like this was unthinkable and yet she was allowing it to happen. She shivered slightly as Annie's fingers gently slid up her leg and slowly began peeling off her stockings.

Annie helped her in to the warm scented water then placed a little pillow behind her head. She turned on the jets of the jacuzzi and the water bubbled up around her.

'Oh, this is fabulous,' Katherine sighed. 'Thank you, Annie. This is just what I needed.'

Katherine looked down at her pink-tipped breasts bobbing in the rippling water and sighed; this was heaven. She let her head sink back on the pillow. Her lips parted. She moved her body sensuously as she luxuriated in the warm scented water. Just visible through the bubbling water, her dark bush swayed to and fro like some exotic plant in the ocean tides.

Annie went about her business quietly and efficiently then slowly poured some rose scented oil on to her hands.

'I'm going to give you a little massage now, miss. It will help you relax even more.'

Overcome by the wine, the perfume and the soothing effect of the bubbling bath water, Katherine was too tired to protest even if she had wanted to. She murmured her thanks and continued to sip her wine. She sighed deeply as Annie's cool hands, slick with rose oil, slid on to her shoulders and began kneading her aching muscles.

'That feels so good,' she murmured, as Annie's hands moved down between her shoulder blades then up around her neck and into her hair. The tension was oozing out of her now and under Annie's skilful hands ripples of released energy began to flow throughout her body.

Next, Annie turned her attention to Katherine's arms which were lying submerged in the water. Slowly, she lifted one arm and then the other and stroked them. She trailed her fingers lightly up and down, stopping now and then to draw lazy little circles in the sensitive hollows of her elbows. Moving down to her hands, she stopped and caressed the palms then slid her fingers in between Katherine's own. Then she made a little circle with her thumb and index finger and proceeded to slide this up and down the full length of each of Katherine's slender fingers.

'What are you doing?' Katherine mumbled, squirming deliciously in the warm bubbling water.

Annie remained silent and continued her slow sensual massage. As she continued to work her magic, Katherine squirmed beneath her touch. The sensations were exquisite. Gradually, Katherine realised she was becoming aroused. She could feel her nipples hardening into stiff little points and a warmth was gathering between her legs. She was amazed at the way she was responding. After all, Annie was just giving her a massage. She had made no sexual overtures at all.

'Just relax, Katherine,' Annie whispered in her ear, addressing her more casually for the first time. 'You're doing just fine. Let yourself experience whatever it is you're feeling. Don't fight it.'

'Oh, God,' Katherine sighed loudly as Annie moved down to her feet and began rubbing each individual toe with her smooth oily hands. She could hardly bear the sensations that were radiating up to the juncture between her legs.

Annie dried Katherine's feet then bent down and took the big toe in her mouth and started to suck on it. Katherine squealed in surprise but immediately gave herself over to the exquisite torture of Annie's long wet tongue. She gasped as it began moving up and down the thick fleshy shaft of her big toe. Then Annie began to suck and pull on it until it was on fire.

Annie moved on to the other ten toes. 'Can't leave out all the others, can I, Katherine?' she said, a new tone creeping into her voice.

'This little piggy went to market – '

'Oh, Jesus,' Katherine cried as Annie slithered her tongue in between her other toes and began to probe between each one. She then closed her mouth around them and sucked greedily on each one in turn.

'And this little piggy went wee wee wee wee all the way home,' she added, then took all the toes on one foot into her mouth at once.

Katherine squealed with delight as Annie's mouth engulfed her toes and her tongue began to forage between each of them, sliding back and forth, sending little tingles racing up and down her body. The sensation was exquisite, at times almost unbearable. How delicious this is, she thought. Who would have guessed I would be so turned on by this sensual assault? Annie was playing her like a musical instrument and Katherine was responding in spite of herself.

'You like that, miss?' Annie asked, reverting to the more formal mode of address.

'Oh, God, yes,' Katherine sighed loudly as tiny electric shivers raced up and down her body.

Katherine could hardly believe how aroused she was. She didn't want Annie to know how much; she was much too embarrassed. But it was no use. Her nipples betrayed her and she was squirming in the tub now, splashing the scented water over her swollen breasts. Her breath was coming faster and she ached to be touched in more intimate places. A long sigh escaped her lips.

'I know what you want, Katherine,' Annie replied crisply.

Katherine gasped as Annie slid her soapy hands over her breasts and began massaging them. She wanted to stop her but she couldn't. She knew she was giving herself over to a complete stranger, a woman even, but she couldn't help it. She was so shocked and so excited she couldn't even speak. She was horrified at what she was allowing this woman to do to her. Yet she couldn't stop herself. She had never felt so overwhelmed by such naked sensuality. She felt dizzy – drugged almost. There was no way she could resist. In spite of herself, Katherine arched her back offering her nipples to Annie's expert touch.

Annie continued caressing Katherine's breasts. Her soapy fingers snaked across the swelling white mounds, circling her nipples and teasing them until they rose in aching little peaks. Katherine's hips jerked in a spasm of pleasure as sexual thrills coursed down into her loins where a hot demanding energy was slowly building. She writhed against Annie's fingers, hungry for more.

'You like this, Katherine? You want more?' Annie's voice whispered in her ear as she started fondling and palming her breasts more vigorously.

'Annie,' she moaned, unable to put her feelings into words.

'That's OK. I know just what you need. Bend forward,' she added abruptly, her voice more commanding now as she took the wine glass from the edge of the tub and set it down on the floor.

Intoxicated with sensations, Katherine obeyed her order. Feeling rather light-headed, she sat up and bent forward, her breasts completely submerged in the bubbling water. She felt overwhelmed and aroused to a fever pitch.

Annie trailed one hand down Katherine's back then reached into the water with the other and trained one gentle jet of water on Katherine's nipples and another on her vulva.

Katherine's high pitched cry told Annie she had done exactly the right thing.

'Oh, yes, yes,' Katherine moaned, as the fine spray of needles sent shock waves of sexual energy coursing down to her pussy lips – which were already swollen and open with desire.

She gave a sharp cry as Annie's hands slid down over her rounded behind. Her fingers stopped just short of the crease between her buttocks where they began drawing tantalising little circles. Katherine felt almost delirious. This was heaven. But there was fear mixed in with her joy. She did not want Annie to go any further. God, she couldn't allow that!

Annie's hands didn't go any further. They just lingered there, softly stroking and teasing her secret cleft, her long nails occasionally raking gently over the sweet dark indentation. Katherine experienced a sharp pang of disappointment when Annie stopped and laid her back against the tub but she felt relieved too. She was caught up in so many conflicting and confusing feelings, she didn't know how she felt any more. What other delights did Annie have in store for her?

The beguiling young maid reached down into the bath water, picked up one of the detachable water jets and started running it up and down Katherine's legs, making sure to come close but never touch that aching area which demanded attention. Thrills of pleasure pulsed through Katherine as the jets stimulated her even further. The feeling of the little ripples of water caressing her legs was almost unbearable at this point and she didn't know how much more she could stand. The fiery heat that had been building between her legs was now a roaring furnace. Once again, Annie seemed to know just what she needed. In a deft movement, she adjusted the water jet to a more delicate setting and slowly aimed it at Katherine's vagina. As the jet assaulted her throbbing pussy, her clitoris reared in response. It was stiff and rigid and pulsing wildly. The sensation of the fine spray flooding into her vulva sent her into a frenzy and her hips bucked wildly in spasms of pleasure. But still she had not peaked.

'Not yet, miss, not just yet,' Annie whispered in Katherine's ear.

Katherine moaned in frustration and thrust her hips as high as she could, splashing the water over her breasts and over the edge of the tub. She was wild now, on fire, and desperate to find the release her body craved.

Ignoring her wild gyrations, Annie reached down into the water and began manipulating the jet so that one minute it was trained directly on her sex and the next it was taken away. In that way, Katherine was brought to the edge of orgasm but not allowed to climax just when she was ready to tip over the edge. Katherine was soon caught up in a continual pulsing effect which mimicked to perfection her own aching rhythms.

'Oh, please, Annie, please.'

But Annie would not oblige. 'Wanting is pleasure,' she stated in a crisp, matter-of-fact tone of voice. 'The agony of waiting is part of the pleasure. Begging for pleasure increases the joy of release. Can you do that? Can you allow yourself to admit what you want and ask for it?'

'I want you to bring me off. I want you to suck my breasts and lick my clit and stick your finger up inside me,' she whimpered.

'That is good, Miss Katherine,' the maid replied calmly. 'Perhaps that will happen later but right now, *you* will have to finish off what I've started. You will have to pleasure yourself and you will have to do it right in front of me.'

Katherine's wail of disappointment rang out loudly in the steamy bathroom. She couldn't wait any longer. Desperate and beyond shame, she jammed her hand down into the bubbling water and grabbed her throbbing sex. Feverishly, she slid her finger up and down the shaft of her clitoris then flicked the rigid little head, erect now beneath its silky hood. Her vagina opened even wider and she rammed two fingers inside her moist tunnel and began plunging them in and out. She ground her hips down on her foraging fingers, clutching at them with her inner muscles.

Finally, everything in her seemed to dissolve and her legs tensed. She shuddered as her climax burst upon her and waves of pleasure radiated through her body. Her moans of agonised delight echoed in the room until, spent and exhausted, she fell back into Annie's waiting arms. As she lay there panting and shaking in the aftermath of her orgasm, she could feel Annie's cool hands soothing her swollen breasts and raw nipples until finally she began to calm down.

After about fifteen minutes, Annie helped her out of the bath and laid her down on the soft black carpet where she proceeded to dry her off with a big fluffy bath towel. Katherine felt dazed. She could hardly believe what had just happened. How could she have pleasured herself like that in front of a complete stranger? And yet, even as she asked herself this question, she knew there had been no choice. Something in her had responded to Annie's soft caresses, something that had remained hidden for too long.

'You did well, miss. So, I have a little reward for you, a surprise I guess I should say. Anyway, you still seem quite agitated. So, if you like, I can arrange for something that will help calm you.'

Katherine could only nod her assent.

'Good, then let's go into the other room in front of the fire. You'll be nice and warm there,'

Annie wrapped her in a towel and almost carried her into the bedroom. She led her over to the fireplace and helped her to lie face down on the black fur rug.

'Now, I'm going to get that surprise I told you about,' Annie announced calmly as she reached up and yanked on a velvet bell pull.

In a few minutes the door to the bedroom opened and a young blond man walked in. He closed the door softly and silently and approached the two women.

'This is Jimmy, Katherine,' Annie explained. 'He's going to finish off your massage. I know you'll really enjoy it. He's got great hands.'

Jimmy reached into his pocket and pulled out a little phial of coloured liquid which he poured into his left palm. The scent of lavender immediately filled the room.

'This will help you relax, miss,' Annie quickly explained. 'Lavender is good for that. I know you'll love it. It always works wonders with me. I have to go now but I'll be leaving you in Jimmy's very capable hands. You'll be as well taken care of with him as you were with me,' she added, as she saw the apprehension in Katherine's eyes.

Before Katherine could say a word in protest, Annie slipped out of the room. For a second, Katherine felt the old anxiety creeping back but when Jimmy began moving his oily hands in long soothing strokes up and down her back, she relaxed under his touch. He did have wonderful hands, she sighed inwardly. She groaned softly when he slid his hands over her buttocks then down her legs toward her feet. As she inhaled the pleasant scent of the lavender oil, Katherine allowed herself to relax and enjoy the firmer, heavier touch of Jimmy's strong male hands. She loved the feel of them on her skin and the scent of lavender was intoxicating. Not until this moment had she realised how potent the scent of essential oils could be. It made her feel very sleepy just as if a fine champagne had gone directly to her head. Jimmy continued massaging her back and legs until he felt Katherine's muscles give up their tension.

'Turn over now, Katherine,' he told her, as he emptied the rest of the phial into his hands. 'I want to finish up so you can get some rest. How are you feeling now?'

'I feel wonderful,' Katherine said sleepily, turning over on her back, her voluptuous body bathed in the flickering firelight.

Gently, Jimmy covered her with a bath towel and continued the massage. His large oily hands moved over her neck and shoulders, sliding easily down her arms then back up again to the upper portion of her chest. He kept this up for a few minutes until she was totally relaxed. Just below his large square hands, her breasts rose and fell beneath the towel, the hard nubs of her nipples obvious beneath the thick terrycloth towel.

'I think you are ready for more now,' Jimmy whispered in her ear.

Slowly, he pulled the towel down over her breasts, then he cupped them in his oily hands and began rolling the nipples back and forth between his thumb and his forefinger. Instantly, they responded to his touch and elongated into sharp points.

Katherine cried out in protest but the pleasure was

too acute to deny. 'Oh, God, Jimmy, what are you doing? Annie said . . . I mean . . . I can't –'

'Now, miss, you don't have to worry about a thing,' he reassured her in a soothing voice. 'You had to make yourself come before. Now, I think you deserve to lie back and let someone else do it for you.'

Katherine was stunned but, before she could speak, Jimmy's hands were on her again, massaging her breasts and worrying her nipples.

'This won't take long,' he whispered. 'You're so ready and you're so hot. I know all about what happened with you and Annie in the bathroom. I was watching through a two-way mirror.'

This revelation caught Katherine completely off guard and she stared at him in shocked amazement.

Noting her reaction, Jimmy hurried on. 'Your first orgasm took a long time to come. And then, when it did come, it didn't last very long. So you ended up feeling sort of tense. The one *I* give you will come soon but it will last a long time. You'll love how delicious and dragged out I can make it for you; that is if I have your permission.'

Katherine was incredibly excited by the thought that Jimmy had been watching Annie stroke and caress her in the bathtub. Her sex tingled at the idea of his peeking at them and the heat between her legs intensified. She was amazed at herself. She was letting another stranger fondle and play with her. But the sensations flooding through her once again would not be denied. She arched her back and jerked her hips, giving Jimmy permission to feast on any part of her he desired.

Jimmy's oily hands were slithering all over her now, slipping and sliding into every crease and crevice of her body; moving sensuously up her legs then stopping to graze and draw circles in the sensitive area behind her knees before moving further up to the tender flesh on the insides of her thighs. Katherine shuddered and the lips of her vulva contracted. She was in ecstasy again, only this time it was slow and gentle and not harsh like before. She had never dreamt that sex could be so textured, so multi-layered. And now she could feel that familiar hot energy building deep inside again.

Jimmy ran his hands over Katherine's breasts. He lingered there for a moment then allowed them to snake their way down over her mound and tangle themselves in her dark wet bush. Katherine groaned aloud as his fingers grazed on her pussy. She raised her hips, silently begging for more. Her juices were oozing out of her and her dark passage ached to be filled.

'Are you ready, miss?'

Katherine smiled and drew up her knees. Then she let her legs fall wide apart, revealing her retracted outer lips and her fully engorged clitoris which protruded proudly from beneath its silky hood.

'Mmm,' you are ready, aren't you?' he said, giving her aching nipples one last tweak. Then, slowly, he slid two fingers inside her and began twisting and turning them as he jabbed them in and out.

Gyrating beneath his touch, Katherine ground and jerked her hips to match the exquisite rhythm of his fingers as they relentlessly probed the deepest part of her. Her hands groped for her breasts and she began flicking her fingers at her nipples.

Jimmy rolled his thumb over Katherine's clit as he continued scything his fingers in and out of her. When her inner muscles began milking his fingers, Jimmy knew it was time to move on to the next phase. Without any warning, he scooped her up in his arms and carried her over to the bed where he gently deposited her on the cool ice-blue satin bedspread. In a flash, he had secured her arms and legs with white satin ropes and placed a silken pillow beneath her hips. Katherine cried out sharply and struggled against her constraints. Suddenly, she was fully awake and aware of her situation. However, the more she struggled, the tighter the ropes got and the more aroused she became. She was wild with desire. Her juices were flowing out on to the pillow and, with her hips elevated and her legs spread wide, both her sex and the dark rose of her puckered arsehole were totally exposed to Jimmy's hungry gaze.

Katherine gasped as Jimmy used his two index fingers to part her plump labia and briefly explore her delicate inner folds. At his touch, she caught her breath, straining once more against the silken ropes that held her captive. Once again, her struggles only drove her to a higher peak of arousal.

'That's it, girl, that's right,' he crooned to her. 'You're very close and you're very ready. And now I am going to make you come until you scream for me to stop. Would you like that?'

'Oh, God, Jimmy. I want to come, please,' Katherine begged as she writhed and pulled against her restraints. 'I can't stand any more.'

Jimmy responded instantly to her agonised pleas and slid his fingers deep into her. Slowly, he began twisting and turning them in all directions, flicking constantly at her clitoris. Then, when he knew she could wait no longer, he quickly and effortlessly slid the third finger of his other hand deep into her bottom hole and up inside her anus. Then, very gently, he began a slow thrusting movement in and out, some-times moving both fingers in the same rhythm, sometimes moving them in a counter motion. Moving his fingers in and out, he foraged and ravaged every part of her until she was begging for release. Then, as she teetered on the brink, he made one last expert move and started the chain reaction that would send her over the edge.

Lost in a sexual haze, Katherine's whole world was now centred on the exquisite sensations of Jimmy's probing fingers. Finally, she could hold back no longer. A low growl rose up in her throat as her orgasm seized her. She twisted and turned on his fingers, trying to wring every ounce of pleasure out of them that she could. Her vagina and anus lurched and convulsed together as her climax blazed through her. Her whole body seemed to be dissolving. Every part of her was climaxing. Her clitoris surged endlessly and her anus contracted matching its rhythm. Deep inside her, the walls of her vagina pulsed in little spasms of excruciating pleasure. She went spinning over the edge and out into some dark, starry place she had only dreamt about.

Jimmy stayed with her all the way. Not once did he stop his plundering fingers. Finally, sated with passion, Katherine begged him to stop.

'Well, how did it go, Jimmy?' Martha asked anxiously.

'It went real well, Miss Martha. She's a hot one all right. All she needs is someone who knows how to pleasure her the right way, that's all. She even let me go for the whole ball of wax.'

'Did she now? Well, that's very hopeful.'

'Oh, yes, ma'am. You've got a live one this time.'

'All right, Jimmy, that's enough. You do your job well, but you're not here to comment on the guests. That will be all for now. I'll take over tomorrow.'

Chapter Three

Katherine stretched languidly then snuggled further down into the warm cosy bed, a satisfied smile on her face. She felt sleek and sated like a cat who had just finished a big bowl of cream. She basked for a moment in the rays of morning sun that streamed in through the tall, graceful windows and cast a warm golden light over the room. That had been quite a dream, she thought, sighing deeply as she ran her hands over her breasts. Then her eyes flew open. That had been no dream. That had really happened! Her cheeks flushed as the details came flooding back. How could she have allowed herself to be coerced like that? And by a man *and* a woman! She was stunned at her behaviour. And yet she had enjoyed it too much to feel guilty. Even as she tried to chastise herself, she could feel herself getting excited again.

Memories of the pleasure she had experienced flooded through her and she knew she had done nothing wrong; nothing wrong could feel this good. She had learnt something too: by allowing Jimmy and

Annie to do what they wanted with her, she had ended up having an incredibly hot time. And yet, in a strange way, she had been the one in control. After all, they had been the ones who had had to find out what turned her on. All she had had to do was lie back and enjoy it. She blushed as she remembered the water jets and Annie's oily hands. And then there had been that incredible massage with Jimmy. My sex life certainly seems to be changing for the better, she thought, with an impish grin. She had been here only one night and already she had pleasured herself in front of a complete stranger and then had given herself over like a wanton to the expert ministrations of another. She had never before allowed herself such indulgence. But, yesterday, she had given herself with total abandon, allowing complete strangers all kinds of liberties. Her pussy tingled as she remembered. Annie and Jimmy – and indeed Rolf – had satisfied her in ways she had never dreamt possible but she realised that she too had played a very important part in this experience. She didn't have it quite clear yet but somehow she knew that by allowing herself to be dominated, she had gained a subtle kind of power in the situation. This insight excited her and she felt determined to explore it further. She pulled herself back to the present. She had to get up. Breakfast was at nine and would be followed by her interview at ten.

She glanced over at the timepiece on the bedside table. It was only seven o'clock; far too early to get up. She slid back down between the satin sheets. If only she had a lover with her right now. She would tell him exactly what she wanted. Until her wild experience with Rolf, she had never had a really exciting sexual encounter with a man. And she had always thought it was because there was something wrong with her. Now she was starting to know better!

The men she seemed to meet were never quite right. They were either really intelligent with minimal sex appeal or randy jocks without a brain who only knew how to fuck. Then there were all those other guys who just didn't know how to please a woman.

Katherine closed her eyes and the image of her dream lover appeared in her mind's eye. He was tall and slight but superbly proportioned. His skin had an olive cast to it, his hair was thick and black, his dark, shining eyes slightly slanted. He had sensitive hands and long, tapered fingers like an artist, hands that knew how to bring her to ecstatic peaks of pleasure. She could see him leaning over her now, his full, sensuous mouth pressing down on hers.

Katherine stuck two fingers in her mouth and began sucking on them. They felt just like his warm hot tongue. She would let him spear his tongue into her mouth and then she would suck on it and snake hers around its long warm hardness. She ran her other hand over her breasts and began playing with her nipples. Instantly, they hardened. She took her fingers out of her mouth. They were warm and slick. She saw her lover bending over her. His warm mouth began kissing her belly, his tongue lapping her naked flesh in little circles until finally he reached her lower abdomen. Now he would do exactly what she told him. He stopped licking her and slid his hand over her pussy and started rubbing her until she was moaning softly.

Katherine opened her eyes and looked at her reflection in the mirror hanging above the bed. She was sprawled naked on the rumpled bedclothes with one hand on her breast and the other buried in the dark tangle between her legs. She groaned and gyrated her hips. She closed her eyes and urged her lover to move more quickly now. She wanted to come. It had been a long time since he had been able to pleasure her the way she wanted. She wanted him to make her come the way he always did, with one finger rubbing her clit and the other deep in her dark tunnel. As she eased her fingers into her warm, moist sex, she could hear him whispering her name. She arched towards him and led his hand to the head of her aching clit. At first, he began fingering her softly, then he increased the pressure. He took two fingers of his other hand and slid them easily into her. She thrust her hips up to meet his touch and began moving in time to his probing fingers. She ground her hips and tightened her buttocks, reaching for her orgasm. She guided his fingers so they moved more urgently, intensifying her pleasure. Then she felt it. Her legs tensed and her clit stiffened and she moaned loudly as she came in a series of short hard spasms.

At that moment, the alarm clock rang out harshly and Katherine started violently. Her fantasy was over; now she had to wake up to reality. Her fantasy man had been part of her life for such a long time she had started to feel he really existed. If only she could find a man like him, a man who could fulfil all her desires and leave her panting for more.

It was eight o'clock. Breakfast was at nine. She dragged herself out of bed and headed for the shower. In a half an hour, she was dressed and on her way downstairs. She paused for a moment in front of a mirror at the top of the stairs to check her appearance; she looked great. Her eyes were bright and her skin was glowing. She had dressed casually in a navy skirt, a white silk blouse, and thong sandals. Her long hair

46

was tied back with a red and white scarf and she had kept her make-up simple. She felt ready for anything.

Breakfast was a pleasant affair. The people at her table were all rather nice and had motioned her to sit with them when she had walked into the breakfast room. One woman, whose name was Karen, was slim and dark. The other, Jasmine, was a voluptuous blonde. They were both in their mid-thirties. There was also a very handsome young blond man named Alan and a black man named Steve.

However, the one who really caught her eye was a handsome, middle-aged man who looked Arabic. He was incredibly good looking, distinguished even, with dark hair, tinged with grey at the temples and olive skin. His eyes were ice blue, a startling contrast to his swarthy complexion and, when he smiled, his full, sensual lips parted to reveal a row of evenly-matched white teeth.

Katherine's heart was pounding in her chest and she could hardly breathe. Except for his eyes and his age, he looked exactly like her dream lover. She shook herself and tried to regain her composure but she couldn't stop staring at him. The resemblance was so strong she had to remind herself that his hands had not been stroking her pussy an hour ago. She took a deep breath and tried to calm down.

He was devastatingly handsome. His gaze seemed to burn her skin as it flickered over her breasts and down the full length of her body. When their eyes met, she felt a strange sensation in her stomach, similar to the one she always got when a lift descended too quickly. She felt her breath coming in rapid little gasps. When he rose to introduce himself, their eyes met and she shuddered inwardly. In spite of the bemused smile that hovered at the corners of his mouth, there was a hard glint in his eyes.

'Delighted to meet you, Miss MacNeil,' he murmured, bowing to kiss her hand. 'I am Assam Aswabi.'

The touch of his mouth seared her skin like a burning coal and she recoiled involuntarily.

He threw her a questioning glance then sat back down and smoothly continued the conversation. He spoke a little about himself. He was a businessman from the Middle East who was here on a stopover before returning to his country. He would be staying for a few days for a well-deserved rest and he was looking forward to socialising with the other guests.

Katherine could barely hear what he was saying. She was violently attracted to him and was having a hard time hiding the fact. She knew he was attracted to her too. In fact, it seemed he couldn't keep his eyes off her. Every time she looked over at him, his cold blue eyes were staring back at her, stripping away any pretence she might like to set up between them.

Katherine liked the feeling of power she got when she knew a man was attracted to her. She liked the idea that her mere physical presence was enough to cast a spell over him and hold him captive. But there was something about this man that was different. She couldn't quite put her finger on it. Somehow she knew he would be nobody's pawn and that whoever got involved with him would be putty in his hands. A delicious shiver skittered over her skin. Maybe her dreams were finally going to come true.

Alan seemed interested in her too, but he didn't electrify her the way Assam did. She smiled inwardly. Two men drawn to her at once. This certainly had not happened in a long time. A wild fantasy rose up in her mind. She was sitting at the table naked while Alan and Assam caressed her. One was kneeling between her legs, licking her pussy and the other was standing behind her, toying with her nipples. Then Alan lifted her up off the chair and eased her down on to the table. Using his knees to part her legs, he mounted her and shoved his short, thick penis deep inside her. She raised her hips to meet him. To her right, Assam looked on with interest as Alan serviced her. He was smiling and, in his hand, he had a small white whip with silken thongs. He bent over her and gave her nipples a quick little flick. She gasped out loud and almost came right there at the table.

In an instant, the fantasy dissolved. Katherine glanced around quickly at her breakfast companions. Had they noticed anything? The conversation seemed to be proceeding smoothly without her. She sighed with relief but, when she looked up at Assam, she knew he was on to her. From the ill-concealed laughter in his eyes, she knew he understood exactly what had just transpired. She blushed violently under his knowing gaze and squirmed uncomfortably in her seat.

Luckily, at that moment, Jasmine turned and asked her opinion about something and she got back into the conversation. The rest of breakfast was a blur and before she knew it Assam was saying his goodbyes to the rest of the people at the table.

When he rose to leave, her heart sank with disappointment.

'You're not leaving so soon?' she blurted out.

'Forgive me, everyone, but before I can settle into my holiday here, there are some very important business matters I really must attend to. I apologise for breaking up such a pleasant gathering. Perhaps, after dinner this evening, we can get reacquainted over coffee in the blue room? Until then . . .' he added. With a bow, he was gone.

When he left, the life seemed to go out of Katherine and she withdrew into herself.

The sound of Alan's voice brought her back. 'Hey, Katherine, come back. You're a million miles away. Listen, it's time you saw something of the place. How about meeting me in the library later? We could have tea and browse through some of the old tomes. It's a wonderful room and it's got the most unusual books. I'm sure you would enjoy looking through some of them.'

'Thanks, Alan. I'll have to think about it,' she murmured half-heartedly. 'I have an interview at ten and then I'm not sure what I want to do. How about I call you in your room later and let you know?'

'I wish you would come. I have a feeling you would really enjoy it. I know I always find the library so relaxing,' Alan continued, his eyes lingering on her erect nipples, which were clearly visible through the thin material of her blouse.

Katherine grew hot beneath his gaze and mumbled something to the effect that she loved foraging around in second-hand book stores in search of interesting old books. However, her remarks were half-hearted and somewhat forced. She was still thinking about Assam.

'I'm sure you'll find something to your taste in *this* library,' Alan persisted, his voice full of meaning.

For some reason, the others seemed to find his words very amusing and burst out laughing. Katherine felt like the odd woman out as the others exchanged knowing glances. The atmosphere at the table had changed suddenly and they were staring at her strangely. She felt uneasy. The conversation

seemed full of double meanings and sexual under-
tones. She felt agitated yet intrigued. She jumped
nervously when Alan slid his hand on to her thigh
and gave her a little squeeze.

'Relax, Katherine,' he purred smoothly. 'You're
going to be fine. Nothing ever happens here without
your permission. Look, think about getting together
later. I'm going to spend the afternoon browsing and
relaxing in the library. You can meet me there or not,
whatever you wish. If you decide you want to meet
me there, check with the front desk first. If there's
been a change in my plans, I'll leave a message for
you.'

Katherine agreed to this arrangement but she felt
confused. One minute he was squeezing her thigh and
the next minute he was acting as if nothing had
happened. She felt bewildered by his remarks and
stunned at his audacity but the others at the table
didn't seem to give his actions a second thought and
continued chatting. However, she could feel their
furtive little glances aimed in her direction as they
tried to gauge her reaction. She scanned their
expressions closely and tried to figure out what they
were thinking. Their faces looked just like smiling
masks and the meaning in their eyes was veiled.

She blushed deeply. She was angry that someone
had taken liberties with her like that – and in public
too – but she was also sexually excited by it and
everybody at the table knew it. She was in a public
place and yet she longed to rub herself or better still,
have someone at the table do it for her. She wriggled
in her seat. She was astonished at the state she was in.
For years she had dedicated herself entirely to her
work. Now, after being away from it for only two
days, she could think of nothing but sex.

She looked up with a start. Alan was staring at her. His expression was polite and there was a smile on his face but there was a look of naked lust in his eyes. Katherine knew that look. She knew he wanted to do to her exactly what she had been fantasizing about a few moments earlier.

She tore her eyes away, stood up, and got ready to leave. The atmosphere in the breakfast room was so tense and sexually charged that she had to get out and clear her head. Besides, it was almost time for her interview. She wanted to make a good impression and get there on time. She excused herself from the group and turned to leave the room.

'Call me later and let me know whether you want to meet for drinks,' Jasmine called out to her from across the room.

'Okay, I'll get back to you later this afternoon,' Katherine replied with a smile, noting to her dismay that Alan's arm was now draped over Jasmine's shoulder and his hand was buried deep inside her blouse.

What the hell was going on here? She fumed inwardly as she made her way across the foyer. Those people seemed to know something she didn't. They also seemed to feel quite free to act on their sexual impulses whether they were in public or not. She shivered as she remembered Alan's hand snaking across her thigh. The thought of a visit alone with him sent tingles of trepidation down her spine. Perhaps she would cancel. She could always use the excuse that she was still tired from her trip. And yet, she had to admit there was something about him that intrigued her. Perhaps there was no harm exploring things with him a little further, she told herself. If he turned out to be a bore, she would nip it in the bud.

Using a map of the hotel she had found in her room, she followed the winding hall leading off the main foyer. In no time she was there. The name was on the door: Martha Hind. Katherine knocked firmly and a voice told her to come in.

The moment she opened the door, a tall, attractive, grey haired woman came forward and held out her hand in welcome.

'Welcome, Katherine. I hope you've enjoyed your stay with us so far. Please sit down and make yourself comfortable. I'd like to discuss your reasons for being here and any ideas you might have concerning your personal programme.'

Katherine was impressed with the woman's powerful aura and forthright personality and immediately felt at ease.

'So, what do you want out of life, Katherine?'

Startled by such a direct approach, Katherine had to pause for a moment, searching for the answer to such a difficult and complex question.

'Power,' she blurted out finally. 'Power and sexual fulfilment.'

Martha seemed pleased by her response. 'And do you have it?'

'No. I don't.'

'Why not?'

'I don't know.'

'What are you prepared to do to get it?'

'Anything,' she replied without thinking, amazed at her quick, unedited responses.

'Anything?'

'Yes.'

'You're not happy at work, your sexual relationship is dull and boring and you feel blocked and incomplete, right?'

Astonished at her correct assessment, Katherine could only nod in agreement.

'Well, you've come to the right place. I know we can help you.'

'Help me?' Katherine asked, feeling confused at the direction the conversation was taking.

'Why, yes. Didn't Phyllis Manion explain what we do here? We're a sex therapy clinic. We help people get through their sexual blocks so they can live more fulfilling lives.'

'What!'

'That's right. I'm surprised Phyllis didn't tell you. She knew so many intimate details of your past, I naturally assumed you told each other everything. Oh well, no matter. The important thing is you're here. And you couldn't have picked a better place to work out your problems. I know you're here at Phyllis's suggestion. She's been very concerned about you for a long time. In fact, she was the one who told me the details of your case.'

'My case?'

'Well, perhaps that's being a little too clinical. I'm sorry. Listen, Katherine. Let's put it this way. You need a place where you can reflect on your personal needs and we provide an environment where you can do just that. It seems like a good fit to me. And from all reports, it seems you've settled on some kind of plan already.'

'Well, yes, I have actually, but I didn't know; I mean, I thought this was a place where I could have a bit of a rest and sort things out for myself. I thought I could even let my hair down a bit seeing as I'm so far from home and everything. But I'm certainly not interested in some rigid therapeutic situation where I have to be analysing myself every minute of the day. That's not my idea of a holiday.'

'I agree with you. I think you should be perfectly free to do exactly as you please. We offer people that option here. We also give you the chance to gain some perspective on your life as well. And, if needed, we provide guidance, advice, or whatever you feel is appropriate. However, this isn't always necessary. Some of our guests just need privacy and the opportunity to explore their sexual needs in their own way. We also offer people that possibility. I think this option would suit you best. It would give you more freedom. At the same time, you can feel secure knowing that we're here to support you in any way you need. So, please feel free to call on us at any time. Now, let's get down to it, shall we?' she continued, abruptly changing the subject. 'How do you feel after last night with Annie and Jimmy?'

'You mean they . . .?'

'Yes. Annie and Jimmy are on the staff here. Rather good, aren't they?' Martha smiled, slyly.

Katherine blushed. She felt ashamed but she felt angry too.

'Listen, Katherine, you haven't got time to be embarrassed or upset. Your stay here will be brief. However, if you put your mind to it, you can accomplish a great deal in a short period of time; that is if you open up and try to enjoy yourself. We're here to help you do that. It's clear from the way you answered my questions this morning that you know what you want. You just don't know how to get it. Well, I do. I can offer you the run of the place so you can find out what makes you tick sexually and what is stopping you from enjoying sex to the full. All you have to do is stay open and go with your instincts.'

'I . . . uh . . . well, yes, all right. Actually I had sort of decided on my way here in the car that it was time for me to try something new.'

A sex therapy clinic, Katherine thought, astonished. That certainly explains a lot. She still felt somewhat out of her depth and was relieved that Martha seemed to approve of her plan to experiment and explore. It actually looked like she was being given *carte blanche* to do as she pleased. What an amazing situation! She had come here thinking she was going to have some rest and relaxation and maybe get some of her priorities straight. She never dreamt she would find herself in the middle of a sex clinic that was offering her access to limitless sexual possibilities!

'That's the spirit,' Martha continued. 'You need to broaden your sexual base, have different experiences, break free, find out what you really like to do and not just what you think you should do. There are all sorts of ways to express ourselves sexually, you know. And all of them are appropriate, provided, of course, everyone involved is willing.'

'So, I can just go ahead and do what I want?' Katherine asked, her voice eager with anticipation.

'Absolutely. In fact, I think that's the best thing you could do. You have been much too rigid. You have worked to the exclusion of everything else and have denied yourself the pleasures a woman needs to be happy and healthy. You don't need therapy really. What you need is to be surprised, to be seduced, to have a variety of sexual encounters. And this is the ideal place to do that. You are safe here and our staff are here to help. Also, each guest is guaranteed complete confidentiality. That way, you won't be inhibited by worrying that people at home will find out. So, relax and follow your instincts. See how it goes. Then, later, if you like, we can meet and assess how things are going. If need be, I can always arrange a little scenario for you. Our clients find that very useful.'

Katherine looked at her in amazement. 'You mean, you can help me fulfil my fantasies?'

'That's right. As long as you never violate another person's wishes. We don't force anyone to do anything against their will here.'

Katherine felt a surge of relief. No matter what she chose to do or have done to her, she could relax in the knowledge that she would be absolutely secure. It was like a dream come true. She was free to indulge every secret sexual desire she had ever had. Maybe this was her chance to really start enjoying life instead of working like a madwoman all the time. Maybe now, she could give free rein to some of those outrageous fantasies she had never had the nerve or the opportunity to explore. She felt excited and filled with a growing sense of confidence. In fact, she felt so much better, she decided to keep that date with Alan in the library after all.

'We have all manner of devices and situations here at the clinic to increase our pleasure,' Martha was saying. 'You will find whatever you need as you explore the house and the estate. You might like to try the butterfly for starters and see how you like that.'

'The butterfly?' Katherine asked.

'Annie will explain everything. I have another appointment in fifteen minutes and, while you're here, I would like you to watch a few short scenes on the TV monitor behind you. Afterwards, you can tell me which one excites you the most. This will give me an idea of some of your preferences. Then, if you like, I can set up a scenario for you later on down the road.'

Katherine turned in her chair and watched as the first scene came up on the television screen. Two men and one woman were making love. It was a hot, steamy scene and she liked it but even though she found it exciting, it didn't turn her on.

The screen flickered and the scene changed. Two naked women were wrestling. Their holds slowly turned to erotic poses as they flaunted their voluptuous bodies in front of the camera. They ended up wrapped around each other in the sixty-nine position licking and sucking each other. Katherine liked this a lot and her nipples stiffened. Still, there was something missing.

The next image came on the screen. A woman was tied down on a bed and was struggling wildly against her constraints. The fact that her movements were curtailed seemed to excite her and she was moaning in pleasure. A man was gently whipping her. He kept flicking the leather thongs over her breasts and thighs then would stop and snake them down over her quivering vulva. Her legs were spreadeagled so that her sex was in full view and her wiry pubic curls were dark and wet from the juices that oozed from her swollen pussy. The more she struggled, the more aroused she became until she was groaning and writhing under the relentless flicking of the whip. Katherine was aroused too and began squirming in her seat.

The final scene portrayed an older woman strapped down to a metal table. Her legs were spread wide apart and her ankles were secured in leather cuffs. Her arms were stretched above her head, manacled to chains that were anchored to the floor. A young blonde woman stood in front of her, brandishing a small silver whip which she used to flick and tease the older woman's quivering sex. Then she took the handle, slid it inside the woman's crease and began rubbing it back and forth over the head of her clitoris. The close-up shots showed that her pleasure bud was erect and protruded from her swollen pussy. The older woman wriggled and groaned with delight as the whip moved down towards the entrance of her vagina. Slowly, the blonde inserted the tip and began churning it in small clockwise circles. The older woman writhed under the delicious torture. Then, very slowly, the blonde removed the whip. The woman whined for more but her tormentor paid no attention. Instead, she flicked the whip lightly over her victim's breasts and her swollen sex, teasing her until the woman on the table was trembling beneath its silky bite. After a few moments, a man walked in. He was dressed completely in black. He approached the younger woman and opened his flies. His huge cock sprang free. Without a word, he mounted her from behind and slid deep inside her. She tossed her head and arched her back towards him. Then she began jerking her hips to match his slow penetrating thrusts. As she allowed herself to be impaled on him, she went on teasing and torturing her willing captive with light flicks and brushes of the whip. Soon the three of them were caught up in a vortex of pleasure and their moans increased as their passion began to peak.

'Let's leave them to it, shall we?' Martha suggested, her voice breaking the sexually charged silence. She turned off the TV monitor and looked over at Katherine.

Katherine didn't answer. She couldn't; she was caught up in her own lust, completely indifferent to Martha's presence. One hand was rammed between her legs and the other was pulling and teasing her nipples.

'I'm so near but I can't come,' she cried out in frustration.

'I thought you would like that video best,' Martha said calmly.

She got up quickly and walked over towards Katherine. 'Tell me what you liked about that last video, Katherine.'

'I can't,' Katherine said as her hips writhed beneath her frantic touch.

'Stop playing with yourself and tell me,' Martha commanded brusquely.

She took hold of Katherine's hands and forced her to look into her eyes. 'You won't be able to come until you tell me why that last video got you so hot.'

The change in Martha's language to a tougher kind of talk hit a nerve and broke through Katherine's natural reserve.

'I can't. Leave me alone,' Katherine snarled, her polite façade completely melting away. 'Can't you see I'm going crazy here and I don't know why? I want to come and I can't. You're the therapist. Help me.'

'I'm not going to help you and I'm not going to let you touch yourself either, not until you tell me what was so exciting about that scene.'

Katherine struggled to free herself from Martha's iron-like grip but she couldn't.

'You can do it, Katherine. Come on, tell me.'

Martha realised she had to use more drastic tactics and changed her tone completely.

'You're a bad girl, Katherine. You're a very bad girl. You've been touching yourself and trying to make yourself come. You know that's forbidden. You will be punished for that. And you will also be punished if you don't tell me why you're so hot! Now, spit it out!'

Martha's strange words electrified Katherine and, as she screamed out her answer, she climaxed violently, her hands still locked in Martha's firm grip. As her orgasm seized her, she yelled out words that didn't make sense to her. Then she began shaking from head to toe and collapsed in Martha's arms.

Martha held her steady and led her over to a couch where they sat down. She put her arm around Katherine and held her close for a few moments.

Dazed, Katherine fell back against her, still shaking from the force of her totally unexpected orgasm. What had set her off? How had she been able to come without even touching herself? Martha's strange words rang in her ear and, once more, she felt her clit tighten and her pussy start to throb. Martha's hand moved up and down her body, stroking her breasts and feathering over her quivering thighs and throbbing sex as they tried to soothe and calm her fevered body.

'That's enough for now, Katherine,' Martha said crisply, as Katherine pushed against her hands, still wanting more. 'You've made an excellent start. Our time is up now but remember, we are here to help you in any way we can. So, please feel free to take advantage of that. I want you to try to relax and enjoy yourself. Now I really must get ready for my next appointment. Good luck and I'll see you soon.'

Barely recovered from her extraordinary experience, Katherine mumbled her thanks to Martha, pulled herself up off the couch and wordlessly stumbled out of the room.

* * *

When she had gone, Martha sat thinking about the scenario Katherine had picked. The disconnected words the younger woman had yelled out still echoed in her mind.

'It's the power. They can do whatever they please. I want that too. They have it all. I have nothing. I lost everything a long time ago. I want it back.'

Martha sat listening to the words echoing through her mind. Yes, my dear Katherine, she thought to herself, but if you really want the power, you have to experience the pleasure of giving it away. With a sigh, she sat back in her chair and waited for her next appointment.

Back in her room, Katherine looked at herself in the full-length mirror. She looked tired. She felt completely drained by the experience in Martha's office but she felt strangely liberated, too, as if she had admitted something very important. She didn't understand what had happened but she really didn't care at this point. All she wanted to do right now was shower then have a nap. She was exhausted and she wanted to be fresh for her appointment with Alan.

Her thoughts were interrupted by a knock at the door and then Annie walked in. She handed Katherine a little package.

'It's the butterfly, isn't it?' Katherine asked excitedly.

'That's what it is. I can tell you how to use it if you like.'

'Oh, yes, please.'

'Well, it's a great little device. You wear it between your legs and it keeps you aroused all day. When you walk, it moves on you just like someone's tongue or fingers. You strap it on to your upper thighs and it's rigged out with little suction cups that keep it glued to your pussy. Inside, there are little rubber stalks of varying lengths which stimulate your clitoris and your entire genital area. While you walk around doing other things, you can get all the sexual stimulation that you want. You can wear it any time you want, doing the dishes, out shopping, wherever. And nobody is any the wiser.'

'Good Lord, what an incredible idea,' Katherine gasped.

'Do you want to try it?' she teased.

'I think I'll wait for a while. I've had a pretty wild morning already and I'm meeting Alan in the library later. So, I won't really have time today.'

'Hey, there's no pressure to wear it, Katherine. Try it if you feel like it but I guarantee that if you do, you'll be very pleasantly surprised. I know. I used to wear it a lot. It's a really nice way to warm up for the main event, if you know what I mean. Also, it's a great way to give yourself a good time when there's no one else around to do it for you.'

'Did it help you, Annie?'

'You bet it did. I love to wear it. As a matter of fact, I'm wearing one right now. Do you want to see?'

Before Katherine could say a word, Annie lifted her skirt, walked over to the fireplacae, pulled down her panties and lay back on the *chaise longue* with her legs spread.

Intrigued, Katherine followed her and looked down at Annie's exposed sex. There, in the centre, was this brightly coloured device that looked exactly like a butterfly. Katherine could see that Annie was wet and that her pussy was swollen with excitement.

'It feels so great,' Annie continued. 'You could

always try it before you meet Alan. I guarantee you'll be primed and ready for anything if you do.'

'Well, maybe,' Katherine murmured, fascinated by the small device that was obviously giving Annie so much pleasure.

'Have a nice time this afternoon, Katherine. And remember, try to take advantage of every opportunity that comes your way if you can, no matter how unusual.'

With those enigmatic words, Annie crossed over to the door and opened it to leave.

'Thanks for the butterfly, Annie. I think I'll wait to try it. I'm not quite up for it today.'

Annie smiled and blew her a kiss then closed the door behind her.

Katherine walked over to the bed. She picked up the little box and put it carefully on her bedside table. She would try this later, she decided. Right now she wanted to concentrate on getting ready for her date with Alan. She would wait and see how things developed between them. It was premature to wear the butterfly right now. If she wore it, she would be too aroused and therefore too vulnerable. She didn't want to feel that way during her first encounter with Alan. She wanted to be in charge and she had the strangest feeling that Alan wanted it that way too.

She headed for the bathroom and took a long hot shower. Afterwards, she felt revitalised and ready for anything. She was determined to take Martha's advice and follow her instincts. She felt like getting dressed up for her meeting with Alan. She opened the wardrobe and took out her favourite black leather skirt and a low cut, white knit top which accentuated her breasts to perfection. She finished off the outfit with sheer black stockings and black leather high heels. She applied some bright red lipstick and tied her hair up in a knot. When she checked herself in the mirror, she liked what she saw. With her heart beating wildly in anticipation, she hurried downstairs to join Alan in the library.

Chapter Four

When Katherine arrived at the front desk, there was a message waiting for her that Alan had been detained and would not be able to keep his engagement. She was disappointed but decided to go to the library anyway. She had heard so many fascinating things about the place, she couldn't wait to see it for herself.

She made her way across the foyer. She smiled at some other guests who were going out for a stroll then she headed down the hall just to the right of the great circular staircase. According to her map, the library should be just around the next corner.

When she got there, the doors were closed and the glass panels were heavily curtained which prevented her from seeing inside. She decided to explore the room and hoped she would be on her own. She opened the door and walked in then sighed with relief when she saw that the room was deserted. She really wanted some time by herself. Her heels sank into the deep pile of the moss-green rug as she strolled over to the centre of the room and looked around. Tall French doors looked out over a tiny walled rose garden which looked secluded and inviting. One of the doors was open and the heady scent of roses wafted in on the warm air.

The room was comfortably furnished with easy chairs and couches covered in dark brown leather. Bookcases lined the wall and behind their glassed-in shelves she could see tomes of every description.

Then she noticed another book. It was lying open on a table in the centre of the room. Intrigued, she walked over to take a look. It was very old and bound in soft black leather. It seemed to be a book of etchings and paintings of some kind; some in colour, some in black and white. When she bent over to take a closer look, she gasped. Every page was full of drawings and paintings. They were set in exotic, faraway places and depicted times both past and present. Some were watercolours, others had been done in oils. They showed people indulging in every kind of sexual and erotic pleasure imaginable.

Women with white-painted faces knelt in front of men whose robes gaped open. Their huge erect members protruded through the folds of their robes right into the eager red mouths of the women who lapped at their cocks greedily as if they were sucking on sweet lollipops. One man's eyes were rolled back in ecstasy.

Another picture showed a man with his long rod buried up to the hilt in a woman's vagina while his anus was being licked by a second girl.

Then there was a man lying on a silk bedspread with his legs wide apart. A beautiful young woman was lowering herself on to his huge penis, her juices in plain view as they oozed out of her.

There were women lying naked on beautifully

manicured lawns, with men's faces buried between their legs; long snake-like tongues speared deep into their dark slits. As they enjoyed the services of the men, their fingers played with each other's breasts.

In another, mysterious veiled women wearing gossamer pantaloons and flimsy tops were being undressed and fondled by huge eunuchs while other men licked their lush red nipples.

Another picture showed a woman sprawled naked on a table with each hand clamped around the penises of two black men who stood at either side of her. Another man had his penis deep in her throat and, in between her legs, someone else was spearing her with his short thick cock.

Katherine tore her eyes away. Her breath was coming in quick harsh gasps. She was so aroused she could hardly breathe. Her nipples were pushing painfully against the confines of her bra and the crotch of her panties was wet with dew. She squeezed her thighs together to try to get some relief but it didn't work. She was incredibly excited and she wanted to keep on looking. In spite of herself, she turned the pages and feasted greedily on the lascivious poses and actions of the characters in the erotic paintings.

On one page, a woman dressed in a peculiar leather harness was ramming a shiny black dildo into the vagina of her partner – who was kneeling in the doggie position with her fingers buried between her labia. Her head was bent down to one side so she could look back at the one who was servicing her. The look in her eyes sent shivers of excitement directly to Katherine's own clitoris, which reared in response and began to throb.

There was another picture of a man down on all fours, his bottom raised, his arsehole in full view. His buttocks were being whipped by a woman wearing a dark red dildo. Another woman was lying underneath him sucking his cock while a man hovered over the gaping crease in his buttocks, his tongue poised for action.

Katherine could hardly stand any more but, when she saw the next picture, she knew she had to go on. She couldn't believe it; it was the same picture she had seen hanging in the main lounge. Well, almost the same. There were slight but significant differences. It was the same woman, all right, and she was wearing the same sheer white gown. However, in this picture, one of her full creamy breasts was exposed and this time you could see what she was holding in her hand. You could also see what she was going to do with it. The man in black was waiting in anticipation for her to begin. In this picture, he had taken his fully aroused penis out of his pants and, with both hands wrapped around it, was offering it up to her ministrations. Given what she had in her hand, it was clear what he wanted.

Katherine was horrified but fascinated at the same time. She tried to turn away from the picture but she couldn't.

The woman was holding a small black whip with a silver handle. She was brandishing it just above the man's swollen penis as he knelt before her, begging her to bring the lash down on his erect member.

'Would you do something like that for me?' a voice whispered in her ear.

Katherine started violently and squealed with terror as the unknown intruder pressed up against her buttocks.

'I've got one of those darling little whips too. Would you like to feel it?'

Katherine gasped. He was lifting her skirt up over her buttocks. She tried to wriggle away but he held her tightly against him. She trembled violently as he slid a long smooth object in between her legs and began to slide it back and forth over the slippery crotch of her panties. It must be the whip. Her knees almost gave way beneath her. He was rubbing her with the whip. It was the same whip that was in the picture; she knew it was. Just the thought of it turned her legs to jelly and her juices started to flow. She moaned and gasped for air. She loved the touch of the instrument as it skimmed smoothly over the silky crotch of her knickers, sending delicious little thrills dancing down into her crease.

He snaked his other hand around her, slipped it inside her bra, and quickly palmed her nipples until they were long and hard.

Katherine reached behind her, trying to make some kind of contact with him, but he wouldn't allow that.

'Take the whip,' he said, pushing it against her sex and through to the front where she could grab hold of it.

She couldn't say no. She was caught up in something that had a life of its own. She couldn't resist. She had to go along with it and see where it led. She took the whip in her hand and looked down at it. It was black and silver just like the one in the picture. She moaned softly.

'You know what to do with that, don't you?' he asked.

He turned her around to face him. He was masked and dressed in black. He pulled her breasts out of the low, scooped neckline of her top and mouthed them briefly.

Katherine gasped and thrust her hips forward.

70

Almost as if he were silently willing her, her hands reached down and opened his flies. She slid her hand inside and pulled out his inflamed cock; it twitched in her grasp. He sighed at her touch and knelt down before her, offering his penis just like the man in the picture.

Katherine looked down at the whip in her hand and at the man begging for its bite. She felt wildly excited. He wanted her to take charge, to respond to his pleas. He wanted her to take the upper hand. Suddenly, she knew she wasn't going to hold back. She raised the whip slowly and gently flicked it over his penis. He thrust upward towards its tiny black tip. A wave of dizziness swept over her. She feathered it over his penis again, this time a little harder. He groaned and licked his lips. Her breasts swelled and her nipples flared out into agonizing points. She ran the whip slowly along the seamed underside of his shaft and then wrapped it around and pulled upward. Then she pulled it off and brought it down again on his member, this time a little harder.

'Stand up,' she commanded, hardly recognising her voice. She led him across the room to one of the big leather chairs. 'Sit down here. No, don't lie back. I want you sitting on the edge. You will have to wait until I decide what *I* want you to do.'

Her own words titillated her even further. She knelt down in front of him and took him in her mouth, snaking her tongue around the shining purple head and probing the tiny opening with the tip of her tongue. As he thrust against her mouth, moaning softly, she grazed him with her teeth along the full length of his shaft. When she looked up at him, his eyes were half shut and his hips were thrusting forward, ramming his penis in her mouth. She pulled her mouth away and raised the whip then gave his swollen penis another flick. Then she made the whip dance along the top and curl around the underside, pulling him up and down. The low, animal sounds escaping from deep in his throat inflamed her lust and she smiled at the results of her handiwork.

She was relentless and she knew this was exactly the way he wanted her to be. She led him on in an agonising dance; teasing and taunting him but never letting him come. She stopped once and slid her hands between his legs and cupped his testicles; they felt heavy with passion and cold to the touch. She weighed them in her hand for a moment then gave them a little pinch. He flinched, then groaned as the pain turned to pleasure. She licked her hand and clamped it around him. She began sliding her hand up and down his cock, pulling and squeezing as she twisted him in many different directions. He grunted and panted and reached for her but she wouldn't be touched. She would flick him and service him until he came the way he liked to come, she thought. He was going to get what the man in the picture was never able to have and she was going to be the one to give it to him. In her mind, clouded now with passion, she was convinced that by her actions she would be altering history.

Katherine was feeling a little crazy now, caught up in some drama that had been frozen in time a long while ago. She bent her mouth to his cock and began lapping and nipping the full length of him. Then she let him go and feathered the whip over the tender flesh on the inside of his thighs, dragging it slowly over his penis then flicking him lightly. He was shaking from head to toe and moaning in ecstasy.

She liked to see that. It made her feel powerful and

incredibly excited. She took the tight, throbbing head of his swollen cock between her lips again and sucked him hungrily.

She let him go and looked up at him with a smile. 'I'm going to make you come. Would you like that? Would you like to come for me?' she asked.

She slipped the handle of the whip into his mouth and held it there. In a frenzy, he began sucking and pulling at it. Her free hand closed around his quivering rod and began milking him. Finally, he fell back in the chair exhausted, thrusting forward over and over but still unable to come.

Instinctively, she knew he would not be able to come until she said the words he needed to hear.

'You will have to get down on your knees and beg,' she whispered.

He fell on his knees and lifted his cock up towards the whip she was holding over him. 'Please,' he begged. 'Please. I have to have it.'

He moaned as she played the whip around his penis over and over again, lightly flicking and teasing him into a frenzy. Then she took him in her mouth one last time and grazed his quivering length with her small, white teeth for a few moments before stopping to admire her anonymous plaything.

'Now, you can come. You can come now because *I* give you my permission,' she whispered.

With a strange, high-pitched wail, he jerked forward and climaxed, his penis surging in spasm after spasm as it spurted his seed across the room.

As he reached his peak, Katherine used one hand to flick his penis with the whip and the other to palm her breast. The minute he collapsed back in the chair, she turned the whip towards herself and slid the cold silver end deep inside her aching pussy. For a moment, her inner lips recoiled from the icy touch of the metal, then fluttered crazily against it. She waited a split second then slid it over her clitoris. The minute the cold metal touched the hard pulsing nub, she came in a quick harsh climax that left her breathless. She collapsed panting on the floor.

She could hardly believe that she had just taken part in this strange yet deeply exciting experience. She was stunned at the way she had acted but, at the same time, she was filled with a kind of intense satisfaction she had never felt before.

Later that evening, she and her companions from breakfast were gathered in the blue room having after-dinner coffee. For some reason she did not dare to admit, Alan kept staring at her. Katherine felt mildly flattered but somewhat irritated. After all, she thought, this isn't school. If he's got something he wants to say, why the hell doesn't he just come right out and say it? She decided to ignore Alan's peculiar behaviour. She was much more concerned about Assam. He was nowhere to be seen. At breakfast, he had said he might meet them here. So far, he had not put in an appearance.

She started to pace restlessly back and forth in front of the fireplace, nervously sipping her coffee. At one point, she caught a glimpse of herself in the large mirror that hung over the mantelpiece. She had to admit she looked stunning. Her skin was glowing and was dramatically offset by her dark red evening gown. It was a designer's original made of the finest satin. The yards of material in the full-length skirt billowed out from her tiny waist in soft voluminous folds, giving her a very romantic look. However, underneath her magnificent gown, Katherine didn't feel romantic;

she felt entirely different. This evening, she had decided to wear only her red suspender belt and sheer black stockings. She felt deliciously naughty walking around with no knickers underneath her long gorgeous dress. She loved the way the smooth, cool satin caressed the tangle between her legs every time she moved. The strapless bodice could barely contain her magnificent breasts which looked lush and inviting as they swelled out over the skin-tight top. She had worn this dress on purpose. She had wanted to dazzle Assam. Now it looked like he wasn't going to show up after all. Dinner had been over for a half an hour and still he hadn't appeared. She couldn't deny the sharp pang of disappointment in the pit of her stomach. For her, the whole evening would be a waste if he didn't show up.

The others were getting ready to leave and she didn't know what to do. Should she wait for him and then feel like a fool if he didn't make an appearance? Or should she just call it a night and forget about him? People began drifting out into the hall. Not sure what to do, she just stood staring into the fire.

She felt a light touch on her shoulder. She jumped nervously and whirled around; it was Alan. In that brief second when their eyes met, she suddenly knew for sure what she had suspected. He was the man she had met in the library that afternoon. The one she had controlled with such relish! Her stomach muscles tightened and she fell backward a few steps in utter amazement.

'That's right, Katherine,' he murmured, seeing the realisation dawn in her eyes. 'May I say, you were magnificent. Perhaps we can meet again soon?'

Without waiting for her response, he turned and left her standing by the fire in a state of shock. She was instantly transported to her wild encounter with him that afternoon. The memory of the powerful sex they had shared overwhelmed her and she began to tremble uncontrollably.

It was at that moment that Assam chose to enter the room. He saw the state she was in and quickly led her over to a chair where he helped her to sit down.

'My dear Miss MacNeil, whatever is the matter? Is there anything I can do to help?'

His obvious solicitude calmed her and, before long, she regained her composure and her legs stopped shaking. 'I'm not sure what it is,' she stalled.

What a time for him to walk in, she fumed inwardly. Now what was she going to do? She was at a disadvantage right from the start and she didn't like that one little bit.

'You look pale. I think you should get some air. Come. We can go out into the rose garden. It's not far from here.'

Wordlessly, she followed him out of the room. Maybe some air would calm her nerves, she thought, cursing Alan for his timing. When they reached the French doors, Assam took her arm and led her outside.

She drew a deep breath. The night was enchanting. The garden was bathed in the soft silver light of a full moon and the air was fragrant with the scent of flowers. She sat down on a small, white wicker couch and tried to relax. She was calming down now and was starting to feel more than a little foolish.

'I'm sorry,' she murmured. 'I really don't know what came over me.'

'Please don't apologise. Sometimes, life can be quite stressful even when one is on holiday.'

He smiled at her and she gasped inwardly at how magnificent he looked in the moonlight. He was wearing a tuxedo and his neat frame filled it out to perfection.

'You are very beautiful, Katherine. May I call you Katherine?' he whispered, as his hand reached out to stroke her shining black hair which she had swept up into an elegant French knot for the evening.

She nodded but said nothing. She was surprised at his touch but she did not pull away. It felt like the most natural thing in the world to be touched by him. She sighed and let him caress her hair. Maybe something was going to happen between them after all. She lay back against the couch and sighed. His hands felt so wonderful. She relaxed under his touch and gave a long deep sigh.

'May I touch you?' he asked.

Startled by this direct approach, she could only give silent permission and watch in fascination as he moved his hand down over her breasts. She drew in a sharp breath as he gently trailed his fingers back and forth over the smooth material of her dress, concentrating on the area directly over her nipples. She loved being caressed through material like this. It always excited her so much and now was no exception. She sighed softly as he moved his hand on to her bare flesh and trailed his finger down into the deep valley of her cleavage.

'Your bodice is very tight,' he murmured. 'It is hard to do what I want. Sometimes though, being restrained only adds to the pleasure, does it not?'

He ran his finger along the edge of her bodice. Beneath the material, her nipples were hard nubs.

'You like the way I touch you, don't you?' he whispered, gazing down at her nipples which were straining against the blood-red satin of her dress.

Katherine was so overwhelmed she couldn't speak.

She could only watch as he reached out and gathered up the folds of satin that surrounded her nipples and rolled the hard tips between his thumb and forefinger. She had never reacted to someone's touch like this before. She moaned and licked her dry lips. She was on fire. His fingers were like tiny little flames, burning and searing her skin right through her dress. She felt him reach for the clasp at the back of her bodice and did nothing to stop him. Instead, she moved a little closer so he could reach it. He undid the clasp at the top of the zip which eased the bodice a little but he didn't pull the zip down any further. Confused, she looked up at him. He smiled and said nothing. Quietly, he reached inside her dress and pulled out her left breast. It glowed like white alabaster in the moonlight. He ran his hands over its creamy fullness, cupping it, then massaging it lightly. She moaned and lay back against his arm as his thumb rubbed her taut, aching nipple.

'I think you are an instrument I might just like to play,' he whispered, lowering his mouth to her nipple.

She cupped her breast and offered it to him, her whole body pulsing with the nearness and the male smell of him. He touched her nipple very lightly with the tip of his tongue. Wild shivers of pleasure skittered over her skin and a long sigh escaped from her lips. He kissed her lightly on the engorged tip, pulled it softly between his lips and sucked on it once, hard, then stopped. She let out a little cry and her eyes flew open, a wild question in their velvety depths.

Without a word, he picked her up and carried her to the low stone wall that surrounded the garden. Very gently, he sat her down on the edge of the wall. Sitting like that, her knees were level with his face. When he started inching her dress up her legs, she trembled in anticipation. When it was finally up around her thighs, he spread her legs very wide then stood back and stared at her for a long time. She knew how she must look sitting there half-dressed, her naked crotch barely hidden in the shadows of her dress.

Slowly, he walked up to her. Then, very slowly, he slid his hand in between her legs and spread his fingers among her damp curls.

Katherine gasped at this sweet invasion into her most secret area. One of his fingers inched its way along her crease then gently began scratching her quivering labia. She shuddered and groaned softly. As he played with her pussy he looked straight into her eyes.

'You are plump and luscious, just like a ripe fig; all swollen and tender, oozing sweet juices,' he murmured huskily, then licked his lips. 'I would very much like to taste this fruit that is so ready for the taking.'

Katherine gasped at his obvious intent and she lurched forward.

He reached out and caught her before she fell. She could hear him telling her to hang on to the edge of the wall with her hands. Then she watched as he took up his former position between her thighs and slowly slid his hands up her long shapely legs, so inviting in their sheer black nylon stockings. She shuddered violently when his hands touched her and her legs began to tremble.

He smiled at her reaction. Then, very slowly, he snaked his hands even further up her legs. When he reached the top of her stockings, he moved closer so he could slide her legs underneath his arms. Then he eased her dress further up her legs so the tops of her stockings and the areas of thigh flesh above were exposed.

She sighed deeply as he lowered his mouth. She felt drunk with his attentions and the heady scent of roses. She tensed her legs under his waiting mouth. His soft lips kissed the tops of her stockings and the naked space above. When he stuck out his tongue and licked her bare flesh, she gasped aloud. His mouth was so near her pussy, she could feel his hot breath on her. She squirmed under his ministrations. She loved his touch. She wanted more. She wanted him to touch her pussy again. He electrified her. The feeling of his mouth so near her sex sent delicious little thrills dancing over her skin. She trembled under his exquisite touch and his tantalising nearness. When he bared his teeth and took a few sharp nips, she cried out in delight. She tried to touch him but he gently pushed her hands away.

'Not tonight,' he murmured. He reached down and began taking off her shoes.

Katherine was completely overcome with his sensuality. He was caressing her feet now, running his nails over the soles and pushing his fingers in between her toes. She felt so overwrought, she couldn't contain herself. She felt the tears well up in her eyes and she threw her head back and clutched the edge of the wall. Her entire body was quivering from head to toe.

'I knew you would be like this,' he whispered.

He lowered his mouth to the top of her stockings again and ran his teeth along the edge of them, sucking and nipping as he went. She could hardly breathe; she was awash in a sea of aching sensuality. She shivered as he slid his hands up and down her silky legs. When he reached the top of her stockings, he stopped. His fingers plucked at the parts of her suspender belt which held up her stockings. He opened his mouth and started to suck on them, every now and then stopping to lick her naked flesh.

She felt his fingers tugging at the little clamps. She had never been teased and subjected to such wanton sensuality. Her senses were reeling and her body was still quivering with excitement. He moved at an agonising pace. She wanted him to hurry but, at the same time, she did not want to give up this slow delicious torture.

He unfastened first one stocking, then the other. When they were both undone he turned his attention to only one. This he began to peel off her leg, bending to kiss and nip at her skin as he slowly pulled it down. Finally, he eased the stocking over her foot. Then he brought it up to his mouth and inhaled deeply.

'Your scent is overpowering,' he said as he let the stocking fall in a soft little pool on the grass.

Katherine was trembling so hard, she thought she was going to faint. He was playing her like a master plays his instrument and she was responding with eager abandon.

She looked down at her body. Her breast was on display, her left leg was bare and her dress was thrown up around her waist, exposing the dark tangle between her legs: she looked like a wanton. This thought aroused her even further and she could feel her dew soaking through the back of her dress. She looked down at the man between her legs. He was holding her bare leg in his hands and was kissing and sucking the naked flesh in the hollow just behind her knee. As he kissed and licked her flesh, he kept running his fingers up and down the silky surface of her other leg. The contrasting sensations were delicious and she fell even deeper into a vortex of sensual pleasure. She felt sated, heavy, her senses reeling, but still she was hungry for more.

'Do you now know incredibly sensual you are?' he muttered against her leg. 'Perhaps, after tonight ...' his voice trailed off into the warm night air.

She cried out in protest when he turned from her suddenly and walked over to the other side of the garden. To her relief, he returned in seconds, carrying some soft green ferns and one red rose.

Before she could guess what he was going to do, he feathered the ferns over her breasts. She sighed deeply as he dragged the soft wisps over her naked flesh and began teasing the aching nub of her inflamed nipple. Every now and then, he would lower his mouth and kiss the tip of her nipple or give it a little nip with his teeth and she would groan and thrust her breast towards him. She did nothing to stop this dizzying assault on her senses. She couldn't. She was completely under his spell and that was exactly where she wanted to be.

As the evening wore on, her moans of ecstasy echoed in the still night air as he initiated her further into his secret world of sensual delights. Not once did she ask him to stop and not once did he find an end to her intoxicating charms.

It was almost midnight when she heard him speak for the last time. She was lying on the cool grass, her dress bunched up around her waist, her hair loose and flowing down over her bare breast. Some of the shiny dark strands were tied around her nipple and her arms were bound above her head with long strands of ivy. On her mound, sprigs of violets and shreds of rose petals were woven in and out of her dark pubic curls.

'You look like a precious flower in that dress,' he

whispered, as he bent over her and very lightly brushed her curly tangle with his lips.

She caught her breath as he picked up a rose and traced the outline of her lips. When her lips began to tremble, he slipped the flower down to her cleavage then feathered it over her naked breast, circling then flicking the tight point of her nipple. She was in another world now, a world where only pleasure and sensation existed. She didn't allow herself to think who she was or where she was at this moment and she didn't care. She felt overwhelmed by the exquisite scent of the flowers and by Assam's relentless touch: those long slender fingers that probed, explored and ornamented her with flowers. Now, she could feel him dragging the soft silky rose over her naked breast. He trailed it lazily over the tip of her nipple then slid it down her arm, across her mound, then down in between her legs to the tender flesh on the inside of her thighs. She strained at the ivy that bound her, groaning softly as her sensitive skin responded to the silky rose petals. Her pussy lips quivered. She caught her breath as he snaked it up and down her inner thighs, sometimes brushing over the dark bush between her legs, sometimes hovering just above it.

'This rose has a thorn,' he whispered. 'All beautiful things do. I am willing to guess you have thorns too, Katherine. Only they are not on the outside like this one. I think I would enjoy exploring those thorns with you sometime.'

She tried to speak but she couldn't seem to find her voice. She stared at his hand moving the rose up and down her skin.

'You please me greatly,' he announced calmly. 'I think soon you will be ready to spend an entire night with me. I'm afraid all this has been a bit too over-whelming for you. I apologise.'

He untied her hands and laid her across his lap. Then he stuck his finger in her mouth and slid it back and forth over her tongue a few times. A long drawn out moan escaped her lips as he pulled his finger out of her mouth and slid it deep into her vagina. She was completely under his spell, in a dream state where the only thing that mattered was his touch. What was he doing to her? It was glorious exquisite torture. She never wanted him to stop, never. She couldn't believe what he was doing. He was so calm, so confident. She had never felt so moved by a sexual encounter. His fingers were deep inside her, rubbing her in places no other man had ever explored; places which yielded up intense, agonising delights. She felt as if her whole body were dissolving. This can't be happening, she thought. But it was happening and she was almost fainting from the sensations washing over her.

After a few moments, his expert ministrations started a series of deep pulsating waves that rose and fell deep in her vagina. Her mouth opened in a silent scream as they peaked and flooded through her body, inundating her entire being with a pleasure she could not name.

Her cries were still echoing in the warm night air when he untied her hands, bowed, and walked out of the garden – leaving her lying on the grass like a crushed rose in the moonlight.

Chapter Five

Katherine rode into the courtyard at a good clip then stopped in front of the stable and dismounted. Her hair was wildly dishevelled and her eyes were sparkling. She felt wonderfully exhilarated after her long ride through the grounds of the estate. She had never ridden an animal so responsive. She reached down and stroked the silky coat of the white Arabian mare. What an extraordinary horse and such a dream to ride! She was light and fast like the wind. It was like riding on a cloud of mist. She more than lived up to her name: Highland Misty.

As usual, after a long ride, there was a delicious throbbing between her legs. The movement of the horse beneath her always stimulated her and by the end of a ride, she was usually in a state of sexual excitement. But she didn't mind. This had always been part of the pleasure of riding for her. And today there had been an added feature. Memories of her breathtaking encounter with Assam the night before kept coming back to excite her even further. Was she

85

ever going to see him again? she wondered. She shivered as she remembered his touch. It was intoxicating. His fingers had set her senses on fire. He had driven her wild, slowly and expertly bringing her to the edge of ecstasy over and over until she thought she would go mad. Then, finally, when he had brought her the release she craved, she had been totally swept away by the force of her response. He had been so selfless throughout their late-night tryst. He hadn't once released his penis from the confines of his trousers and must have retired to his room with a fierce hard on. She remembered the feel of his hands and his mouth on the most intimate parts of her body and her nipples stiffened. She ached to see him again.

She wrenched her thoughts away from him and led her horse into the stable where the groom was waiting for her.

'Did you have a good ride, Miss MacNeil?' he asked with a friendly smile, taking Misty by the bridle and leading her into her stall.

'The best ever, Johnny. I really appreciate your choosing Misty for me. She was wonderful.'

'I knew she would be perfect for you, miss,' he replied, his eyes dropping to Katherine's breasts and lingering there for a few seconds.

Katherine's cheeks burned. She knew her nipples were tight and pushing against the sheer fabric of her riding shirt.

Silently, Johnny continued grooming her horse. The atmosphere was suddenly charged with sexual tension.

'She's wild, just like you,' he said suddenly.

Katherine was at a loss for words and her breath started to come more quickly when he sauntered slowly over in her direction. He stopped right in front of her, blocking her view of the rest of the stable.

'My stallion, Thunder, services that little mare every chance he gets,' he drawled. 'And she's such a hot little thing, she lets him do it whenever he wants. She whinnies and gives those high little shrieks. It just sends shivers through you. And then when he fucks her, she snorts and tosses her head real wild like. It's a sight to behold, it really is. It gets me real hot and bothered sometimes.

Katherine stood motionless, stunned at his crude talk. She could hardly believe her ears but when she looked into his dark eyes, she knew he wanted her and that he was determined to have her right then and there. She tried to move away but he stepped closer.

'The first time I saw you, I knew you were wild and beautiful just like Misty here. I knew if someone gave you a good ride, you would cry and whinny just like her. I know you pretend to be all cool and ladylike but underneath you're hot, miss – real hot. I can tell.'

Repelled by his barnyard talk, Katherine tried again to step around him but he blocked her way. In a panic, she tried to push past him but he didn't budge. Her breasts brushed against his arm. This seemed to ignite the situation and, before she could stop him, he swept her up in his arms and started walking towards one of the empty stalls.

'What do you think you're doing?' she gasped, wriggling in his arms. 'Put me down this instant. You have no right to . . . Johnny, stop.'

'Oh, now, don't waste your time pretending with me, miss. I know what you want and I'm just the man to give it to you. I'm going to give you the ride of your life. Pretty soon you'll be tossing your head and whinnying just like Misty here. We're going to have a fine time together. Just you wait and see.'

Katherine struggled in his arms but it was no use. He was a magnificent specimen of a man with a well-developed muscular torso, lithe tapering hips and a grip like iron.

'Please put me down, Johnny,' she whimpered, squirming in his arms. 'I don't want this. I don't feel that way about you.'

'Oh, come on now, miss,' he said, smiling down at her. 'I know you want what I've got. If it wasn't so obvious, I wouldn't bother.'

He kicked the stall door open, set her down on her feet, and pushed her up against the wall.

When she felt his hard maleness grinding into her, Katherine felt something give way inside her. Suddenly, she didn't feel like struggling. She was amazed at herself. In spite of her weak protests, his lewd, rather brutish approach was actually getting to her and her breath was coming quick and fast.

Johnny looked her right in the eye and continued talking to her as he held her against the wall with his lower body and placed his big square hands on her breasts. Slowly, he began to massage them and flick her nipples with his thumb.

'I bet they feel even sweeter without that shirt,' he muttered, reaching for the buttons.

Katherine wriggled against him but this only served to inflame him further and he ground his pelvis into hers. One by one, he loosened the buttons of her shirt until it was open to her waist. He stood for a moment gazing down at her full breasts swelling in luscious mounds over the half cups of her bra. Then he grasped them with both hands and began moving his thumbs over the material that covered her nipples. Katherine moaned as they peaked under his touch. Then, very slowly, he pulled the material of her bra down, exposing the hard jutting tips of her nipples.

'Oh, miss, your nipples are so hard,' he groaned.

He undid the front clasp of her bra and her heavy breasts tumbled free into his waiting hands. She could feel her juices flowing into the crotch of her panties as he continued to whisper his special kind of sexy talk in her ear.

As his desire became more urgent, he pressed harder against her. She gasped when she felt the bulge in his pants and her mind went wild with images of what he looked like naked.

'Your breasts feel so heavy, just like ripe fruit ready for eating,' he whispered in her ear.

Katherine arched her back and thrust her breasts forward to meet his touch.

He lowered his mouth and began raining little kisses on her breasts, darting his tongue over her puckered nipples. Then he clamped his mouth down on one of the tight little peaks and began to suck it until it was taut and fully extended. Katherine wriggled in his arms, grinding her pelvis against the bulge in his pants and moaning aloud as he turned his attention to her other breast, which swelled and quivered under his knowing fingers.

'Oh, it feels so good,' Katherine said and dug her fingers into his hair. His mouth was hot and wet, his tongue was skilful. She could hardly bear the sensation as he moved it back and forth over her swollen breasts. She gasped out loud when he pulled away and stood looking at her.

'I can't stand here playing with your beautiful breasts all day,' he muttered, his breath coming faster now. 'I want to be inside you, miss, deep inside. I want to feel your hot pussy around my cock. And I want us to do it right here in the stall, standing up like horses. I'm going to be your stallion, miss. And you're going to be my mare. You're going to have a ride you'll never forget.'

Very slowly, he slid one hand down to her waist and loosened the opening to her jodhpurs. They fell down around her ankles revealing her voluptuous hips. She shuddered as his gaze travelled the length of her body. She knew how she must look standing there, her full breasts naked, her damp pussy hair escaping in little tendrils around the crotch of her flimsy bikini panties which were soaking now with her dew. She ached for him. She wanted him to stick his cock deep inside her and she wanted him to do it to her right here in the barn just like an animal in heat. She strained her hips toward him. Her pussy was hot and she ached to feel his fingers part her delicate folds and stroke her clit.

Slowly, he inched his hand down inside her panties. 'You're so wet, miss, so ready,' he said as his huge hand cupped her entire vulva. His palms were rough and calloused but she loved the feel of them on her smooth, sensitive flesh. Slowly, he began rubbing her, moving his hand in slow circles, grazing her tender skin with his sharp nails.

She writhed beneath his touch. She felt drunk with his male scent and the pungent odours of the barn. She felt like a wild horse who had just been captured by a dark gypsy man who was now using all his tricks to tame her and make her his. He kept talking to her, touching her, teasing her until she was crazy with excitement.

He eased her panties down over her hips and let them fall in a soft little heap at her feet. She was now naked from the waist down. Johnny stopped for a moment and ran his eyes up and down her trembling body. Then he slid his hand back into the warm wet valley between her legs and gently ran his nails back and forth along her quivering pussy lips, tickling and teasing her until she was gasping for breath. Her wiry pubic curls were wet and slick with her dew. He wound them around his finger and gave them a little pull. Then he dragged one finger slowly back and forth along her moist crease, playing with the soft fur that rimmed the entrance to her secret pleasure centre. She gasped softly when he drew her outer lips apart and, very slowly, insinuated his fingers into her silky folds. She was wet and hot and his fingers slid easily along the shaft of her clitoris.

'Oh, yes, Johnny, yes.'

'You're so wet, miss,' he said. 'So wet with your sweet honey.'

He knelt down in front of her and pressed his mouth up against her sex. She could feel his hot breath on her and went weak at the knees then thrust her hips forward in anticipation. He stuck out his tongue and ran it slowly along her dark moist cleft then began lapping her in long, deliberate strokes. Katherine moaned as he licked her, tossing her head from side to side as he slid his tongue deeper and deeper, exploring and discovering every inch of her delicate flesh. Slowly, he dragged it back and forth along the shaft of her clitoris. Her hips were trembling so violently he had to clamp his hands on either side of her to hold her still. Then his tongue found the head of her clitoris. It was swollen and protruding proudly from beneath its hood. It was pulsing against his tongue. He closed his mouth around it and began sucking and pulling on it until she was gasping for breath.

'Oh, God, it feels so good, so good, oh God,' Katherine moaned, thrusting her hips forward to meet his hot foraging tongue. She was aflame now, all thoughts of resistance long gone.

'That's enough now,' Johnny muttered, lifting his head from her moist sex. 'I can't stand any more. I've played with you long enough. I want to feel your sweet pussy around my cock and I want it now.'

He stood up and unzipped his flies. His penis sprang free from the confines of his tight pants. She looked at him and shuddered. He was huge. His cock was thick and stubby, twitching with passion. He took her arms and put them around his neck, then lifted her so that her legs went around his middle.

When she was in position, he pushed past her outer lips and entered her fully. He slid easily into her wet tunnel, penetrating her so deeply that she gasped out loud. Slowly, he began pumping. She rammed her hips forward to meet the thrust of his hard shaft and groaned loudly when he almost hit the back of her womb. She sucked in her breath; he was enormous. He filled her completely, stretching her, probing the very depth of her. He penetrated her deeply, slowly, thrusting back and forth, each time sliding more deeply into her. She wanted him to ride her long and hard. She felt wild, like a horse being tamed under its master's touch. He continued whispering his explicit intentions in her ear until she felt crazy with passion.

'Oh, you feel so good, miss, so good,' he said as he scythed his penis in and out. 'You're so hot and tight. You hold me just right. I love the way my cock feels way up inside you and the way your pussy sucks on me. Oh, God, you're such a hot little mare. I'm just the stallion you need to help put out your fire'

With each word, he pumped faster and faster. Katherine was moving with him now, grunting out her pleasure as he plundered the deepest part of her. Automatically, her vaginal muscles closed around him and she began milking him as hard as she could.

Katherine felt transported. She didn't care about anything. Her whole world had narrowed down to Johnny's penis and the pleasure it was giving her. She knew they were both near the edge and could feel her orgasm beginning to build. She couldn't believe she was going to come so fast but she didn't want to wait; she wanted to come now.

'Make me come, Johnny, make me come now,' she panted, rubbing her swollen breasts against the coarse wiry hair on his chest.

Johnny placed one hand on her buttocks and pressed her hard against him. His cock penetrated so deeply it seemed to graze the back of her womb. Katherine threw her head back and arched her back as she thrust and ground her hips on his pulsing shaft. He reached down in the space between them and inserted his finger into her cleft. Her clitoris was swollen and rigid. He pinched it gently. Katherine gasped and bucked wildly against him as he rammed his cock into her up to the hilt.

Then her orgasm grabbed her and her whole body seemed to dissolve. A flood of pleasure filled her and her inner muscles grabbed at his pulsing rod. With a shudder, Johnny surged within her and they were both swept away in the enveloping tide of their mutual climax.

Gasping and panting, Katherine clung to Johnny. She was too weak to stand on her own and his big strong legs provided the support they both needed as their bodies continued to shake and tremble in the aftermath of their orgasms.

After a few moments, Johnny whispered in her ear, 'Now we're going to do it horsie style.'

Keeping her legs wrapped around him, he walked over to the middle of the stall then pulled her off him and laid her gently down on a pile of sweet-smelling hay.

'When you were out getting hot riding your horse this afternoon, I was in here cleaning out this stall so it would be all ready for us when you came back.'

Katherine looked up at him standing over her and stretched sensuously. She enjoyed the feel of the soft prickles of the hay on her naked flesh. She knew what she must look like lying there, her breasts swollen, the wiry curls in her dark tangle damp from their love making.

Johnny stood looking down at her, feasting his eyes on her luscious body. Then he picked up a little piece of hay and knelt down beside her. Very slowly, he trailed it over her naked breasts, circled the tender flesh around her nipples, then teased the raw tips ever so lightly.

She trembled beneath his touch, intoxicated by the male smell of him and the sweet fragrance of the newly mown hay.

He feathered the hay strand over her mound and slowly inched it down her abdomen until it was between her legs. She moved lasciviously beneath his touch and spread her legs even wider. He smiled knowingly but continued moving at a snail's pace. She moaned in anticipation and lifted her hips in invitation. But Johnny would not be rushed and proceeded to tease and tickle her legs and lower belly just above her bush, lowering the piece of hay inch by inch until he reached the sensitive skin on the insides of her thighs.

Katherine was whimpering and moaning, her hands feverishly pulling on her nipples. Gently, Johnny ran his nails up and down her legs and across her abdomen – each time stopping just short of her damp pussy curls. She sighed as he teased and tickled her quivering flesh. She was desperate to feel him part her swollen outer lips and slip his fingers deeper into her pleasure centre.

'Please,' she begged. 'I want to feel your fingers inside me.'

She gasped as he used his fingers to part her outer lips. He inserted the little piece of hay and began gently jabbing and probing her most sensitive flesh with its rough tip. Exquisite little points of pleasure danced over her delicate folds and radiated deep into her vagina. When it was clear she couldn't take much more, he put down the piece of hay and ran one finger along the moist lips of her sex. She was desperate to feel his thick cock inside her again. She felt drugged with his teasing. Every nerve in her body was pulsing, screaming for more.

'It's time to stop playing, miss, and get to it,' he murmured, his voice thick with lust.

He turned her on to her stomach and, using his legs, urged her up on her knees. She responded to his touch and quickly got up on all fours. Instinctively, she arched her back, revealing her pouting sex. Her heart was beating wildly and she could hardly breathe. She was acting like a barnyard animal; a female animal that wanted only one thing and was determined to get it.

He mounted her quickly. He felt for the wet swollen

lips of her sex, put his cock between them, and slid into her once more. She arched her back to meet him as he penetrated deep into her. She caught her breath again at the size of him; he was so thick and hard.

'Oh, God, Johnny, do it. Do it,' she whimpered as she felt the hot dry hardness of him thrusting inside her.

'I'm so lucky you came here this week, miss, so lucky,' he said as he pumped his penis in and out. 'You're a real lusty little mare. I'm going to fuck you long and hard like a good stallion should until you whinny just like Misty,' he panted.

With each word, he penetrated more deeply. She grunted out her pleasure. She was moving with him now, her head tossing from side to side as she slid back and forth on his pumping cock. Her passion had been reignited very quickly and she could feel the tides of an orgasm rising in her again. She knew they were both ready to come. She didn't want to wait any longer. She reached down and rubbed the fleshy head of her clitoris with one hand and fingered her nipples with the other. Her legs tensed as her orgasm began to build. As it seized her in its searing grip, she squeezed down on Johnny's penis as hard as she could.

Johnny roared his pleasure and she shuddered as she felt him pulse and surge inside her. Panting and groaning, they climaxed in unison then fell breathless in the soft hay.

A few moments elapsed before either of them made a move. Then, slowly, Johnny rolled over on his back and stretched.

They must have dozed for about half an hour and Katherine awoke feeling wonderful. Tingles of pleasure radiated through her body and still she yearned for more. Johnny had opened the floodgates and nothing was going to stop her until she was completely satisfied. She looked over at him lying on the straw. His big penis, only half erect now, was protruding from his open fly. Her mouth began to water. Then, out of the corner of her eye, she saw a small riding crop hanging on the wall. Feeling a new sense of excitement, she got up and walked quickly across the stall. She slipped the crop off the hook and walked back to Johnny's reclining figure.

Without a word, she pulled his legs apart and slid her hand inside his flies. When her fingers closed around his penis, it reared in her grasp. In a matter of seconds, it had elongated under her touch and was twitching and pulsing in 'her hands. She gently ran her finger along the length of his rod, raking her nails through the hair at its base. Her fist closed around him and she squeezed and milked him quickly, bringing grunts of satisfaction to his lips. Then, slowly, she took him in her mouth. He felt big and thick and velvety smooth. She lapped the full length of him then ran her tongue around the ridge of the head, teasing and flicking, then pushing into the tiny little hole at the very tip. His groans and cries egged her on as she reached further inside his trousers and cupped his balls, opening and closing her hands to exert a varying amount of of pressure on them. Johnny panted loudly and began thrusting between her lips, grunting low animal sounds. She loved to hear the effect she was having on him. It made her feel powerful. She was in control. She was the one making things happen. He was in her power now; his pleasure was totally dependent on her. This knowledge acted like an aphrodisiac on her and she sucked him even harder.

Just when it seemed like he was about to come, she

withdrew her mouth and grabbed at his pants. He raised his hips and she pulled them off.

'Now, I'm going to ride *you*,' she muttered.

She straddled him and slowly lowered herself on to his penis. She threw her head back and took a long deep breath. She loved the feel of his wonderful hard cock. She began riding him, looking straight into his eyes, her hands playing with his nipples then teasing her own. She arched back, pulling on his inflamed organ. He cried out at the delicious torture. She rose and fell on him, pleasuring herself, making sure it touched her in all the right places. She angled herself so that her clitoris rubbed against his stalk, tangled her hands in his thick pubic hair and clenched her fingers around the base of his penis and began squeezing. He was going wild beneath her. She rode him harder and harder, finding endless ways to increase their pleasure. The feel of his cock sliding in and out of her wet tunnel, grazing her clit when she moved in just the right way, sent thrills of sexual ecstasy racing through her. This was what she had craved for so long and now she was going to savour every moment of it. Then, with fiendish delight, she stopped and rolled off him. He cried out in protest.

'Not yet,' she crooned. 'Not just yet. Now, I want *you* to get up on all fours. You can be *my* horse now.'

She knew he didn't want to do this but she also knew she could make him do whatever she wanted. He was very near his climax and she was the only one who could give him that release. She loved the feeling of being in control. It acted like an aphrodisiac on her and she shivered in delight.

With a flourish, she picked up the little crop that was lying beside her on the floor of the stall. He was kneeling in front of her now. She ran her hands over his firm buttocks then slowly inserted the handle of the crop into his bum crack. He recoiled and cried out sharply but she would not be deterred. Slowly, she began rubbing it back and forth across his puckered arsehole, egging him on as if he were her mount. She knew this would drive him crazy and she was right. She smiled as he began to grind his buttocks to match the movement of the crop. Then, very slowly, she eased its hard leather tip into his hole, shoving it deep into his anus. He cried out sharply with a mixture of pain and pleasure then began thrusting his buttocks in time to the rhythm of her skilful hands. She twisted and churned the short leather handle in and out until he was moving wildly and growls of pleasure were wrenched from his throat. She knew he was almost ready to come but she was not going to allow that. Not yet.

'Now I'm going to give you the ride of your life,' she whispered. 'Turn over.'

He moaned and fell over on his back. His cock was long and hard, a glistening little drop on its inflamed tip. She put down the crop and straddled him again. When she lowered herself on to his rod, she leant close to his mouth so that her heavy breasts grazed his lips. She stayed like that for a few seconds and let him suck her nipples, then pulled away and, arching her back, began to ride him. She could feel the tides of her passion rising once more and she began to move more quickly. She rolled her nipples between her thumb and forefinger and slid her fingers down over the hard nub of her clitoris. She stroked and caressed herself as Johnny pumped faster and faster. She could feel her climax building. She looked down at his face which was suffused with passion and smiled.

'I'm going to give you a climax you'll never forget,' she whispered, as she pinched one of his nipples.

She tightened her vaginal muscles around him again and grabbed the base of his cock with her hands to exert the faintest pressure on this sensitive spot.

'Oh, Jesus,' he moaned, reaching for her breasts.

Katherine smiled at his reaction and rode him even harder. Then she felt him tense beneath her. With a growl, he began to climax. Gasping with her own mounting pleasure, she rode him through it, impaling herself on his surging member over and over until her own orgasm engulfed her. When it was over, she fell panting and sated on his chest.

After a few moments, she got up and dressed. Then, after kissing him lightly on the mouth, she whispered goodbye and walked out of the barn, leaving him sprawled naked in the stall behind her.

The sex had been great but she felt no desire to stay and talk. There was no real connection between them except for the terrific chemical attraction and she felt no need to pretend there was. She was sure Johnny felt the same way.

As she walked, her thoughts turned to other matters. So much had been happening to her lately. She had to have some time alone to reflect and assess her situation. Instinctively, she headed down to the beach. She needed to be by the sea. She always did her best thinking by the water.

The beach was deserted. She lay down on the hot sand and tried to clarify her thoughts. She had taken advantage of a lot of opportunities lately and had entered into every one of them wholeheartedly. She felt alive and vibrant, more relaxed than she had felt in a long, long time. She realised now she had been starving for good sex for years. For some reason, she had continued this deprivation right up until the present moment. All she ever did was work, work, work. Well, there were going to have to be some drastic changes and the sooner the better. She was already on her way to a more adventurous pesonal life. Why, just in the last few days she had had some wonderful sexual encounters. She knew now how much she had been missing. So far the sex had been exciting and unusual. She had realised too that she enjoyed sex with both men and women. To her surprise, she felt quite comfortable with this fact. Also, much to her astonishment, she had discovered that she liked dominating her partners from time to time. She also found being dominated unbelievably exciting; she enjoyed both the passive and the aggressive role. Each offered their own special kind of sexual excitement. She was pleased with the way her experiment was going and she felt sure things could only get better.

Still, there was something deep inside her that had not been touched and she longed to find out what that was. She felt she had to talk to someone about this feeling that kept tormenting her, the feeling that she was being cheated somehow, that there was some secret door that had to be unlocked before she could really feel free to enjoy her life in all aspects. For years now, she had tried to analyse and understand her feelings but she had always failed.

She realised now that someone else would have to help shed some light on this enigma. She was glad Martha was available and had offered her services. She knew she would talk to her when the time was right.

However, now wasn't the time. Not yet, she told herself. There were still new areas she wanted to explore by herself. Her talk with Martha could wait a little longer. Right now, it was time to stop and just let the sun and the sea breezes work their magic on her. She stretched languorously on the soft warm sand and ran her fingers over her breasts and down over her belly until her fingers were buried between her legs. She caressed herself lazily for a few moments. Delicious, she thought, as the old familiar thrills ran down her legs. Then, with a contented sigh, she closed her eyes and fell into a deep sleep.

Chapter Six

Katherine awoke with a jolt. For a moment, she didn't know where she was. Then she smiled. Oh, that Johnny, she thought. Her nipples stiffened as she remembered the feel of his hands and his mouth on her. She had loved every minute of her time with him. It had been wild, wonderful, but quite exhausting. No wonder she had fallen asleep. She sat up and stretched. She was hot and covered with sand from sleeping on the beach. A swim would feel so good right now, she thought. She looked around. The beach was deserted and the sea looked inviting. She decided to go for a quick dip. In moments, she had stripped off her clothes and was running into the ocean. She gasped as the cool water splashed her hot skin. She took a deep breath, then plunged into an oncoming wave and began swimming vigorously, her body tingling with the sudden change in temperature. She was a strong swimmer and she loved the way her body knifed through the waves. She swam a long way out before she thought about turning back. When she knew she was getting tired, she stopped and turned over on her back and floated for a while. When she felt rested, she did the back stroke for a while then turned over on to her stomach and swam at a leisurely pace back to shore.

When she got near the shore, she saw a woman waving to her from a little way down the beach. It was Jasmine. Katherine stood up in the shallow water and waved back then ran up the beach to meet her. When she remembered she was naked, she stopped dead in her tracks.

'Hi, Katherine. Looks like you're putting your holiday time to good use,' Jasmine exclaimed, her eyes flitting over Katherine's naked breasts.

Katherine smiled back at the blonde woman then walked over to the spot where she had left her clothes. If only she had her bathing suit with her. It would be so much more appropriate than her jodhpurs and blouse which were hot and gritty from lying on the sand. Jasmine had the right idea. She was wearing a skimpy red bikini that barely covered her voluptuous figure.

When she had dressed, Katherine walked over to Jasmine who was sunning herself on a blanket.

'You're right, Jasmine,' Katherine said, plonking herself down beside her. 'I am having a wonderful time.'

Katherine had no intention of sharing any details of her sexual encounters with her blonde acquaintance and decided she would keep the conversation pleasant but non-committal.

'Well, I think you're doing marvellously,' Jasmine continued. 'I know, for me, well, it's always been hard to let go and really follow my instincts. I envy you, Katherine. You don't seem to be having any trouble at all in that area. And you're so independent. I wish I could be like that.'

Katherine smiled but said nothing.

'And now, you have that gorgeous Mr Aswabi under your spell,' Jasmine continued petulantly. 'Hell, I've been coming here for years now and I haven't been able to get the time of day out of him. But you, you're here one day and already he can't take his eyes off you.'

Katherine bristled slightly but her curiosity was piqued. 'What do you mean?'

'Oh, come on, you know what I'm talking about. At breakfast, of course. All the time he was talking to us, he kept staring at you. And when he left, you were the one he directed all his remarks to, you know, about meeting later and everything? Of course, he never did show up after dinner last night, did he?' she added with a triumphant little smile.

Katherine's heart leapt. She was amazed how much Jasmine's words affected her. So, others had noticed his attraction to her. It wasn't just her wishful thinking. It was true he had kept staring at her at breakfast. And, of course, later that evening he had done more than stare, she thought, shivering at the memory of their time together. However, just because they had shared some amazing sex, it didn't mean he was serious about her. It could just have been a casual interlude for him.

Katherine sighed. If only he were here with her right now. She was surprised how much she missed him; he had made more of an impression on her than she realised. The mere mention of his name set her heart racing and her cheeks burned as she remembered his fingers moving deep in her vagina. She glanced quickly at Jasmine to see if she had noticed her reaction but she was staring wistfully out to sea.

Katherine decided she was not going to discuss Assam with Jasmine. The woman seemed just a little too interested. In fact, she seemed to have developed a thing for him herself. It wouldn't do to say anything that might hurt her or make her jealous. Besides, Katherine didn't know what, if anything, was going to happen in the future. She was determined not to spoil her special time with him by gossiping about it with Jasmine. And she certainly wasn't going to build it up to be anything more than it was – either in her mind or in the mind of others.

It suddenly occurred to her that Jasmine had mentioned seeing Assam before. How could that be, she wondered. Was Assam a regular guest here? She was just about to ask Jasmine about this when she saw a man come running up the beach. When he got closer, she saw it was Alan.

'Where have you been?' he exclaimed, directing his question to Katherine. 'Karen and I have found something really fantastic. Come on. I'll show you.'

'Oh, I know what it is. It's that . . .' Jasmine began.

'Don't spoil it for her, Jasmine,' Alan exclaimed impatiently. 'Just because you know – '

'Know what?' Katherine asked, her curiosity piqued.

'I'm not going to tell you. You'll have to come and see for yourself,' he teased.

Katherine felt annoyed at Alan's juvenile tone and decided not to take the bait.

'I really don't know if I'm up to it, Alan. I'm tired and I want to rest for a while. Why don't you come to my room in about a couple of hours and I'll see how I feel then?'

She knew from the look in his eyes that he was

disappointed but she was tired after her swim and the sexual workout with Johnny and she longed for the peace and quiet of her beautiful room.

'OK, I'll see you then,' Alan replied. 'Have a nice rest.' With a wave to both women, he turned and walked off down the beach.

Katherine said goodbye to Jasmine and strolled back up to the house. The minute she got to her room, she put the Do Not Disturb sign on her door then lay down on the bed and tried to sleep. However, after tossing and turning for about fifteen minutes, she knew it was no use. She was much too agitated to sleep. Jumbled images of Assam and Johnny fondling and caressing her were racing through her mind. Finally, she gave up trying and decided to watch some TV in the hope that she would get drowsy and drift off. She reached for the TV remote control and clicked the on button.

To her amazement, the first picture that flickered on to the screen was of a young man and woman making passionate love. The woman's legs were draped over her lover's shoulders and his head was buried between her thighs. The woman moaned loudly as the man licked and sucked every inch of her pussy.

Katherine squirmed against the pillows. What was this? How did this get on the TV screen? Fascinated, she watched as the man wound the woman's dark pubic curls around the tip of his tongue then flattened it out and began licking her pussy lips. When he slid it past her dark crease and shoved it deep inside her, Katherine groaned aloud. She could see the hard nub of the woman's clitoris swelling and sticking out from beneath its hood. The man saw it too and, when he clamped his lips around the fleshy bud, the woman cried out in delight.

Katherine couldn't tear her eyes away from the screen. The woman was panting and writhing. The top of her dress had been pulled down to reveal her full white breasts. They were swollen with passion and her dark nipples were long and tight. Every inch of her gorgeous body was taut with sexual excitement. She kept tensing her legs, stretching them out over her lover's shoulders as she ground her pussy hard against his mouth.

He continued lapping the hard nub of her clitoris, flicking it over and over as she squirmed and panted beneath him.

'Oh, God, yes,' she whimpered as his tongue moved off her sensitive bud and slithered down towards her dark slit.

He hesitated for a moment at her opening and greedily lapped at her juices. The woman groaned as he drank her in then cried out sharply as he slid his tongue inside her, penetrating deep into her vagina. Shuddering, she bucked and ground her hips as his tongue pushed deep into her love tunnel. As she grunted her pleasure, her hips lurched forward to match his rhythm. She cupped her breasts and offered them to his hands as they snaked their way up her belly, blindly reaching for her nipples. With a knowing skill, he fingered her taut peaks until they elongated even further with desire. She was mad with passion, her body shaking and quivering under his relentless touch.

'You taste so good, baby, so good,' he panted, his voice heavy with passion as, once again, he impaled her on his tongue, thrusting it inside her as far as it could go.

His mouth and tongue began moving more quickly on her, bringing her closer and closer to her climax. He was in a rhythm now, spearing his tongue in and out of her slit, then sliding it out to lap the head of her clitoris then returning once again to her dark tunnel. He repeated this glorious torture over and over until she was thrashing on the seat beneath him, her breath coming in short harsh gasps.

Katherine was totally caught up in the passionate scene being enacted before her. Her hands were grabbing at her breasts and rubbing her pussy which was moist now with her flowing juices. As she rubbed herself, she imagined herself to be that girl in the car. She ached to feel her lover's cock part her swollen labia and push deep into her. She wanted him to fill her, to pin her to the seat of the car with his rod, she wanted –

Suddenly, the screen went dark. Katherine gasped in shock. What had happened to the picture? She felt stunned by the sudden interruption. It was as if someone had cheated her of her own orgasm, as if she had been forbidden to experience it. Suddenly, she felt peculiar. She felt as if something very familiar were lurking at the edge of her memory, as if she had experienced all this before. However, try as she might, she could not remember. All she knew was that she felt cheated, thwarted somehow. And then there was the other feeling too, familiar, tantalising, just beyond the reach of her understanding. It was unnerving not to remember. She was hot too, aroused and titillated. For the moment, she didn't have the energy to dwell on the elusive memory. All she knew was she had to get some relief or she was going to go crazy.

She turned off the monitor. It was only then she realised that the programme must have been on the hotel's closed circuit television system. Why would that particular scene have appeared on her monitor? There had been no menu to choose from or anything like that. It had just appeared. It was almost as if someone had planned it, as if someone knew exactly what would get her excited. But how could anyone know that when she was just beginning to find out for herself? Her mind raced with unanswered questions.

She decided to take a shower and headed for the bathroom. The water would wash off the salt from her swim and it would cool her body – which was feverish and overstimulated. Then she remembered Alan. He would be here soon. She decided she would go with him and see what all the fuss was all about. Anything to distract herself from her wild sexual longings.

She had just finished dressing when there was a knock at her door. She went to answer it. It was Alan.

'Have you decided what you want to do?' he asked, his eyes shining like a little boy who had just discovered a jar full of cookies.

Katherine smiled in spite of herself and nodded. 'Lead me to it. I feel ready for anything,' she announced, forcing herself to smile as she stepped out of her room and joined him in the hall.

Silently, he led her down a series of winding corridors into parts of the house she had never seen.

'Where in the world are we?' she asked, bewildered by all the twists and turns.

'I'm not really sure,' Alan answered. 'Karen and I went exploring this morning. We just followed our noses. Wait until you see where we ended up!'

As he spoke, he stopped in front of a huge mahogany wardrobe. He opened the door and pushed a hidden button and the back wall of the wardrobe opened to reveal a secret staircase. He climbed inside and motioned to Katherine to follow him up the steep stairs. She went in after him and began climbing the staircase. There was a musty smell in the air as if no one had been there for a long time. When they reached the top they were in a small room with a huge wooden door. The key was in the lock.

'This is just the way we found it,' Alan explained as he opened the door and ushered her inside.

The moment she stepped into the room, Katherine stopped and looked around in amazement. It was a spacious well appointed room with mirrors on every wall. In front of a huge fireplace, there was a leather armchair and, on a huge bed near the far wall, lay piles of clothing from every imaginable period of history. Karen was standing by the bed, trying on some costumes.

'Look at all this stuff, Katherine,' Alan exclaimed excitedly. 'Isn't it incredible? We've been trying things on for hours. There are clothes from the twenties and all the way back to heaven knows when. Elizabethan times even.'

Katherine was intrigued. Costumes of every description lay in profusion all over the room. The doors to all the closets were open and clothes were spilling out of half-open drawers and draped over the backs of chairs.

'It's like a playroom. You can dress up and pretend to be anybody you want,' she breathed excitedly. 'How did you find this place?'

'We were bored and didn't have anything better to do so we decided to go exploring. We found staircases hidden behind closet doors and secret corridors. It was fantastic. Anyway, we just followed wherever they led and we ended up here. As I said, there was a key in the lock of the door. So, we just walked in,' Alan explained.

'Yeah, we've been having lots of fun, haven't we Alan?' Karen chimed in, pirouetting in front of the mirrors in a dazzling flapper dress.

Katherine was delighted with the vast array of outfits before her. There were dresses from the Edwardian period, with low-cut necklines, some without any bodice at all, clearly designed to display a wide expanse of bare bosom; there were hoop skirts and pantalettes from the antebellum time in the southern United States and velvet gowns in styles dating from the time of Elizabeth I and Mary Queen of Scots.

'What a fabulous place,' Katherine exclaimed. 'You could spend all day trying on these clothes.'

'That's exactly what we have been doing, among other things,' Karen added, smiling mysteriously as she struck a coquettish pose in a velvet bonnet with long satin ribbons. 'Oh, look at this,' she cried, as excitedly as a child, pointing to a red leather bustier, black leather boots, and silver slave bracelets lying in a heap on the bed. 'Now, this is more like it. I'm going to try these on right now.'

Katherine watched as Karen tore her clothes off and poured herself into the skin-tight leather outfit. She had never seen clothes like these but she found them very alluring.

'Hey, Katherine, try this one,' Karen urged her, handing her a black leather bustier with cut-out holes for the breasts. 'With breasts like yours, you would look absolutely fantastic in something like this.'

Katherine took the outfit and held it for a few minutes, studying the design. It was made of a fine soft black leather and decorated with silver studs. Gingerly, she placed it on the bed and began to undress. She felt slightly uncomfortable taking her clothes off in front of the other two because she knew they were watching every move she made. Quickly, she got herself into the costume. When she looked at herself in the mirror, she could hardly believe her eyes. She looked like a totally different person. The black leather enhanced her dark good looks and her luscious breasts protruded boldly though the holes in the tight top.

'All you need now are breast clamps on those big nipples of yours,' Alan said softly. 'But maybe that's better left for another time.'

Katherine cried out as he bent over and licked one of her soft pink nipples.

'Mmm, I love the way you taste. Hey, Karen, come over here and see what our breakfast companion looks like,' he cried, taking another lick at Katherine's nipples which stiffened into hard little nubs.

Katherine moaned in protest but she loved the feeling of Alan's tongue on her and didn't really want him to stop. She felt hot and was trembling from head to toe. All the sexual excitement she had been trying to contain since she had watched the TV programme came bursting upon her. She felt overwhelmed and slightly out of her depth. This situation was much different from any of her other encounters up until now and she didn't know exactly how to conduct herself. However, it seemed she didn't have to worry because Karen and Alan knew exactly what to do. She closed her eyes and gave herself over to their expert ministrations.

Karen was already behind her, holding her firmly around the waist and fondling her breasts while Alan stood in front of her, running his hands over the skin-tight leather that flared over her voluptuous hips.

Katherine opened her eyes. She saw herself again in the mirror. She was startled at the way she looked. The leather outfit accentuated every curve of her gorgeous figure and the thick tangle between her legs was clearly visible. She watched in the mirror as Karen massaged her breasts and moaned softly as her fingers played with their jutting points. With a sigh, she arched her back and ground her buttocks back into Karen's crotch. Then Karen moved around in front of her and took one of Katherine's breasts in her mouth. She sucked and pulled on the pink tip until it elongated even further.

Katherine squirmed with pleasure as Karen's mouth moved to her other breast and began licking and sucking her sensitive flesh. Then Alan was behind her, moving his hands over her naked buttocks. Katherine wriggled sensuously under his touch and swayed her hips in time to his exploring fingers. She cried out sharply when he slipped his hand along her crotch and used his surprisingly long nails to graze the sensitive skin below her soft pussy hair. She was wet and aching. Between her thighs, her clitoris was hard and tight. Her legs were trembling so hard she thought they were going to give way beneath her. She had never been touched like this by a man and a woman at the same time. But, somehow, it wasn't just that. She was also being caressed by the soft lining of the leather outfit. And the way Alan and Karen were reacting to her was inflaming her so much. It was the way they fondled her breasts and stroked her pussy. It was being held in Karen's firm grasp while they played and toyed with her.

Alan drew his nails along her plump pussy lips in a slow scratching motion and her sex quaked as his fingers raked her sensitive flesh.

'Now, to complete the outfit, you must put on black stockings and those high-heeled boots over there,' Alan suggested, as he dragged his nails over her pussy one last time.

He handed Katherine the stockings and a pair of black leather boots and told her to put them on. When she tried to put her foot in the stocking her hands were shaking so badly she couldn't do it.

'We'll help you with that,' Alan said, his voice husky with passion.

He whisked her up in his arms and carried her over to the bed where he laid her down on a pile of clothes. Karen was there waiting for her. She slipped the stockings up Katherine's quivering legs then fastened them to the suspender belt which was an extension of the bustier. Then Alan slipped the boots on her feet. They were a perfect fit. He closed the long zip on the inside of her legs then stood back to admire the total effect. He bent over her again and ran his nails up her legs stopping just short of her thick tangle. He pulled gently on her pussy curls, damp now with her dew. She wriggled lasciviously on the bed and spread her legs even wider. She was wet and her sex was throbbing. She ached to feel his fingers part her pussy lips and slide into her dark wetness. Suddenly, she felt Karen lift her arms and pin them in a vice-like grip. She was now held firmly in the woman's grasp. She couldn't get away even if she wanted to.

'I told you she would look great in this outfit,' Karen said huskily, tightening her grip on Katherine's hands.

Katherine felt bewildered but deliciously aroused. She became even more excited when she realised she couldn't move. She revelled in the fact that she was letting Alan and Karen do whatever they pleased. She wanted it this way. She liked being in their power. She liked being restrained while Alan toyed with her pussy and Karen licked her breasts. She was letting them control every move she made and she was loving every minute of it. She realised too that the more she struggled against Karen's restraining hands, the more aroused she became.

'Okay, Katherine, stand up and show us how you look,' Alan said. 'But wait, there's just one more thing I want to do,' he added softly.

Karen continued to hold Katherine's arms tightly above her head while Alan spread her legs and used his strong arms to pin them down on the bed. Katherine knew she was helpless to stop them but this only added to her mounting excitement and she ground her hips as she felt her juices begin to flow. Alan positioned himself between her legs then lowered his mouth to her crotch. When she felt his hot breath so near to her sex, she moaned loudly in anticipation. He hovered over her squirming hips for a moment then sucked her entire pussy in his mouth. He held her like this for a few moments then slid his tongue along her crease, nipping and sucking her outer lips until she cried out in delight. She loved the feel of his mouth eating her, sucking her. It was so hot, so wet, so all-engulfing. She wanted more. She wanted to feel his tongue licking her clit. She wanted to feel his lips pulling and tugging on her pulsing bud.

Alan slipped his tongue past her dark cleft. Slowly, he began lapping her soft silky flesh with long deliberate strokes. She was writhing beneath him now as his tongue discovered every part of her. She gave a long low moan when he flattened out his tongue and moved it over her rigid clitoris. Then he stopped and clamped his mouth hard around the fleshy bud.

'Oh God,' she gasped. 'That feels so good, so good. Don't stop. Please.'

Alan had no intention of stopping and his mouth moved more quickly on her now, sucking and licking her clit, foraging among her tender folds until Katherine was thrashing beneath him, ramming her crotch against his mouth wanting more and more. Then, just when she thought she could bear no more, Karen bent over her, forced a piece of leather into her mouth and told her to suck it. Greedily, Katherine bit down on the leather and began sucking and licking frantically, moving her tongue deliriously back and forth over the slick smooth surface until, in some strange way, she felt she was licking her own pussy. She could feel her orgasm building now as Alan continued devouring her, his tongue darting and flicking at her tight, aching clit. Then, finally, it was upon her and her hips jerked upward reaching for the ultimate pleasure. Her body shuddered violently as her orgasm blazed through her. Again and again she surged panting and moaning as it carried her on waves of agonising pleasure.

When, finally, it was over, Karen and Alan lay on either side of her gently kissing and caressing her until she was calm again. Then Karen broke the silence.

'Sorry, but we have to stop now,' Karen said abruptly.

Katherine whined in protest as they helped her off the bed. Her entire body was still quivering from her climax and she could hardly walk. She wanted to savour the aftermath of her orgasm a little longer but Karen and Alan weren't going to let her bask in the afterglow one minute more. They had other things in mind.

As if in a trance, Katherine let them guide her across

the room to a full-length mirror. When she looked at herself, she couldn't believe what she saw. The sheer black stockings and the stiletto-heeled boots rising high on her thighs made her legs look even longer and more tantalizing than ever. The white flesh of the exposed skin above the dark tops of the stockings gleamed like alabaster. She looked fantastic in this leather getup, like a stranger she had never met, except perhaps in dreams she had always tried to ignore.

Karen slipped a little black whip into Katherine's hand and clamped silver slave bracelets around her upper arms.

'There. The finishing touch,' she announced proudly, standing back to gaze at her handiwork. 'Come here, Alan. Come see our beautiful vixen all ready for action.'

When Alan saw Katherine in her completed outfit, he fell to his knees and, with a groan, began licking and sucking the boot leather.

Katherine was shocked and tried to pull away, but Karen grabbed her from behind and held her tight. As Alan sucked and licked the leather in a frenzy of excitement, little sighs and moans of pleasure escaped his lips. As Karen continued to hold her in an iron grip, Katherine knew in her heart that she didn't really want to free herself. She was mesmerized watching Alan suck and lick her boots and was becoming increasingly aroused by his groans of pleasure.

'He might like to suck leather but there's something else he loves to suck too. Remember?' Karen whispered in her ear, as she slid her hand between Katherine's legs and began rubbing her damp pussy.

Katherine's sex fluttered wildly and her legs sagged

beneath her. Once again, the flames of her passion had been rekindled and she felt incredibly turned on. Her clitoris was pulsing insistently and her nipples were so tight they ached.

'It's time for the whip,' Alan groaned, looking up at Katherine with a strange pleading in his eyes.

Katherine's head was spinning. What had she got herself into? Except for that one time in the library, she had never done anything like this. She felt almost drunk with sexual excitement and she knew she couldn't stop. Things had gone too far for that.

'All right, but only a little,' Karen replied cooly. 'Remember she's just a beginner. She's more comfortable playing horsie with Johnny in the barn than she is playing around with us. So, we have to go easy for a while.

Katherine's cheeks burned as she remembered the scene in the barn. How did they know what she had been doing with Johnny? Had they been hiding somewhere watching? Memories of the interlude in the barn came flooding back and she shivered. Had these two been spying on her? This possibility aroused her even more and she ground her hips back against Karen's crotch.

Katherine looked down at Alan writhing at her feet. He had torn his pants off and his bare buttocks were raised, waiting for the bite of the whip. She felt a wave of lust surge through her loins. Without hesitation, she raised the whip and brought it down on Alan's waiting behind. At the first bite of the whip, he moaned in pleasure and sucked more vigorously at her boot. Katherine felt a wetness gathering in her crotch and she lowered the whip again, this time a little harder as she thought of Alan, the voyeur, watching her in the barn. When Alan cried out in a mixture of pleasure and pain, she felt dizzy with excitement. Her clitoris was swollen and pulsing insistently between her legs and her pussy hair was soaking wet. She felt Alan's hand snaking up her legs. She opened them wide to meet his touch as she raised the whip one more time. Alan reached up to her crotch and slowly dragged his nails along her pussy then took the plump flesh between his fingers and pinched her lightly.

Katherine's knees gave way beneath her. Karen held her up in her strong arms and Alan, encouraged by her reaction, stuck out his tongue and dragged it back and forth along her damp cleft. The touch of his tongue sent wild sexual thrills rippling through her body and she responded by flicking the whip once more over his bare buttocks.

Driven into a frenzy by Katherine's cries and the feel of the whip on his naked flesh, Alan speared his tongue past her outer lips and pushed deeper and deeper until it slid up over the swollen head of her clitoris. Frantically, he began sucking and lapping her hard little nub, teasing and pulling on it until he coaxed it out from beneath its hood.

Katherine was mad with lust now and she lowered the whip again and again on Alan's writhing buttocks. Egged on by his muted cries of pleasure and the skilful way he was working her pussy, she had reached a fever pitch of excitement. She flicked the whip again and his buttocks pumped wildly. He let out a muffled groan and clamped his lips more tightly around the rigid bud of her clitoris. He played his tongue back and forth over it for a moment then started to suck on it hard.

Katherine's breath was coming in short harsh gasps. She ground her hips down on his tongue. It felt so velvety smooth on her aching pussy. She wanted to close her swollen pussy lips around his tongue and never let him go. She began moving her hips in slow little circles. Then she brought the whip down hard on his bare buttocks one more time. It was all he needed. With a strange high-pitched wail, he fell back on the floor, caught up in the throes of a wrenching orgasm.

Katherine looked down at the writhing figure on the floor. She felt as if she were in some kind of dream world where she was both the star and the director. She was close to coming again and was wildly aroused, crazy with the feelings that were surging through her. Her pussy was soaking with her dew, her nipples hard and extended. There was a delicious heaviness in her loins but she didn't have the energy to do anything about it. Who would have thought that having her pussy licked by a man she was dominating could be such a turn on? She was so hot. She felt wild. She wanted to come. She wanted to come so badly. She swayed and closed her eyes.

'Now it's your turn,' Karen whispered in her ear.

Without a word of explanation, she led Katherine over to the leather armchair by the fireplace and sat her down. Instantly, Katherine felt her arms being pinned behind the chair and her wrists cuffed in the cold grip of steel manacles. Before she could say a word, a gag was tied around her mouth and a soft leather band put around her head, holding her motionless against the back of the chair. Her upper arms were then restrained by leather straps that circled her from the back of the chair. Her legs were spread wide and draped over each arm rest. Each thigh was strapped down to the armrest and her ankles were then cuffed to long chains attached to rings embedded in the floor. She was now completely immobilised with her most secret parts exposed.

Alan appeared at the foot of the chair and stood staring at her for a moment, a hungry look in his eyes. Suddenly, Katherine felt how totally helpless she was. She struggled against her restraints. This only intensified the throbbing between her legs. Her excitement increased when it dawned on her that she was completely at their mercy. She felt a stab of fear but when she looked deep into Alan's eyes, she knew she could trust him. She remembered Martha telling her to stay open to all experiences, that nothing would ever be done to her against her will. She relaxed and moaned through her gag. She realised with a shock that whatever was in store for her, she wanted it to happen. She wanted it very much.

Being unable to move added an incredible excitement to her sexual arousal. Her breasts were swollen and jutting out of the holes in her bustier, longing to be toyed with. Her dew oozed out of her, soaking her pussy and the seat beneath her. She felt crazy with desire. She struggled again beneath the straps and felt a surge of sexual excitement that was almost unbearable.

'Is she ready?' Alan asked.

Karen inserted one exploratory finger into Katherine's moist sex. 'She's more than ready. I told you she would love this.'

Alan turned and took something off the shelf beside the chair. It was a long black object attached to a cord which he plugged into the wall. It began to hum.

Katherine was suddenly aware of how tightly her arms were tied behind her and how she could not move her legs an inch. Her eyes darted wildly from side to side. Her muffled moans rose up behind her gag as Karen teased and tweaked her nipples. She watched helplessly as Alan approached her. Waves of dizziness washed over her when she saw the long black vibrator in his hand. It was glistening with some kind of ointment. She cried out from behind her gag but she could only lie motionless as he guided the fake penis between her legs. Her hands clenched and unclenched uselessly as he slipped it easily between the lips of her pussy and then slid it deep into her. It began to pulsate and churn within her. The walls of her vagina and her clitoris began to vibrate. Her sex swelled as waves of pleasure suffused her secret core. She wanted to grind her hips, to writhe against the vibrating dildo but she could not move. Her pussy was quivering wildly. Karen bent over Katherine's heaving breasts and swirled her tongue around the jutting points. She raised her mouth from Katherine's raw nipples and began raining kisses all the way from Katherine's belly down to her silky bush. Katherine ached to move her body as the sensations in her loins intensified but she was held too tightly in her restraints. She clenched down on the pulsating shaft, determined to wring as much pleasure out of it as she could, working her vaginal muscles as Alan thrust and churned it deeper and deeper into her. Oh God, this feels so good, so good, she groaned inwardly. She loved the feeling of the hard smooth dildo as it moved in and out of her slit, humming and vibrating, electrifying every nerve in her body. Her clitoris was engorged and heavy. It pulsed crazily as the lewd object sent tingles radiating deep into her sex. She felt she would go mad with delight. Soon, the vibrating cock and Karen's mouth took her to the point of no return. She tensed beneath the leather straps as the tide of her arousal crested in a huge wave and she began to climax. She struggled wildly against her restraints as she came again and again, groaning in ecstasy as her orgasm seized her in its searing grip and flooded her with a pleasure she had never dreamt possible.

Chapter Seven

After her experience with Karen and Alan, Katherine returned to her room feeling deeply satisfied but slightly exhausted. She decided she had had enough excitement for one day and planned to spend the rest of the evening by herself, relaxing and watching TV. After a long hot shower, she slipped into her dressing gown and was just about to call room service when there was a knock at her door. Curious to see who would be calling on her unannounced, she walked quickly across the room and opened the door.

To her amazement, a man in a tuxedo with an elegant opera cape slung over his shoulder was standing there gazing down at her, a faint smile on his full lips. A black mask covered the top half of his face.

Katherine started nervously when she saw the mask. 'What on earth?' Katherine exclaimed.

'I am here to escort you to dinner, Katherine,' he announced in a pleasant baritone voice.

'Who are you? I ... I don't quite understand,' Katherine stammered, feeling at a complete loss. 'You want to take me to dinner? I don't know who you are and uh, I mean I'm not dressed and ... just what exactly is this all about?'

'I was told you were open to new and exciting adventures. So, I am here to offer you a very special one. If you are willing, I will take you with me now and we can begin our evening.'

'But I'm not dressed and I – '

'Everything has been taken care of. All you have to do is put yourself in my hands and I can guarantee that you will experience an evening you will never forget. However, if this is not to your liking, I will leave now. Please don't worry; you won't insult me in any way if you decide to turn down my offer. But I warn you now that this chance will not come again.'

Katherine could hardly believe what was happening. She felt as if she were in the middle of an extraordinary dream. After her adventures earlier that day, why should she be surprised by anything that happened at this marvellous hotel? she asked herself. Everything that had happened to her so far at this place had had something of a dream-like quality to it and it had all worked out very, very well. Why should this invitation be any different? Why not take the chance and go for it? She decided immediately that she would accept the invitation from this intriguing man and, without further ado, took his arm, left her room and strolled down the hall with him to the nearest lift.

It was incredible. Here she was, walking along the corridor in her robe on the arm of a masked stranger as if she did this every day of the week. As if this was the most ordinary of occurrences. For any reason she could care to come up with, Katherine knew she should feel strange, if not downright frightened but, in keeping with many dream realities, she felt as if she were doing something completely normal and proceeded on her way with her mysterious escort with a quiet, inner confidence.

The elevator whisked them up to the thirteenth floor where the doors opened on to a quiet hallway decorated in muted tones of grey. Everything seemed quite unremarkable except for her companion and the fact that she was walking in a public area of the hotel in her dressing gown. They stopped in front of a door marked with the number 13.

'This is where I leave you, at least for the moment,' the man said quietly. 'Your clothes for the evening are laid out inside, along with everything else you might need. I will be back for you in about an hour. Then we will proceed with our plans for this evening.'

With a bow, he kissed her hand, turned, and disappeared down the hall. Now knowing what to expect, Katherine took a deep breath, opened the door and walked in. In the centre of the room was a king-sized bed. On it, her attire for the evening had been laid out for her: a black lace bra with half cups, sheer black stockings, a red and black lace suspender belt, black strappy sandals with very high heels and a long black evening dress with a slit that went up to the top of the thigh. The top was rather demure in that it had a very high turtle neck and long sleeves. The back was fastened with a long zip that went from the top of the turtle neck down to below the waist. Very easy to slip on and off, she thought immediately, then caught her breath as her imagination began to run wild with thoughts of her upcoming evening. Judging from the type of dress she would be wearing, and the formal attire of her escort, it looked like she would be dining in fine style tonight.

She sat down at the dressing table to the left of the bed and began applying her make-up very carefully. When she was satisfied with the dramatic look she had chosen for the evening, she swept her long hair up into a sleek French knot at the back of her head. Then she put on the lingerie that had been laid out for her and slipped into the long black dress. It was very tight and clung to every voluptuous curve, accentuating her tiny waist, flaring hips and magnificent breasts. The slit was so high that the top of her stockings and the bare skin above were revealed when she walked. To complete the outfit, she slid her feet into the high-heeled sandals which flattered her long, shapely legs. When she looked at the final result in the mirror, she liked what she saw. She had to admit she looked absolutely stunning. She had never looked quite like this before, not even on those rare occasions when she had taken her law firm's wealthy clients out to expensive supper clubs. Tonight, she looked like someone else entirely. This excited her. She was pleased with this impression and licked her lips slowly. She was a little intimidated however. This was the first time she had ever worn an outfit like this and she wondered for a moment whether she could carry it off. However, when she looked again at her reflection, she saw how her dark eyes glittered and knew that the sexual fire that burned within her was very near the surface, filling her with a growing sense of power and self-confidence. Her heart was pounding with excitement. She knew she could carry off the dress and anything else that might lie in store for her that evening; she was ready for anything.

A soft knock at the door told her that her escort had returned. What did the next few hours hold? she wondered. She took one last look in the mirror then walked slowly across the room. When she opened the door, he was standing there with a bouquet of red roses in his hand. He bowed slightly, then presented it to her with a flourish. She was delighted to receive such a beautiful bouquet and thanked him quietly while she bent to inhale their delicate perfume.

'How beautiful,' she murmured. 'I believe I saw a vase on the dressing table. I'll just put them in water and then we can go. This was so sweet of you. Thank you. By the way, do I get to know your name?'

'My name is Daniel,' he replied softly. 'However, for the purposes of this evening, I'm afraid that is all I can tell you about myself. You too will be asked to wear a mask and to reveal nothing about yourself to anyone except your name. This is to be a night of mystery. Knowing too many details about each other would only spoil the mood. Names, of course, are necessary. After all, we don't want to address each other as, "hey you" do we?'

Katherine smiled faintly at his little joke.

His well-modulated tones and sophisticated manner pleased her and his description of the evening that lay ahead fired her imagination. Her sense of anticipation quickened. She was eager for the evening to begin. She put on the black, sequined mask Daniel held out to her then walked over to the mirror and, once more, looked at her reflection. It was the first time she had seen herself masked and the effect was immediate. The presence of the mask on her face altered her mood completely. The effect was intriguing. The mask did not just conceal the upper half of her face, it did something much more powerful than that. It provided her with a delicious sense of anonymity, a feeling of freedom, even permission, to do things she might never ordinarily dream of doing.

129

When she had arranged the flowers in a vase, she took his arm and walked out into the hall. After taking a couple of turns, they found themselves in front of a plain black door.

'This isn't the hotel dining room,' Katherine remarked, her breath starting to come more quickly. 'Where are we?'

'This will be our special room for the evening,' Daniel explained softly. 'Two other guests will be joining us. One man and one woman. All in all, a party of four. We thought a private dining room would suit our needs best.'

He opened the door and ushered her into a dimly lit room. As she moved slowly through the doorway, her feet sank into a deep, plush black rug. It took a few seconds for her eyes to get accustomed to the subdued lighting. When they did, she saw a big round ebony table standing at the far end of the room. It was set with gleaming silverware and dazzling white and gold china. In the middle of the table, there was an ornate pewter candelabra with tapering black candles whose flames cast long flicking shadows across the perfectly laid table. Beside the candelabra was a silver bowl, full of red and white roses. The effect was very dramatic and a bit eerie, gothic, almost.

Katherine drew in her breath sharply and looked quickly over at her companion but he was not looking at her. He was concentrating on steering her firmly in the direction of the table. She kept glancing all around her as they walked across the room, trying to take in as much of her surroundings as possible but the light was dim and the shadows that lined the edges of the room were deep and dark. The only thing that stood out at that moment was the table, resplendent with its beautiful place settings and highlighted dramatically in a huge circle of light that shone down on it from above.

When she reached the end of the table nearest to her, Daniel pulled out a chair and motioned to her to sit down. She did and, as she took her seat, she became aware that a fair-haired man and a tall blonde woman were making their way toward the table from the other end of the room. Like Daniel, the man was wearing evening clothes but the mask that covered the top of his face was half black and half white.

The man spoke first. 'Good evening. May I introduce myself? I am Louis and this is my guest, Virginia. She is staying here too. In fact, she arrived only this afternoon and I want to make her first experience with us as pleasant as possible. I think we will enjoy ourselves together. I know we have a lot in common.'

Katherine and Daniel acknowledged Louis' introductions and proceeded to present themselves to their dinner companions. Katherine looked over at Virginia and smiled. She was absolutely gorgeous with golden blonde hair styled in a short pixie cut, eyes so dark blue they were almost violet, and a magnificent body that was poured into a skin-tight, shocking-pink satin evening gown. The top of her dress was strapless and her ample breasts rose in delicious mounds over the top. Her skin was creamy smooth and, when she responded to Katherine's greeting, her voice was soft and husky. Her mask was made of white feathers dotted with silver sequins around the eye openings which were large enough to show off her magnificent eyes to great advantage.

When they were all seated at the table, waiters appeared out of the shadows with appetisers and began silently serving them. The meal progressed in a leisurely fashion and, as the four of them enjoyed the exquisite food and wine that was set before them, they exchanged teasing information about each other's lives and talked and laughed about the current books and movies they had all seen and enjoyed. The food was wonderful: seafood appetisers with a light tangy sauce, an entrée of braised lamb with rosemary, roasted baby potatoes and fresh garden peas: a green side salad with a hint of ginger in the dressing and crème brulée for dessert. With each course, the appropriate wine was served. The taste experience was far beyond anything Katherine had ever encountered – even in the sophisticated restaurants she had frequented both in Paris and New York. If the food was any indication, this evening promised to exceed all of her expectations, she thought, with rising anticipation.

Toward the end of the meal, the pace of the conversation slowed as the delicious food and the different wines that had been served with each course began to take effect. The mood was mellow and, when it was time for after dinner liqueurs, Katherine felt so satisfied she didn't think she had room for another taste experience. However, she was eager to savour everything that was being offered so she went along with the others and had an after dinner Cointreau and coffee.

Ever since the meal had begun, Katherine had had the strangest feeling she was being prepared for something, that she was being transformed subtly, quietly, into a person quite different from the one who greeted her every morning in the bathroom mirror. She wasn't quite sure how this was being done but she knew it had something to do with her clothes, the setting, the fine meal and the fact that everyone was masked. There was a special cachet attached to everything this evening, a feeling in the air that anything was possible. Yet, despite the unusual circumstances, Katherine felt comfortable and completely at ease.

She looked over at Virginia and let her eyes roam over the full white orbs that were spilling over the top of her dress. Was it her imagination or could she see just the tiniest hint of pink nipple peeking out from the edge of the skin-tight bodice? Her eyes flitted over the full breasts. When she looked up, she looked straight into Virginia's violet-blue eyes. Katherine lowered her gaze immediately and a slow blush suffused her face underneath her mask.

'Do you like what you see, Katherine?' Virginia whispered, her eyes shining with amusement.

'Oh, no, I mean, uh, I'm sorry, uh, I didn't mean . . . it's just that well . . .' Katherine could only stutter an attempt at a response, then stopped dead when she realised she didn't know what to say.

'Please don't be embarrassed. I thought it was a very sweet compliment. I can only say that if you want to see and touch, all you have to do is ask.'

Taken aback by Virginia's response, Katherine watched silently as the blonde got up out of her chair and walked around the table towards her. She could smell the other woman's scent and her senses reeled. The food, the wine, and the lush setting, together with the heady scent of Virginia's musky perfume were suddenly overwhelming. She felt slightly dizzy and swayed in her chair. Then, she realised Daniel and Louis were easing her chair out from the table so Virginia could kneel down in front of her.

'Would you like to pull my top down and see my breasts?' Virginia asked, moistening her full lips with the tip of her pink tongue.

Katherine couldn't respond. She was so amazed by this unexpected turn of events, she was speechless.

She watched in fascination as Virginia reached around behind herself and started to loosen the zip that held her skin-tight bodice in place. Very slowly, she eased the zip down and, bit by bit, the pink satin top began to inch its way over her breasts.

Katherine felt paralysed, caught up in the overwhelming sensuality of Virginia's movements and her obvious intent. Her heart was racing and there was a dull throbbing between her legs. Her mouth was dry. She licked her lips. She was vaguely aware of Louis and Daniel but she was totally caught up in the scent of Virginia's perfume, the closeness of her body and the overwhelming urge she felt to reach out and touch the other woman's breasts.

The two women stared at each other hypnotically. Finally, Katherine dropped her gaze and allowed her eyes to feast on Virginia's luscious breasts – almost bare now before her. Suddenly, she couldn't stand it any more. Before she could stop herself, she reached out her hand and pulled Virginia's bodice all the way down to her waist. The woman's smooth creamy skin gleamed warmly in the candlelight. Katherine caught her breath: Virginia's breasts were magnificent. She devoured them with her eyes, lingering for a long time on the pale pink nipples. The feeling in her mouth was driving her crazy. She bent her head.

'Wait,' Virginia said softly and beckoned to one of the waiters who was standing silently in the shadows.

In an instant, he was beside them holding a silver tray. On the tray was a little bottle of pink liquid. Virginia took the bottle and poured a few drops on to her hands. Then she proceeded to rub the liquid on her nipples. 'After-dinner candy,' she said softly. She ran her tongue over her lips, cupped her breasts and thrust them toward Katherine. 'Now suck them,' she added, a harsher, more urgent, tone in her voice.

Without a second thought, Katherine clamped her mouth around one sweet-tasting nipple and began to suck and pull on it as hard as she could. The sensation was incredible. It was strange and yet familiar territory at the same time. She felt as if she were sucking her own breasts. The nipple was soft on the edge and hard in the middle and tasted of strawberries. She groaned as she sucked and licked the hard little nub. She was new to lesbian love-making yet it all felt so natural. The feel of Virginia's nipples under her tongue, the texture of her skin, the way they hardened and peaked even further as Katherine sucked and played her tongue over them was titillating her more and more. Her sex was wet now and her own breasts were swollen and aching beneath the silky fabric of her bra.

Virginia moaned softly and arched her back so that her breasts jutted closer to Katherine's face. Katherine opened her mouth as wide as she could and began licking and kissing first one then the other until both women were breathless.

'I want you to make me come. I want you to suck me until I come,' Virginia said. She ran one hand up Katherine's thighs, found the slit in her dress and slid her fingers in between her legs.

'Oh, you're so wet,' she cried. Quickly, she feathered her fingers over the silky wetness of Katherine's black lace panties, pinching her pussy lips and probing along her crease.

Katherine squirmed sensuously on her chair. The sensations were so delicious, she couldn't help grinding her hips down on Virginia's teasing fingers. She knew the situation was outrageous but she didn't care. She knew this territory was totally foreign to her, almost taboo and, because of this, it was intensely exciting. She gasped out loud as Virginia trailed her long nails over the silky material covering her pussy. She jerked her hips forward in a quick spasm. Then she opened her mouth and dragged her tongue back and forth across the fullness of Virginia's heavy white breasts, kissing and laving her like a ravenous beast. Virginia's loud moans egged her on, inflaming her passions even further.

Virginia was relentless in her caresses. She kept fondling and playing with Katherine's pussy, using her long nails to rake and tease. Then she slid her fingers under the edge of Katherine's panties, tangled them in her wet pussy curls and gently began to pull on them. Katherine took Virginia's breasts in both hands. Greedily, she palmed and massaged them. Then she took both nipples between the index finger and thumb of each hand and began to squeeze and pinch them; gently at first then harder and harder.

'Yes, yes, that's it. Oh, God, I'm coming, oh yes,' Virginia cried out.

Katherine had already known Virginia was close to her climax and she felt a strange sense of power knowing that the other woman's pleasure was under her control. She moved her fingers more insistently then lowered her mouth one more time and pulled Virginia's right nipple long and hard. Virginia cried out sharply as her climax seized her. She came hard and fast with short harsh gasps then fell on the floor in front of Katherine, panting and gasping for breath.

Katherine slumped back in her chair. For a moment, she couldn't account for her actions and then she remembered she had been wearing the mask, that wonderful device which had given her permission to act on impulses that perhaps on other occasions she felt bound to ignore. She was elated, turned on. She couldn't believe the amazing freedom she was experiencing. And she was so hot; her pussy was drenched in her juices.

It had been fun and exciting to play with Virginia's gorgeous breasts and feel the blonde's fingers on her sex but she needed some release of her own and she needed it right now. She looked down at Virginia who was lying on her back now with her legs spread wide apart. The lower half of her dress was rucked up around her waist and Louis' head was buried deep in her pussy. The grunts and cries of pleasure coming from the two of them turned her on even more.

As if reading her thoughts, Daniel appeared out of the shadows and helped her up from her chair. Silently, he led her over to the table which had been cleared and was covered with soft, black leather.

'Where are we going?' she asked.

'It was such a marvellous meal, I thought I would finish it off with my favourite dessert,' Daniel whispered, as he laid her gently down on the table.

Katherine moaned softly as he stretched her out on the leather-covered surface and proceeded to strap her wrists in black leather cuffs. Then he spread her legs and secured them in the same fashion. Before she knew it, she was tied so firmly she couldn't move. Her eyes darted wildly from side to side. When she looked up, she saw her reflection in a mirror that was slanted above the table. She could see herself; her masked face, mysterious, sinister even, her arms and legs spread wide, and her body bathed in the long flickering shadows cast by the many scented candles in the room. She was spread out on the table where

137

they had eaten their meal, lying there as if she were being offered up like some delicious morsel to be savoured and tasted – an after dinner treat to delight the senses. She shuddered and struggled against her constraints. It was no use; she couldn't move. This aroused her even more. She looked over at Daniel who had changed his clothes and was wearing only black leather pants. His chest was bare and she could see dark wiry hair curling in dark clumps all over it. He was still masked and he held something in his hand which she couldn't see clearly. She shivered in anticipation and her breath began to come quickly in short rapid gasps.

Daniel put down the mysterious object and walked over to her. Katherine noticed his eyes were glittering darkly behind his mask as he slid his hands up her legs and pushed her dress up around her waist. When she looked again at the mirror above her, she could see herself spreadeagled on the smooth black leather, her breasts heaving beneath the tight black top of her dress, her black lace panties soaking with her juices, her her red and black lace suspender belt and sheer black stockings contrasting dramatically with her silky white skin which gleamed above her stocking tops. She caught her breath at the sight of herself and arched her body in a long sensual movement as Daniel's hand snaked over her crotch. Slowly, he rubbed his fingers over her mound, gently teasing and scratching her through the thin material of her panties. When he moved his hands up to the waistband of her panties and began to pull them off, her hips jerked forward in a quick spasm.

'You look absolutely delicious,' he whispered, licking his lips. 'I want to taste that sweet pussy of yours so badly. But, you know, I always like to dress my dessert up a little bit before I eat it.'

He reached his hand down into a little silver bowl which a waiter had placed on the table beside him. When he took it out again, Katherine saw that it was covered in whipped cream. Slowly and methodically, he began to lather it between her legs. Katherine let out a long sigh of pleasure. The cream felt cool and silky on her hot flesh and she strained under the leather straps as she felt the thick sweet cream ooze into her sex.

Then Daniel's mouth was on her, greedily licking and lapping at the sweet substance. His tongue burrowed into every nook and cranny of her, tasting every inch of her, searching for every last bit of the sweet cream. He grunted out his pleasure at the contrasting sweetness of the cream and the salty taste of her sex on his tongue.

Katherine felt wild. The insistent throbbing of her pussy was driving her crazy. She wanted to move and grind her hips but she couldn't; she was held too tightly by her constraints. The feel of his hot tongue and the cool whipped cream was excruciating. Her clit felt like it was on fire, ignited by each stroke of his greedy tongue until she felt as if hundreds of little flames were licking at her tight nub.

Katherine could feel her orgasm building. She wanted to thrust and jerk her hips but she was impaled on Daniel's relentless tongue which continued to scoop up every last vestige of the whipped cream. When he had eaten his fill and the cream was all gone, he swirled his tongue quickly over her clitoris then withdrew his mouth. Katherine groaned out loud when he stopped. She was so aroused, she felt crazy. She wanted him to make her come. She wanted some relief. Her moans were quickly silenced when a gag was placed over her mouth.

'No more sounds, Katherine. You can struggle and pull all you want but no more sounds. Not tonight,' Daniel whispered.

The fact that now she could not use her voice or move her body to express her acute state of arousal only increased her excitement. She began thrashing like a dervish, moving her head back and forth, straining against the leather straps with all her might as the tides of her passion built to a fever pitch. She was so close. She wanted to come now.

Daniel realised how close she was and made his move. He flattened out his tongue and ran it in long slow strokes over her engorged flesh. When he closed his mouth hard around the pulsing flesh and gave it one long hard pull, it stiffened beneath his tongue. A low muffled growl rose up in the back of her throat as her climax seized her. She surged again and again beneath his mouth and he continued to devour her pussy until finally the fire within her was quenched.

When it was over, Katherine lay panting and moaning on the table. She opened her eyes and looked over at Daniel; he had something in his hand. This time she could see what it was. It was a small black whip. She shuddered in anticipation and muted cries rose up behind her gag. She tensed as he dragged the whip over her sex. At first, he flicked it softly then harder and harder. She gasped inwardly at the sharp bite of the leather on her tender flesh but soon the pain dissolved into a burning pleasure that rippled deep into her core and ignited her clit. Over and over, he flicked at her flesh, sometimes softly, sometimes harshly, until her whole body was throbbing with a mixture of pain and pleasure.

Katherine's eyes flew open when Daniel suddenly stopped using the instrument. They darted wildly, following every move he made as he reached his hand up under her back and pulled the zip of her dress all the way down. Then he released her hands from the cuffs so he could pull the top of the dress down over her arms and breasts. When her arms and chest were bare, he cuffed her hands again. Then he unfastened the front clasp of her bra and pulled the cups aside so that her big breasts fell free. He massaged them briefly, pulling on her taut nipples and squeezing them between his fingers. Then he picked up the whip again and feathered it gently over her naked breasts, softly at first then with greater force. She squirmed as the pointed tip stung her flesh and she tried to raise her breasts to meet its sting. She felt almost drunk with pleasure, her senses reeling from the contrasting feelings. Pain then pleasure then the two mingling. She felt drugged, sated with sensation. The throbbing between her legs rippled from her breasts deep into her vagina. Hot sharp tingles were igniting every part of her body. She felt as if she were going to burst into flames. She could feel her orgasm cresting. Once more she was coming and Daniel wasn't even touching her. Only the whip was moving over her breasts and pussy again and again, sending excruciating sparks of sexual fire radiating deep into her core. Finally, she could hold back no longer. Suddenly, her orgasm was upon her and the fiery energy in her belly exploded into an exquisite pleasure which flooded through her in great rolling waves, sending her spinning off into dark starry realms.

The next morning, Katherine got up early. She slipped into a pair of old blue jeans, a red roll-necked sweater and some comfortable running shoes then headed out into the gardens. She felt she needed some time alone with nature, time to try to make sense of everything she was feeling. She needed to feel the caress of the early morning sea breeze and to smell the magnificent fragrance of the flowers in the gardens which surrounded the house.

When she stepped out on to the front steps, the sun was just coming up over the horizon. Everything was bathed in a soft golden glow. She stopped for a moment to take in the beauty of the scene then slowly headed down the front path towards the patio which overlooked the beach. It was such a lovely place, she thought. There was a stone balustrade enclosing the flagstone floor and flowering shrubbery and plum blossom trees were spaced artistically between the stone benches, where you could sit looking out to sea. The deep pink of the plum blossom was breathtaking in the early morning light. Katherine inhaled deeply and sat down on one of the benches. The sea was twinkling on the horizon and the waves were gently rolling in on the beach below. Katherine closed her eyes and breathed in the invigorating salty air.

'Good morning, Katherine. You're an early bird this morning, too, I see.'

Katherine opened her eyes and looked around. Martha was standing there wearing a smart, navy-blue jogging suit. There was a healthy glow on her face and she was breathing quickly.

'I've just been jogging,' she exclaimed a little breathlessly. 'I love this time of the day when everything is new and fresh. Morning is such an important time, don't you think? I mean, it seems to set the tone for the rest of the day. That's why I do my jogging and meditation early in the morning. That way, I'm ready physically and emotionally to handle whatever the rest of the day might bring.'

'Martha, how wonderful to see you. It seems ages since we last talked. And yes, I absolutely agree about morning. It's my favourite time too,' Katherine replied with a friendly smile.

'How are things going, Katherine? Do you feel you're getting the most out of your stay here so far?' asked Martha.

'Oh, please, I don't want to interrupt your morning routine,' Katherine replied quickly.

'Nonsense, you're not interrupting at all. I've finished jogging and I was just going to take a stroll through the back gardens before breakfast. Why don't you come with me. We can talk as we walk.'

Katherine accepted eagerly and both women turned back towards the house. Silently, they walked down a narrow flower-lined pathway at the side of the house. As they turned a corner, the path broadened out into a wider stone walkway that wound its way through one of the big flower gardens on the west side of the house.

'I have left you to find your own way here, Katherine,' Martha said softly. 'If you remember, in our first interview, I said I thought that would be best for you. I felt you needed the freedom and the time to orchestrate your own experiences and to pick and choose from those that were offered to you. Was I right in that decision?'

'Oh, yes,' Katherine replied quickly. 'I did what you said and tried to stay open to as many experiences as I could, no matter how unusual or bizarre they seemed at first. I was surprised actually at how easily I was able to enter into the spirit of things. I thought I would be much more inhibited than I actually was. In fact it was quite the opposite, I found that quite amazing.'

'Not so amazing to me, Katherine,' Martha said with a knowing smile. 'You see, I don't think you are inhibited so much as cut off from your true sexuality. You have been in a kind of denial of your true sexual nature for a long time. Also, your environment back home did not offer you the opportunities you needed to get in touch with your sexuality and you were too shy to try and seek them out. That's why I thought you would do so well here because, here at the clinic, you would be given the chance to explore your sexuality in a totally natural and unthreatening environment where you wouldn't feel ashamed or shy. I'm sure you have noticed by now that, no matter how fantastic your sexual adventures here have been, they were always presented to you in a real and natural way. When sex is handled that way, fear, shyness and any inhibition that might be standing in the way is immediately short circuited and pleasure wins out.'

'That's exactly right,' Katherine exclaimed excitedly. 'I have had the most amazing encounters but, no matter how wild and wonderful they were, I've always felt safe and quite comfortable. The whole atmosphere of the clinic is conducive to relaxing and just being able to let go without fear of being censured or criticised.'

'Criticism and censure are things you will have to deal with head on before you feel completely free to live your sexual life the way you want to, Katherine,' Martha said softly. 'However, from the reports I have been receiving, it seems to me you are well on the way to breaking down those barriers. I'm sure that, before you leave here, you will understand where all that comes from and why.'

'There is still that feeling that always haunts me,' Katherine began tentatively. 'I can never pin it down. It's not as strong as it used to be and certainly, since I came to the clinic, it has been fading quite dramatically. But it's still there. I want to know where it comes from and how to deal with it.'

'What feeling is that?' Martha asked.

'It's that feeling I always get after sex,' Katherine began somewhat hesitantly. 'It's like I hardly have a minute to enjoy the afterglow before this feeling of being cheated rears its ugly head and I feel that something very dear has been taken away from me. Pretty soon I feel just awful. I can't explain it any better than that. It always happens after I've had sex with someone. Before I came here, it got so bad, I decided I wasn't going to have sex at all any more.'

'I think that feeling is very important and I'm sure that before your time here is over, you will get to the bottom of it. We will talk more about this at our next meeting. Now I don't want you to worry too much about this. Just monitor the feeling and how you react after sex but keep on enjoying all the opportunities that come your way. I think this is the way to get to the bottom of this. But now, tell me, how have you enjoyed your sexual encounters?'

'I can't believe how much fun I have been having,' Katherine replied. 'I have been amazed at how many different kinds of sexual adventures I've had and I've been really surprised at how eager I've been to enter into them. Whenever I got frightened or anxious or anything like that, I always remembered your saying I should stay open to all experiences and, if I did this, I could solve whatever it was that was spoiling my sex life for me. I have felt really encouraged and empowered by that advice, Martha, and I have felt free to respond to all the opportunities the clinic has presented to me. I'm really grateful to you and the rest of the staff. I know I'm making progress. I can feel it. I can feel myself getting better every day.'

'Marvellous! I knew you would respond positively to our environment here. And I wouldn't be at all surprised if, at our next visit, you get to the bottom of that feeling which always spoils things for you. In fact, I know you will. You're intelligent, you're determined and you're hot blooded. No secret can withstand a combination like that for long, Katherine.'

'Thank you, Martha, you're so encouraging and supportive,' Katherine said with a grateful smile.

'Nonsense,' Martha replied somewhat gruffly. 'That's what I'm here for. Now, I really must run. I have a breakfast meeting with some of the therapists and then client sessions until lunch. I'll be in touch with you again soon, Katherine. Keep up the good work and you'll be out of the woods in no time. Goodbye for now and remember, have fun.'

With a quick smile and a wave, Martha walked up the garden path and disappeared around the side of the house. Katherine watched her go and smiled happily to herself. She felt so much better after her talk with Martha. She looked at her watch. It was almost time for breakfast. She was ravenous. She started back towards the house. She had just enough time to change and get down to the breakfast room for a cup of that wonderful coffee they made here and some of those delicious cranberry muffins that were baked fresh every morning.

* * *

Later that afternoon, Katherine was sitting out on the beach. She had just finished a long cool drink and was sunning herself in a *chaise longue* which she had set up facing the sea. She felt wonderful. In fact, she felt more relaxed than she had done since she had arrived here. This place was working wonders on her and the sex was getting better and better with every encounter she had. With a sense of growing pride, she realised that she was allowing herself more and more pleasure and was succeeding in remaining open to a variety of unusual and very exciting sexual activities. Coming here had been the best thing she could have done. She gave herself a long stretch then ran her hands down over her breasts. Her nipples crested instantly. She smiled to herself and slid her hand between her legs. Dreamily, she stroked her pussy through the thin cotton of her shorts. She ground her hips slightly and closed her eyes. Yes, she was in the mood again and this time she wanted to try something different, something wild and primitive, maybe even ... Her thoughts trailed off as she heard someone call her name.

She looked down the beach. In the distance, she could see two figures silhouetted against the brightness of the sun. They were too far away for her to make out who they were but it was clear from their gestures that they were trying to get her attention. Katherine just smiled quietly to herself and lay back in her seat. She felt in no rush to respond; they would be here soon enough. For now, she was going to continue to luxuriate in the warm rays of the sun. It was early afternoon and the sun was high in a clear blue sky. Its warmth felt marvellous on her skin and the sound of the waves crashing in on the beach had lulled and soothed her into a deep state of relaxation.

She sighed contentedly and glanced again down the beach. The people were getting closer. She smiled when she realised it was Jasmine and Rolf. Both were wearing skimpy bathing suits which showed off their fit bodies to perfection. Little tingles danced over the surface of Katherine's skin at the sight of the young chauffeur. Instantly, her mind was flooded with the images of their incredible time together. She hadn't seen him since then. She realised suddenly how much she had missed him. She let her eyes roam the full length of his body. He looked marvellous and, as he strode across the sand towards her, his taut muscles rippled sensuously beneath his smooth, tanned skin. He was looking especially handsome today in his tight black trunks which left absolutely nothing to the imagination. Katherine's pussy stirred as her eyes followed the contours of the big bulge in his bathing suit. She sighed softly as she remembered how he had pumped that big cock of his in and out of her sex, how he had made her come over and over. Her breath started to come faster. She was amazed she still felt so turned on by him. The fact was that she wanted him just as much today as she had that first day in the limo.

She looked over at Jasmine. The young blonde woman was walking jauntily along the beach beside him carrying a small package in her hand and a tote bag in the other.

'Hi, Katherine,' Jasmine called out as she approached Katherine's chair. 'Do you want to go for a walk along the beach with Rolf and me? We thought we might explore one of the big caves at the far end of the beach, maybe even go for a swim. It's a great day for it. What do you say? And you can wear this,' she added, holding out the small package to her. 'I saw this in the village and I thought of you immediately. I just couldn't resist. I hope you like it.'

Curious, Katherine took the small package from her blonde friend and looked inside. She removed the two small pieces of cloth and held them in her hand. It was a hot-pink thong bikini. She had always wanted to wear one of these but had never quite worked up the nerve. It wasn't that she didn't have the figure for it; she knew she did. It was just that she had never felt comfortable exposing so much of her body in a public setting like a beach. She knew she would not welcome all the stares and leers her presence in such a skimpy outfit would provoke. Here, however, she was among friends. She certainly didn't have anything to hide from Rolf, she thought with a smile. He had already explored and savoured much of what would be barely concealed beneath the flimsy little bikini.

'Oh, Jasmine,' she exclaimed. 'It was so sweet of you to remember me like this but I don't know. I mean, it's quite a walk back to the hotel and I would have to go all the way back to change and . . .' Her voice trailed off and she blushed, imagining herself in the scanty bathing suit.

'You don't have to go all the way back to the hotel, Katherine,' Rolf said quickly. 'See that big rock over there? You can change behind that. No one will see you there, you'll be fine. Also, the beach is completely deserted right now so you could change right out in the open and still there would be no one around to see you. Come on, Katherine, say yes. It's a perfect day for a walk.'

Rolf's smile was so warm and inviting, Katherine couldn't resist. She smiled and, with a nod, accepted their invitation. The sand was so hot it burned the soles of her feet as she ran quickly across the beach.

When she reached the rock, she ducked down behind it and slipped into the tiny bikini. When she had put it on, she gasped when she looked down at herself. Her full breasts were practically tumbling out of the bra top and the small triangle barely covered the thick bushy tangle between her legs. She took a deep breath and stepped out from behind the rock.

'Well, how do I look?' she asked shyly.

'You look great, Katherine, just great. Now come on, let's go. I don't want to stand here on the hot sand one minute longer,' Jasmine cried, scampering quickly down to the water's edge.

Rolf's eyes lingered on Katherine's breasts which were swelling in luscious mounds over the half-cups of the bikini top. Then he let his gaze move up and down her body a few times before speaking. 'You look great, Katherine, really hot. Almost good enough to eat,' he remarked gruffly, sliding his tongue over his lips.

Katherine blushed at his words and walked silently with him down to the water's edge where Jasmine was waiting for them. Then, without further ado, the three of them started walking along the edge of the water, laughing and shouting as the big breakers rolled in and splashed their legs, soothing the burning soles of their feet and cooling their hot skin.

As they walked along on the hard sand at the edge of the ocean, Katherine could feel the thong of the bikini bottom rubbing inside her bum crack and along her crease. The panties were just a little small for her and were irritating her sex in the most delicious way. The heat of the sun relaxed her, acting on her like an aphrodisiac, while the memories of her last interlude with Rolf continued to excite her. Her nipples tightened and she threw her head back to bask in the rays of the sun as the light breezes blew through her long black hair. She did not have a tan yet and the creamy colour of her skin contrasted dramatically with the shocking pink of the bikini.

The three of them continued on their walk, quieter now, enjoying the sounds and smells of the sea. Finally, they reached the mouth of the cave which was huge, dark and mysteriously inviting.

'Come on, let's go inside,' Rolf said eagerly, putting his arm around Katherine's bare shoulders as he urged her forward into the dark interior.

Katherine shivered slightly at his touch and moved forward into the cave, following Jasmine who had taken the lead. Once inside, they were completely blinded for a few moments and they all came to a standstill, waiting until their eyes grew used to the gloom.

Soon, they became accustomed to the dim interior and ventured further into the cave. The sand was cool and hard beneath their bare feet and the roof of the cave was far above their heads. As they made their way deeper and deeper into the cave, their small talk echoed strangely down through the twists and turns of the labyrinth that was leading them deeper and deeper into the earth. At one point, Jasmine reached into her tote bag and took out a small pocket flashlight to better light their way.

Finally, they turned one last corner and the path suddenly opened out into a small circular clearing. Katherine gasped out loud at what she saw. They had reached a part of the cave which was deep in the rock but, to her surprise, it was not dark. High above, there was an opening through which streams of muted sunlight shone down, bathing the entire cave in a golden light and giving it an almost magical, other worldly quality. Huge granite rocks jutted out everywhere, creating ready made places to sit and footholds to climb. The floor of the cave was partly rock and partly hard-packed sand. In the middle of the cave, there was a small pool of crystal clear turquoise water and, at the far end, emptying into the pool, was a small waterfall. Behind that, a shadowy alcove could just be made out.

'What a magnificent spot,' Katherine breathed in wonder.

'It's a natural formation,' Rolf explained. 'We think it might have been used by pirates a long time ago. And, in even more distant times, we think it could have been used for other purposes,' he added mysteriously.

'What other purposes?' Katherine asked, intrigued.

'We think that once, long ago, it could have been a place of sacrifice or worship or something like that. Also, there are manacles and chains embedded in the rock here and there. So, we think at one point it might even have been used as a prison,' Rolf explained. 'The presence of chains and restraints seems to indicate that people might have been kept prisoner here.'

His words sent shivers down Katherine's spine and, for a moment, a sinister pall hung over the startling beauty of the place.

'Oh, Rolf, don't be so melodramatic,' Jasmine broke in hurriedly, dispelling the gloomy mood. 'Katherine doesn't want to hear depressing stories like that. Besides, I think that's just your imagination working overtime. There's never been any proof those stories were true.'

'OK, OK, but you have to admit this is no ordinary cave. Anyway, Katherine, what do you think of the place? Isn't the water a fabulous colour? It's the special minerals and plant life which make it look like that.'

'It's glorious,' Katherine replied excitedly. 'And it looks so inviting. I can't resist. I think I'll take a dip.'

Without waiting for the others, she slipped into the water and began frolicking and playing, diving under the water then jumping up and diving under again. When she got tired of playing, she rolled over on her back and began to float. 'This is heavenly,' she cried. 'Come on in.'

Before they could respond to her invitation, Katherine swam across the pool to the far end where she climbed up on the rocky ledge and stepped under the waterfall, allowing the cool clear water to rush over her body from head to toe.

'Ooh,' she squealed,' this is wonderful. It feels like a thousand little hands all over my body.'

Rolf watched her for a moment then dived into the water. When he reached the other side of the pool, he heaved himself up on the rocky shelf where Katherine was standing under the waterfall. Her head was thrown back and the water was splashing down over her breasts in clear rivulets which streamed down into her deep cleavage. Her nipples were long and tight and clearly visible beneath the material of her wet bra – which clung like a second skin to every contour of her voluptuous breasts.

Rolf joined her under the waterfall, reached his arm around to the small of her back and pressed her to him, thrusting his pelvis hard against her.

'I want you. I want you right now,' he groaned into her wet hair.

Katherine started nervously at his sudden presence but when she felt his erection pressing against her, she responded instantly by grinding her crotch against him and raking her nails over his buttocks – which were rock hard beneath his tight wet bathing suit.

'You feel all cool and slippery,' she whispered softly, darting her tongue over her parted lips. She stretched her torso away from him and out of the way of the flowing water and slid her hands down over his bulging crotch. She smiled as Rolf caught his breath and thrust his pelvis forward to meet her touch. 'I had forgotten how big you are,' she whispered huskily. She slid one hand under the crotch of his trunks and cupped his hairy balls. Encouraged by his grunts of pleasure, she grazed them gently with her nails. They felt cool and soft to the touch. Her mouth watered. She wanted to lick them, take them in her mouth and run her tongue over them but, first, she had to get his trunks off. She slipped her fingers inside them and began inching them down over his hips.

Rolf groaned as his huge cock sprang free and the full intensity of the water flowed down upon it. The delicious sensation of the cool water on his enflamed member was soon replaced by the fiery heat of Katherine's eager mouth as she knelt in front of him and took his penis deep in her mouth. Greedily, she began to lick the full length of him with long hungry strokes.

'You taste so good,' she moaned, as she licked and sucked his jutting penis. Relentlessly, she worked on him, flicking him with her tongue and nipping him ever so gently with her teeth. Then she nudged his legs apart as wide as she could and slipped her head up close to his balls. She opened her mouth and ever so gently took one of them in her mouth. It felt just the way she imagined it would; all cool and soft with a light covering of very fine hairs.

Rolf began thrusting back and forth under her

expert ministrations. When she released him from her mouth and turned her attention back to his penis, her tongue circled the head of his cock and pushed at the tiny opening in the tip. With a loud growl, Rolf bucked forward in a sudden spasm. Katherine closed her lips hard around him, sucking and milking him, moving her mouth up and down his shaft in such a way that she matched his thrusting rhythm.

Finally, Rolf could take no more. 'Stand up,' he said as he reached for her and dragged her to her feet.

Katherine staggered to her feet and swayed in his arms as he rammed his hard rod full against her. She leant away from him, thrusting her breasts up towards him, begging for his touch. He reacted instantly by cupping her breasts in his hands, gauging their heaviness, and gently running his thumbs back and forth over their hard pink tips. Aroused even further by her little cries of delight, he pushed the flimsy bra up over her breasts and bent his head so he could enclose the tips of her breast in his mouth. At first, he sucked them lightly, then began nipping them gently with his teeth.

Katherine wriggled and squirmed in his arms. His hot mouth and skilful tongue were driving her crazy. She reached blindly for his cock. Feverishly, she began pulling on him and jerking him as hard as he could, crooning his name over and over again, egging him on to higher and higher peaks of pleasure. She wanted to get him so hot that he would stick his rod inside her. That was all she wanted. That was all she could think of. She wanted Rolf's cock in her now, right now. She didn't want to wait one minute longer. No more fooling around. Her juices were oozing out of her and her clitoris was tight, swollen and aching for release. She felt so light headed and weak at the knees, she didn't know how much longer she could stay standing up.

'Fuck me, Rolf. I want it now,' she cried, rubbing herself against him as she grabbed his twitching member in her hot feverish hands.

With an animal-like growl, Rolf dragged her out from under the waterfall and into the little alcove that lay behind. Panting with lust and hardly able to contain themselves, they pawed each other frantically, using their hands to tease and titillate each other, nipping greedily at each other's flesh with their teeth and dragging their nails over their most sensitive areas.

Katherine had lost all control. 'I want you inside me,' she said. 'I want you to stick that huge cock of yours right up me until it can't go any further.'

Rolf sighed and slid his hands in between her legs. The crotch of her bikini was smooth and wet. He ran his fingers back and forth briefly across the slick material then stuck his fingers inside the waistband and dragged it down over her writhing hips. When it lay in a little heap at her feet, he cupped her vulva in his hand and fluttered his fingers lightly back and forth along her furry cleft. She moved lasciviously beneath his exploring fingers, gyrating her hips in slow sensuous circles as he insinuated his fingers inside her swollen pink folds. Slowly and deliberately, he began toying with her clitoris, rubbing it back and forth, pressing ever so softly then pressing down a little harder.

Katherine was soaking wet and more than ready for him. She whimpered softly as he backed her up against the wall of the alcove and grabbed her buttocks, urging her to entwine her legs around him. Katherine locked her legs around his waist. She could feel his huge member probing at the entrance to her vagina. Unable to wait a second longer, she impaled herself with one sharp thrust on his rod. Caught up in her own lust, she began riding him like a mad woman, thrusting her hips back and forth, grunting and giving sharp little cries of delight.

Rolf's muscular legs supported them both as he matched her wild gyrations with deep penetrating thrusts, spearing into her again and again. As she bucked and pumped, little words and incoherent phrases escaped her parted lips as he continued his skilful assault. This was so good, so raw, she thought wildly. It was just what she wanted. She loved the feel of him ploughing her over and over again, making the walls of her vagina quake and surge in delicious pulsating waves. Thrills of sexual electricity skittered through her. Her loins were heavy with pent-up sexual energy that was screaming for release. Soon, she was transported to that place where nothing existed but his rampaging cock and the pleasure it was giving her.

She leant back and pressed her hands against his shoulders, positioning herself in such a way that each time he penetrated her, he irritated the shaft of her clitoris.

Then, suddenly, everything stopped. Katherine caught her breath and opened her eyes. She felt shocked and disoriented. What was going on? Slowly, Rolf disengaged himself from her and set her down gently on the ground. When she looked around, she saw that Jasmine had joined them in the alcove. She was leaning against the wall watching them. One of her hands was inside her bikini top massaging her breasts and the other was between her legs, frantically rubbing her mound.

'I want some too,' she whispered, her voice heavy with desire. 'I bet you would like it better with two anyway, Rolf,' she added, her eyes sliding down his naked body until they reached his erect penis.

Katherine was so turned on she could hardly think straight and now Jasmine had brought things to a screaming halt.

'What are you doing here?' Katherine mumbled through her sexual haze.

'Let's show her how it's done, Rolf,' Jasmine said softly. She began walking toward them, pulling her bikini top off to expose her pink-tipped breasts as she got closer to them. Rolf stood quietly by, watching her with hooded eyes as she came closer and closer. By the time she reached them, she was totally naked. He licked his lips as his eyes ran down the full length of her voluptuous body. His big penis was erect, jutting upward, the tip still glistening with Katherine's dew.

Katherine had never seen Jasmine naked before and she caught her breath at the woman's beauty. Her breasts were round white orbs tipped with dark red nipples. Her hips curved generously and her belly swelled gently down into a thick golden tangle of pubic curls. Her thighs were sturdy and well-toned, tapering into shapely calves and delicate ankles. Her nipples were hard little nubs and her blonde pussy hair was darkened with her juices. It was obvious to Katherine that Jasmine was as aroused as she was and ready for some real action. Katherine felt Rolf pulling her further back into the alcove then he indicated a raised rock platform. On it, was a thick piece of rubber foam covered by a drape of black velvet.

'This is where I really wanted us to be,' Rolf said with a sigh as he lay down on the silky surface of the spread and pulled Katherine down on top of him. 'I set this up especially for us today, Katherine. I hoped you would agree to come with me to the cave. I was dying to have sex with you again and I wanted us to do it right here on this altar.'

'Altar!' she exclaimed.

'Oh, yeah, I'm sure this was an altar once. People probably used this to offer sacrifices to their gods or something,' he explained. 'What better place for us to do it to each other?'

Katherine felt strangely aroused by the image his words conjured. She was still excited by their love-making of a few moments ago and she desperately wanted some relief. Her nipples were aching and her clitoris was so hard and tight she thought it was going to explode. She had to get some release – and fast. She lay full length against his naked body for a moment without making a move. Then, as her passion began to take hold of her again, she began wriggling and squirming against him, delighting in the feel of his male hardness against her soft flesh. Before long, she knew she couldn't wait any longer. She wanted to enjoy the pleasure of coupling in this unusual environment. Quickly, she straddled him and then slowly lowered herself onto his twitching shaft.

Rolf groaned his pleasure as her hot sex engulfed his cock. Slowly, she began to slide up and down the full length of him. He reached out his hands and began stroking her breasts, his knowing fingers fluttering lightly over the raw pink tips. Over and over again, Katherine sucked and released him with her strong inner muscles then twisted and turned on his penis until he was pumping madly upwards to meet her.

Then Jasmine stepped out of the shadows. In seconds, she had climbed up on to the mattress beside them, ignoring any pretence of sexual ettiquette.

'Would you like to be tied up and sacrificed on the altar, Rolf?' she asked prettily. 'How about offering yourself as a sacrifice to our pleasure? Would you like that, Rolfie?' she cried, bending over his chest so he could suck her nipples.

Muffled groans escaped his lips as she pushed her breasts together and pressed them against his mouth. Immediately, he began to suck greedily on her dark tips. After a moment, Jasmine extricated herself and bent forward over his chest. Slowly and deliberately, she dragged her tongue across his skin, licking him with long lazy strokes. Then she began nipping at his flesh and pulling on his thick chest hair. She closed her lips around his nipples and began sucking and biting them until they were hard and tight.

Rolf moaned loudly and reached out for her but Jasmine was too quick for him and jumped off the bed. In a flash, she produced some leather straps that had been lying on the floor and secured each of his wrists to little iron rings embedded in the rock on either side of the mattress. Then she fastened his ankles in the same fashion. He was pinned now, his arms and legs spread wide, unable to move anything but his pelvis.

Rolf strained against the straps and jerked his hips up and down, driving his penis deep into Katherine who was speechless at Jasmine's antics. She matched him thrust for thrust as he moved wildly inside her. As she continued to ride him, she watched through half-closed eyes as Jasmine climbed back on the bed and straddled Rolf's chest. Now both women were on top of him: Katherine impaled on his cock and Jasmine astride his chest with her pussy rammed right up against his mouth. The fact that the two of them were on top of Rolf wildly pleasuring themselves was so exciting Katherine could hardly breathe. She stilled herself for a moment then began to ride Rolf once more, gently at first then faster and faster. She couldn't see his face because Jasmine was in front of her but she could hear his grunts and groans as he jerked himself forward over and over, spearing so deeply inside her it was as if she could feel him grazing the very centre of her being.

From the sounds of ecstasy escaping Jasmine's lips, Katherine knew that Rolf's tongue was deep inside the other woman's pussy. She could almost feel his mouth on her, lapping and licking, sucking her juices; probing and exploring every inch of her with his long hot tongue.

Katherine's breasts were swollen and her nipples ached. She knew Jasmine would be in the same state and she wanted to savour her delicious body as well as Rolf's. Slowly, she reached around Jasmine's back and began playing with her gorgeous breasts, tweaking and pinching the two hard nubbins. Jasmine arched her back and thrust her breasts against Katherine's fingers. Rolf placed his hands on either side of Jasmine's gyrating hips and pulled them harder against his mouth so he could feast on her hot pussy and drink the juices that were flowing copiously from between the wet lips of her swollen sex.

Jasmine threw her head back and began thrusting and bucking against Rolf's tongue. As she grew more excited, her moans and wild movements ignited Katherine's passion even further. In one long slow sensuous movement, she slid her hand between Jasmine's legs and began rubbing her furry bush. Then, slowly, she teased the sensitive skin underneath with the tips

161

of her nails and explored briefly the very top of her crease. Knowing she could excite and titillate this bold woman even further, she flattened out her hand and moved her palm in slow, deliberate circles over Jasmine's sex. As she kept up this sweet torment, she proceeded to ride Rolf more quickly, matching his rhythm as it rose to a fever pitch.

Katherine and Jasmine were almost drunk with pleasure, squeezing every ounce of delight they could from Rolf's expert tongue and cock. As their passion started to peak, Katherine pumped harder and harder. She threw her arms around Jasmine again and began pulling on her nipples, her touch harder, more insistent this time. The blonde woman groaned and ground herself even harder against Rolf's tongue and he responded by swirling it more quickly over the head of her rigid clitoris. Each stroke, each caress that any one of them performed, directly affected the others, setting up a kind of ripple effect until all three were crying out, their bodies thrashing and bucking, their entire being caught up in the intensity of their lust.

Katherine knew she was close to coming. She could feel her orgasm building deep in her loins. With one hand, she raked the tender flesh under Rolf's pubic hair and with the other tweaked Jasmine's bullet-hard nipples. She rode Rolf harder and harder. The more she rode him, the more he sucked hungrily at Jasmine's clit. The three were now completely caught up in a circle of passion, oblivious to everything but satisfying their escalating lust.

In the heat of his passion, Rolf thrashed and pulled against his restraints. Over and over, he speared deep into Katherine's throbbing passage while he licked Jasmine's pussy and greedily drank her juices. The women's groans echoed in the cave as his tongue and

162

his penis worked together on them like a well-oiled pleasure machine.

The sounds of their moans and cries echoed strangely in the little alcove, driving them to higher and higher peaks of frenzied excitement. They created more and more pleasure for one another, bringing each other to the edge then pulling back, teasing, touching each other softly then more aggressively, keeping each other teetering on the brink until every nerve in their bodies was screaming for release. Then, finally, they allowed each other to give in to their all-engulfing passion. In a wild crescendo, they peaked together in a symphony of groans and cries that rang through the alcove as they came in a series of searing orgasms.

Chapter Eight

Katherine was nervous, more nervous than she had ever been before a blind date. And that's what it was, she reminded herself. Even though she and Assam had shared an intimate experience in the rose garden, she still didn't know a thing about him. She had only seen him in passing since their wild night together. But, every time their eyes met, a raging heat would suffuse her body and she would smile while they made small talk. He would bow and always be very courteous but his eyes would devour her as if he owned her, as if he knew her body from head to toe. And he did, she reminded herself with a delicious shudder. He knew every inch of her body. Her nipples tightened and her breasts suddenly felt uncomfortably constrained beneath the low cut bodice of her black dress. There was something about the man. A little frisson of fear danced over her skin and she suddenly felt very excited. He was handsome, sophisticated, urbane and an amazing lover. Yet, there was something cold and unyielding about him and, in his steely

164

blue eyes, she thought she sometimes caught a glint of cruelty.

One afternoon when she had been strolling in the grounds, they had bumped into one another and he had asked her for cocktails and dinner in his suite. She had accepted and the rendezvous had been set for that night.

Katherine gave herself a little shake and walked over to the full-length mirror. She wanted to give herself a last-minute check before he came to pick her up. Her hair was swept up into a chignon and her make-up, a little heavier for evening, enhanced her large dark eyes and full red lips. Her sheer black stockings and high-heeled sandals set off her black dress perfectly. She took a long critical look at herself and smiled. Very slowly, she began inching her skirt up over her well-toned thighs. Then she eased it up even further over her voluptuous hips. She was not wearing any panties and her dark curly bush protruded boldly from beneath her black lace suspender belt. She imagined Assam's hands on the bare alabaster skin just above her stockings and she shivered. She ran her hands over her breasts. Immediately, her nipples rose in response. She let one of the thin straps of her dress fall over her shoulder. Then she pulled on it so the material over her right breast slid down and one white orb tumbled free. She stared at her reflection for a moment and smiled. She liked the way she looked; sort of rumpled and sexy with one breast bare, her dress hiked up around her waist and her curly bush, dark and inviting, peeking out below below the outline of her suspender belt.

She began striking erotic poses, running her tongue over her lips, fingering her nipples and rubbing her mound as she arched her back and thrust her magnificent breasts forward towards the mirror. If Assam could only see me now, she thought. She pictured him coming up behind her, running his hands down between her legs, stroking her pussy.

God, she was so turned on! She certainly had changed lately. Usually, she was so calm and collected, so in control of herself. And yet, being in control had not brought her much success or happiness. Well, she had certainly done everything she could to change that. She had explored a lot since she had been here. And yet, she knew there were secrets still waiting to be discovered.

A gentle knock at the door broke into her thoughts. After adjusting her dress, she strode across the room and answered it. A tall dark man dressed in an impeccably tailored white suit stood in the doorway, smiling down at her.

'Good evening, Miss MacNeil. Mr Aswabi sends his compliments and asks that you allow me to show you to his suite.'

Katherine felt mildly annoyed that Assam had not come for her himself and tried to ignore a feeling of mild apprehension that had settled in the pit of her stomach. However, she realised there was nothing she could do but follow the man to Assam's suite. She straightened up slightly and smiled at her unexpected visitor.

'By all means. I'd be delighted,' she murmured.

The man bowed and ushered her silently down the deserted hall into the waiting lift. As they made their slow ascent, neither of them spoke. Katherine's heart was beating so wildly she was afraid the man would hear it. Maybe I shouldn't have accepted Assam's invitation, she thought. She was surprised at her unexpected level of anxiety and tried to reassure herself by remembering how wonderful she had felt with him in the rose garden and how his touch had set her on fire.

When the lift doors opened and she walked out into the dimly-lit hall, she caught her breath in amazement. This was nothing like the cool, elegantly furnished lounge on the main floor or the cosy breakfast room with its white wicker furniture and chintz-covered sofas. This was totally different. It was lush and opulently appointed. The lighting was subdued and the air was heavy with the scent of sandalwood and jasmine. The walls were decorated with paintings of men and women of all nationalities in a variety of erotic poses. Where in the world am I? she wondered. This was a part of the hotel she had never seen. She was willing to bet no one else had seen it either, except those especially invited by Assam, of course. She shivered with a mixture of fear and excitement and continued walking down the corridor, her footsteps muted by the thick carpet that covered the floor. The hall was lined with un-numbered doors and, as she made her way through the dim light, she could hear the sound of low voices, muffled moans and the soft sound of stringed instruments.

'Here we are,' her guide announced as he opened a plain black door and ushered her inside. Without a word he disappeared into the hall and closed the door behind him.

Katherine couldn't believe her eyes; she felt as if she had stepped into another world. She was in a huge circular room. The stark white walls were decked with great swathes of peach satin and filmy white gauze which fell in luxuriant folds to the highly polished parquet floor. Placed with great artistry here and there, were exquisite Persian carpets in delicate pastel colours, thick white fur rugs and, contrasting with the overall pastel decor, dark blue and pink scatter rugs with a dramatic geometric design.

The bed was at the far end of the room. It was round and surrounded by a canopy of peach satin drapes which hung from a circular track fixed to the ceiling above it. The drapes had been pulled aside to reveal the huge bed in all its glory. Plump satin pillows of all shapes and sizes were scattered on the bedspread in a profusion of colour. Ice-green, peach, white and mauve. Beside the bed were white satin bell pulls and, directly above, a big mirror slanted at a sharp angle.

Here and there throughout the room were occasional tables of dark rosewood with intricate lattice-work designs and, opposite the bed on the far wall, was an elegant white and grey marble fireplace. On either side of the fireplace, a number of big cushions were scattered around a low round table which was set with bowls of fruit, brass decanters, and samovars with matching cups and wine goblets. At the other end of the room near the window was a huge jacuzzi tub surrounded by racks of thick fluffy towels. The floor was carpeted in a black and white fur rug and near the tub was a comfortable sofa covered in a soft rose-coloured material with matching easy chairs. Beside another door, which she assumed led to the bathroom, was a conversation area where two couches covered in dark blue velvet faced each other across a rose and white marble coffee table. Here, too, there were brass drinking vessels and decanters set on highly polished matching trays along with incense holders and a beautiful rosewood box. The entire room was stunning in its design and colour and had clearly been set up to delight the senses in every way possible.

Katherine could only gaze in astonishment at the exotic decor. This was the setting for their evening together. She shivered slightly then jumped with a start when she felt a hand softly touch her arm.

'Good evening, Katherine. Thank you so much for coming.'

She whirled around. It was him. He was dressed in a dark full-length silk robe and was carrying a single rose in his hand. His eyes cooly appraised her appearance.

'You are looking very chic, Katherine but, unfortunately, not at all suitable for what I had in mind for this evening. Perhaps you would be kind enough to let my attendants prepare you.'

Before she could respond, he clapped his hands twice and two women dressed in pantaloons and silk midriffs appeared out of the shadows.

Katherine gasped. What was going on here? She glanced quickly over at Assam but he only smiled.

You'll be fine, Katherine,' he said in a calm, soothing voice. 'I'll be with you shortly. I'm sure you will enjoy this little preamble to our evening together.'

Before she could ask for an explanation, he turned and left the room. Confused, she turned towards the women, a question in her eyes. They just smiled and silently ushered her into an adjoining room which was equipped with a round sunken tub, couches, easy chairs, something that looked like a massage table and a dressing table with brushes, combs and other grooming tools.

'Why are you taking me in here?' she asked hesitantly.

'You are to be prepared, miss,' one of the women said softly.

'Prepared? What do you mean?'

'Mr Aswabi gave us strict instructions to prepare you for your evening with him. He likes things to be just perfect.'

Katherine didn't know what to make of the situation. She felt apprehensive but intrigued. She reminded herself of her resolve to experiment and be adventurous. Martha's words came back to her. She would never be asked to do anything against her will. She felt secure with Assam. She took a deep breath and decided to go with the situation.

However, she wasn't prepared for what happened next and recoiled instantly the moment the women began undressing her.

'What are you doing?' she gasped.

'You must not be afraid, miss. Everything is being done according to Mr Aswabi's orders. There is nothing to fear. Everything is being done for your pleasure and his.'

They led her over to a huge full-length mirror and proceeded to undo her dress. She watched as they slipped it over her breasts and down over her hips. In a few seconds, she was standing before them wearing nothing but her underwear and her high heels. The women gave her the same appraising look Assam had given her then whispered among themselves.

'This underwear is not suitable,' one of them murmured.

Katherine shivered as one woman loosened the clasp on her suspender belt and slipped off her stockings while the other one removed her sandals. She was naked now in the harsh overhead light. She started violently as one of the women cupped her breasts and admiringly fingered the nipples which instantly stiffened under her touch.

'Beautiful,' she murmured. 'Just a little colour perhaps, after the bath. Yes, very beautiful.'

'Yes and the pubic hair needs grooming. Perhaps, even a little trim. Also, a closer shave under the arms and the entire length of both legs,' the other added. 'After that, I think the bath and the perfume.'

Katherine was so astonished, she could only stand there shivering. She wanted to protest but the words stuck in her throat. The women led her to the massage table and bade her lie down. Silently and efficiently, they went about their work. In no time, one had lathered her armpits and was shaving her there whilst the other worked on her legs. Both were using very small skin-sensitive razors. The sensation was delicious and strangely erotic. She could hardly believe she was lying naked on a massage table allowing two complete strangers to shave her legs and armpits. It was totally unthinkable and yet she was letting them do it. If the truth were told, she was actually loving every minute of it. She had been waxed in beauty salons, but never had the staff insisted on nakedness!

As this process continued, the lights were dimmed and the heady scent of jasmine and the soft strumming of guitar music filtered into the room. Gradually, Katherine allowed herself to be soothed by the music and the sweet-smelling incense. The women's hands were moving all over her and she sighed deeply as two more women came in and began assisted in the process of beautification. One took her hair out of its sleek chignon and began brushing it with long slow strokes. Another removed the polish from her fingernails and began filing and buffing them. Yet another trimmed her toe nails and removed the polish she had so carefully applied earlier that evening. After an initial feeling of disappointment that her own grooming routine had failed to impress, gradually Katherine began to relax under their gentle attendance. Then one of them placed her fingers just above her dark bush.

'What are you doing?' Katherine gasped, trying to sit up on the table and push the woman's hands away.

'You need to be groomed here as well, my dear,' one of the women whispered with a knowing smile.

And, before Katherine could protest, the woman picked up a comb from the dressing table and began combing Katherine's wiry curls. As the teeth of the comb pulled through the dark tangle and grazed the sensitive skin underneath, a thrill raced between Katherine's legs and through her breasts. She sighed and wriggled voluptuously as the woman dragged the comb back and forth but, when she felt the touch of cold metal against her skin, she cried out sharply then watched in disbelief as one of the women took scissors and began trimming her bush. Slowly and methodically, she snipped and trimmed the pubic curls until they were neat and tidy. The feel of the cold blades so close to her sensitive folds excited Katherine even more and she felt the urge to grind her hips. The closeness of the blades and the feel of the cold metal so close to her vulva sent needles of excitement radiating deep into her core. Her whole body was tingling with this exotic preparation and she could feel her excitement mounting.

As they continued to groom and titillate her, the full implications of their ministrations dawned on her. There was a night of sensual and sexual delights waiting for her with the mysterious Mr Aswabi and she was being prepared very carefully for it. In fact, she thought, she was being aroused intentionally so that when she and Assam got together, she would be more than ready for him. Her breath quickened in anticipation as she fantasised about what was in store for her that night.

Katherine allowed herself to be soothed by their soft hands but, when one of them picked up a pair of tweezers and pulled out a pubic hair, she cried out sharply in protest at the painful sting. Two women calmly held her down while another proceeded to pluck excess hairs that had escaped the blades of the scissors. With each hair that was plucked, Katherine cried out at the stinging pull on her flesh. Soon, however, the initial pain gave way to a warm melting sensation. Before long, she was squirming deliciously beneath their restraining hands.

Finally, their work was complete. Her finger nails and toe nails had been cleaned, filed and repainted a gorgeous peach shade. Her bush was a neatly-trimmed triangle with no renegade hairs spoiling the symmetry of its clearly defined shape. Her hair hung loose around her face and flowed down over her shoulders and halfway down her back. She felt wonderful.

The women helped her up and led her over to the tub. She sat down in the tepid water and allowed them to wash every part of her with a rose-scented soap. Their hands were everywhere: sliding over her breasts, slithering down to her mound, down her back and over her buttocks. Her whole body was awakened under their caressing touch. She moaned as one of them slipped a soapy finger into her rear cleavage and lathered her briefly. Another slid her hands over her pussy and began rubbing and lathering her with gentle strokes. Then she slipped one finger inside

Katherine's crease and made sure she was soaped and clean in that most private area as well.

Katherine could hear herself gasping out loud, unconcerned now about showing her mounting excitement. The feel of their hands sliding over her breasts, rubbing her nipples, cleaning and exploring every part of her until they were sure she was completely and totally ready for what lay ahead, had left her senses reeling.

When the women were finished, they helped her out of the tub. She was feeling slightly dizzy now with all the stimulation and the heady scent of roses and jasmine that filled the air. The women led her back to the dressing table again where hairbrushes and combs, small sable make-up brushes, phials of perfumed oil, small pots of rouge and other cosmetics were laid out in preparation for the next phase. She sighed in delight as the women poured the oil into their hands and began anointing every part of her quivering body. Their fingers were everywhere: in the hollows of her elbows, the sensitive area behind her knees, between her toes and in the hollows of her neck. The scent was overpowering and only added to her state of arousal. Katherine felt like the favoured girl in a harem, being pampered before being presented to the Emir. Her nipples were long hard points now, yearning to be touched. As if she could read Katherine's thoughts, one woman extended a heavily oiled finger and lightly lubricated both nipples. Katherine groaned as the woman toyed briefly with her aching nubs then cried aloud as she slid her fingers down into her bush and began pulling the silky curls until they too were well-oiled and sleek with perfume.

Katherine felt so weak at the knees that she asked to sit down. The women agreed but not before one of them had slid an oily finger between Katherine's buttocks and given her anus a few firm strokes.

'There,' one whispered. 'All perfumed and ready.'

Her head spinning, Katherine sat down on a little stool in front of the dressing table. She watched in delight as the women applied some light make-up, accentuated her dark eyes with a few expert touches of kohl and applied a touch of very pale peach lipstick to her full sensual mouth. Then, to her astonishment, one dipped a small sable brush in a pot of peach-coloured powder and feathered it over her nipples. Katherine gasped aloud as the soft brush caressed her sensitive peaks.

When they were finished, she looked at herself in the full-length mirror. She could hardly believe her eyes. She looked incredibly beautiful. Her nipples were swollen and luscious and even more noticeable now that they had been rouged. Her shining black hair hung loosely down her back and her thick bush was a small tidy triangle. Her entire body was fragrant and gleaming with the scented oil.

She was almost fainting from the sensuality of the experience and her mounting sexual arousal. As she stood admiring herself in the mirror, one of the women came up behind her and draped a sheer white robe over her head and down on to her shoulders. It fell around her sumptuous body like a cloud. She caught her breath sharply when she saw herself draped in this filmy garment; it was completely transparent. Beneath its gossamer folds, the deep peach of her rouged nipples and the dark tangle between her legs were visible for all to see.

'Now you are ready for Mr Aswabi,' one woman sighed, looking at her in admiration.

Katherine said nothing as her handmaidens led her

back into the main room. She was in a kind of trance and, at the same time, all her senses were ablaze with desire. Her nipples were hard and tight and she could feel the heaviness building in her loins. They had done their job well.

She didn't hear him when he walked in but the touch of his hand on her arm burned her flesh like fire and she spun round as if her skin had been seared by a live coal.

'Dazzling,' he murmured appreciatively.

Then, without another word, he lowered his mouth to hers and slid his tongue deep into her mouth where it began exploring the sensitive inner lining, snaking around her own tongue, licking and probing until she thought she was going to faint.

Her moans filled his mouth and she started sucking on his tongue, tasting it and lapping at its long thick hardness.

He pulled away and dropped his mouth to her breasts which were tight and swollen, their tips hard pulsing points pushing against the sheer material of her gown. She gasped as she felt his hot breath on her and thrust towards him. He cupped her breasts in both hands, weighing their heaviness. Her vulva clenched as his thumb moved the material of her robe back and forth over her nipples, irritating their raw tips. Delicious waves raced down to her clitoris and a deep sigh escaped her lips. Her knees sagged beneath her as she swayed under the assault of his knowing hands. He held her steady by dropping to his knees and putting one arm around her waist. As she stood supported in his grasp, he let his other hand wander over her body. His fingers tantalised her through the silky material and she could feel his hot breath on her perfumed mound.

'You smell like roses,' he murmured into her soft downy bush.

He slid his hand up under her robe and, when he found her dark silky tangle, he pushed the filmy material up over her waist and buried his face in her sex. His breath began to come faster now as he inhaled the scent of roses and the strong animal scent of her mounting passion. His teeth pulled at her wiry pussy hairs and his mouth sucked them up in little clumps, tasting and savouring them until Katherine thought she would go mad.

His touch was like fire. She was aflame with passion for him. Every nerve in her body screamed out for his touch. She wanted him to feast on her, to tease and stroke her, to explore every part of her body until she could bear no more.

He raised his head from her quivering sex and stood up. Then, in one easy move, he manoeuvred her down on to the soft rug. Slowly, he inched the gown up her body until it was rucked up over her breasts. She raised her arms and upper body slightly so he could reach around her and pull it off over her head. She fell back on to the rug writhing sensuously, giddy with the knowledge that at last she was lying naked before him. Her scented body that had been groomed and beautified in every way imaginable was now revealed before him in all its glory.

She loved the way his cool glittering eyes devoured every part of her. It felt wonderful to know her body could have so much power over a man. She watched him through heavily lidded eyes as he pulled a square of silken material out of his pocket and laid it on her breasts. She shuddered as he began trailing it slowly and sensuously up and down the length of her body.

Back and forth he dragged it, sending delicious tingles dancing over her flesh.

He turned her over onto her stomach and teased her with the silken material, occasionally following the titillating trail of the silk over her skin with little kisses and gentle bites until she was panting and squirming with delight. When he rolled her over onto her back, she was breathless with desire and her dew was oozing out of her.

He dipped his fingers into her juices and slid them along the crease of her swollen labia then grazed her quivering sex with his nails. Then, speaking softly in his own language, he raised his fingers to his mouth, then licked them.

Katherine's sex fluttered wildly when he sucked the taste of her off his fingers. Almost drugged now with this sensual assault, she reached up and rubbed her hands over her breasts in a fever of rising passion. He responded by lowering his mouth to her belly, trailing his tongue over her sensitive flesh, dipping into her navel then continuing up over her breasts, sliding into her armpits and down her arms to her hands and fingers. Katherine writhed and panted beneath his touch, lost in a whirl of passion. She felt weak and vulnerable. Her body trembled uncontrollably as her raw nerves cried out for more.

Finally, he stopped and lay on his side, looking down at her. 'You are truly wonderful and so deliciously uninhibited,' he whispered. 'You were made for pleasure. It is written in every curve of your magnificent body. All you need is a little fine tuning and you will be at the height of your capacity for sensual enjoyment.'

He clapped his hands and a woman appeared carrying a silver bowl which she laid down beside him. He reached into it and took out an ice cube which he placed on the tip of one of Katherine's nipples. She gasped at the shock of the icy cold cube on her sensitive tip but soon her body began to writhe under the sweet torture as he played the frozen substance over her breasts and down her torso until he reached the tender flesh of her inner thighs.

'The contrast between heat and cold can offer much pleasure,' he whispered, as he continued sliding the melting ice cube over her body, intensifying her arousal.

She was breathless from the touch of the ice on her hot skin and almost delirious from the sensations building up inside her. Assam parted her legs then lay down between them. He began moving his tongue up the inside of her thighs, its hot wetness contrasting dramatically with the cold trail of the ice cube. First the cold, then the hot. Katherine felt stimulated to the point of madness when Assam cupped her pussy with his hot hand for a moment then slid the quickly-melting cube deep into her folds. She groaned aloud as her vulva clenched and her overwhelming sexual excitement stiffened her clitoris into a hard tight nub.

'Please, please,' she moaned, almost incoherent now under this relentless but welcome assault on her senses.

'Yes, my darling, it is time,' he murmured.

Silently, he picked her up and carried her over to the bed where he laid her down gently and parted her legs wide. Then he removed his silken robe and stood naked beside the bed looking down at her, his eyes dark with lust.

Katherine was almost delirious with excitement. No man – not even Rolf – had brought her senses to such a peak of intensity. As she lay on the bed trembling and breathless with desire, she parted her legs even wider. She wanted him to see her pussy, the outer lips swollen and retracted, the inner folds glistening with her dew. She felt no shame. She was proud of her body and the state to which he had brought her. She wanted him to see how hot and wet she was. She was lost in a world of sensual pleasure where shame played no part. She felt deliciously wanton and her body cried for more, much more.

She looked up at him standing by the bed. He was gazing down at her, his eyes feasting on her luscious breasts with their long tight points. She writhed sensuously on the satin sheets. Her eyes took in every inch of his body. At the sight of his nakedness, she sucked in her breath. He was magnificent. His body was slight but muscular, well toned and well proportioned. Her gaze slowly went down his belly until its inexorable path reached his penis. It was long and hard and twitching with passion. She moaned in anticipation and thrust her hips forward. She ached for him. She wanted him now. She wanted to feel him pin her with his huge shaft, to feel him stretch her, fill her. She knew from the look in his eyes that he wanted the same thing. Still, he lingered and made no move towards her.

'Not yet, Katherine, not quite yet,' he murmured, responding to the naked desire in her eyes.

'Oh, what are you doing?' she gasped, as he reached over and took her hands.

'More pleasure, Katherine. Much more.'

Quickly, he secured her right wrist in a white satin cuff which was attached to a long silken cord connected to the floor. In seconds, he had secured the other wrist in the same manner.

What is he doing? she thought, fear catching in her

throat. She knew from her experience with Alan that she liked being tied down but, despite herself, she still felt nervous. Again she remembered the rose garden. She had been totally in Assam's power then and he had taken her to heights of pleasure she had never dreamt possible. Now she was giving herself over to him once more. She looked into his eyes and saw an acknowledgment of the trust between them. She relaxed and felt her pleasure intensify as she realised she was now pinned by the silken restraints. She watched through half-closed eyes as he gently circled one ankle then the other with another pair of white satin cuffs which hung from a pulley system in the ceiling.

Very slowly, he manipulated the ropes so that her legs were gently parted and her feet were pulled up towards the ceiling until her legs were at right angles to the bed. Now her most intimate parts were completely exposed. Then, underneath her buttocks, he placed a white satin pillow for support.

'There now,' he sighed, bending to lightly kiss her vulva. 'Now we are ready.'

Very, very slowly, he slid his fingers past her outer labia and gently began to explore her. Katherine sighed loudly at this sweet invasion. His fingers stroked and caressed her until she was writhing beneath his touch. Then he parted the delicate inner flesh, snaked his tongue deep inside her and with slow, deliberate strokes, lapped the hard steely nub of her clitoris.

'Oh, God, yes,' Katherine moaned as she felt his mouth clamp down on her throbbing clit.

Thrills of ecstasy overwhelmed her and she writhed in sensual delight. His mouth was engulfing her, devouring her, sucking and licking every part of her. His tongue snaked up and over her clitoris, slithering back and forth until she was panting and pulling against the silken ties that restrained her. The feeling of helplessness under such a sweet assault, of being restrained and pleasured at the same time, drove her into a frenzy of passion and she thrashed wildly on the bed, her moans of ecstasy echoing through the room.

His mouth was voracious and, as he continued to feast greedily on her, his fingers slid up to her breasts and he began rolling her nipples between his thumb and index finger. Her vagina convulsed and her juices poured forth. She knew she was ready.

'Take me. For God's sake, take me now,' she panted.

Assam would not be rushed nor would he allow her to dictate his actions; that was up to him. And he had other delights in mind for her. From behind one of the satin curtains, he pulled out a small white whip with silk thongs. On the end of these thongs, were heavy little nubs of pink satin which he proceeded to dangle over her heaving breasts.

'What are you going to do with that?' she stammered breathlessly as she watched the little whip swaying nearer and nearer her breasts.

'Remember, Katherine, in the rose garden, I said you had hidden thorns? Well, I do, too. I would like you to taste the sweet pain of one of those thorns right now.'

'Oh, no, you can't . . . you can't mean . . .'

Her words were cut short by the sting of the little white thongs on her nipples. She cried out in sharp protest as the stinging sensation turned into an excruciating pleasure; a wild sexual thrill that raced directly from her raw tips to her wildly pulsing clitoris. He continued lightly flicking the little satin whip over her nipples and the delicate flesh of her swollen breasts. Then he dragged the silken thongs further down her body and gave her a few quick flicks across her pubic mound. His skilful use of the whip sent her into a frenzy and she bucked and struggled wildly against her restraints as her sexual arousal reached a fever pitch.

'That's enough for now, my darling,' he crooned to her, as he put the instrument of her exquisite torture aside and bent to kiss one of her aching nipples.

'One's first introduction to the whip must be brief. It is an acquired taste and one must be initiated slowly into the exquisite delights it has to offer. I hope you enjoyed my little thorns, Katherine. Perhaps, one day, you will allow me to feel the sting of yours. However, more of that later. Right now, I have a surprise for you.'

Slowly, he loosened the ties on her legs and helped her sit up. Her arms remained in the silken restraints. When she was sitting up, he drew her on to his lap and arranged her legs around his waist. Katherine was crazy with desire and felt half drunk with passion. She could not believe he was still holding off. She could feel the hot tip of his member so close to her slit that she felt like impaling herself on it but she could move only as he directed. She strained feverishly against her silken ties.

'Patience, my dear, patience. Surely, you know by now that putting off the inevitable only increases the pleasure,' he added. He turned and beckoned to a figure standing in the shadows.

Katherine started nervously as a young man stepped out into the light. He was naked and his cock was in full erection, bobbing and twitching as he moved towards the bed. Wildly she struggled against her bonds but it was no use. Her wrists were securely fastened and Assam was holding her firmly on his lap. She looked at the young man again. He must have been standing there in the shadows the whole time watching Assam lick and suck her pussy. The thought that he had been spying on them like that electrified her and sent wild sexual tingles radiating through her body.

'Who is this? What does he want?' she cried.

'He wants what you want, darling Katherine,' Assam murmured, his voice smooth and comforting. 'This is Kadir. He's going to make you very happy. Come now, Katherine, admit it. Your body aches for this. You want this just as much as we do.'

Katherine shuddered as her vagina and anus contracted violently. He was right. She knew he was right. Her whole body was clamouring for sex. Every nerve end was screaming for their touch. She wanted him. She wanted them both. She wanted to feel them ravishing every part of her body.

Slowly, Assam adjusted her position on his lap. His member quivered for a moment at the entrance to the source of her pleasure. Then, in one smooth thrust, he slid past her outer ridge into her dark wet tunnel. Katherine held her breath as he penetrated deep into her very core. Finally, he was inside her. Finally, she could feel him, long and hard, sheathed in her hot throbbing passage. She caught her breath as she felt him fill her up, stretch her almost beyond her limit then stop and remain completely still. The feel of him pulsing within her almost drove her mad. He stayed that way, quietly letting her feel the full extent of his passion.

'Oh, God,' she moaned, 'fuck me, fuck me now.'

Assam didn't move. She gyrated her hips in a helpless frenzy, pushing against him, crazy with desire. Then, through her raging lust, she heard him talking to her.

'Feel this, Katherine,' he was saying. 'Let yourself feel this.'

'Oh, God,' she whimpered, as she felt a soft warm tongue snake its way into the cleavage of her behind. She could feel the young man behind her now. He had positioned himself there as she sat on Assam's lap, impaled on his huge penis. She ground down on Assam's cock as Kadir's tongue fluttered back and forth over the puckered brown opening of her anus.

'Let him in, Katherine,' Assam whispered. 'Don't fight it. Let him open you up.'

Katherine shuddered as Kadir removed his tongue. Her buttocks were trembling. Then she felt his long cool well-oiled finger inch its way inside her. She inhaled sharply as it massaged and gently probed the opening to her anus, pushing her to release and open up her puckered little opening. She shuddered when it quivered violently then opened wide to receive Kadir's finger – which he wriggled and pushed deep into her most secret passage. When he began to thrust and churn it deep inside her, Katherine felt herself contract around his finger and begin to milk it. Then Kadir removed his finger and slowly inserted his lubricated, swollen cock into the narrow opening of her anus. At that moment, Assam began to move his penis in a slow thrusting motion back and forth, penetrating deep inside her, until his wild grunts and scything motion set her aflame once again. She made a low animal-like sound, and her hips began to jerk and buck in time with him. His heavy balls hit up against her as he rammed his cock deeper and deeper. His voice crooned her name over and over along with what Katherine presumed were Arabic expressions of ecstasy.

Katherine strained forward and the muscles of her vagina clenched him as she tried to pull him into her very depths. Both men were working on her and she was crazy with passion. Her restraints were still holding her captive; a willing victim to this endless pleasure. Impaled on the two men, she writhed wildly as waves of excruciating pleasure coursed through her. Then, suddenly, her fevered brain lit up with the memory of the woman and the two men in the park she had encountered the night before she had left for her trip. Now, she was that woman. Finally, she was experiencing the wild sensual abandon she had craved that night. Now it was her turn, she gasped inwardly as she pumped and panted in rhythm with the two men. How good it felt to be stretched and plundered by two cocks, to feel them sliding in and out of her, one scything deep into her vagina and the other ploughing her virgin back passage. She tossed her head from side to side, licking her lips, grinding herself on their cocks, and giving herself in total abandon to their expert ministrations. As Kadir continued his pumping motions, he slipped his hands over her breasts and began tweaking and lightly pinching the hard nubs of her nipples.

Overcome with passion, Katherine wailed out her pleasure and jerked her hips even faster, riding the two men harder and harder as they continued to stimulate every part of her. She could feel her climax building deep inside her as the two men speared her from the front and from behind respectively. Her vagina was convulsing, her clitoris aching and swollen. Her anus was now so sensitised by the thrusts of Kadir's huge penis that it was quivering wildly at every penetration. She wanted this to go on forever but she knew she couldn't hold out any longer. Her vagina lurched, sending hot surges of sexual pleasure through her entire body. Her clit felt heavy, swollen, pulsing in wild electric surges as her anus opened and closed in endless spasms.

She wanted it to go on forever, she wanted to savour it endlessly, to teeter deliciously on the brink. Suddenly, there was no question of holding anything in reserve: her whole body tensed as her climax burst upon her. She arched and cried out as her anus spasmed and her vagina clenched around Assam's penis. Over and over she came, bucking wildly on the two rampaging cocks as waves of excruciating pleasure flooded through her, sending her into paroxysms of agonised delight.

Assam and Kadir matched her rhythms, easing in and out of her two passages, and grunting out their climaxes as each in their own way drove her further and further toward the realms of indescribable pleasure.

Katherine's climax left her panting for breath, stunned at the heights of passion she had climbed. She collapsed against Assam, exhausted, satisfied and deeply moved.

They lay in silence for a long time. When she finally opened her eyes, Kadir had left the room and Assam was staring down at her, a tender expression in his steely blue eyes.

'You are a remarkable woman, Katherine,' he murmured softly. 'Are you sure you're from the west?' he added, an amused glint in his eyes.

'I have never felt like this with anyone in my life,' she admitted, blushing deeply.

She was determined not to tell him the full extent

187

of her feelings for him. After all, theirs had been a purely physical relationship so far. She didn't want to scare him away or presume too much about what had passed between them. She knew in her heart that this was someone who matched her in intensity and in intelligence. She had never met anyone like him and, deep in her heart, she was worried that she never would again. He was a man in a million and she would be devastated if she lost him. Assam smiled at her and stared at her for a moment, an enigmatic expression on his handsome face. Then he got up and helped her from the bed. Without a word, he picked her up and carried her over to the jacuzzi.

'I have another surprise for you,' he whispered.

He lowered her into the tub. To her total amazement and delight, she saw that it was filled with cool, lightly spiced milk. And, floating on top, were hundreds of pink and white rose petals.

Katherine caught her breath as the cool milk washed over her hot skin. It was the most delicious sensation she had ever experienced. She settled deeply into the bath and let the smooth creamy liquid and gentle spices sooth and calm her fevered body.

She lay there for a long time, basking in the cool embrace of the liquid and breathing in the spicy fragrance. Then, when she was ready, she allowed Assam to help her out and lead her into the bathroom to the shower where he used the detachable shower head to rinse the milk off her with a gentle spray of tepid water. When he was finished, he dried her off with a big fluffy towel and helped her into a long, white silk kimono.

She felt refreshed and ravenously hungry. When they walked back towards the centre of the room, she saw that a feast had been prepared. The room was dark except for the flickering light of many scented candles and the sound of guitar music could be heard playing gently in the background. He led her over to the round table by the fireplace and motioned to her to sit down on one of the big cushions. He sat down opposite her and together they shared a meal of exotic delicacies and the finest wines. They fed each other fruit and other candied confections. They caressed each other and shared long lingering glances as they tasted and savoured the exquisite meal that had been laid out for them. They talked only when it was absolutely necessary. They knew that the kind of communication existing between them at that point did not require words.

Later, when they did talk, they shared the details and intricacies of their daily lives and their hopes and dreams for the future. For Katherine, it had been a magnificent evening. She was aglow from head to toe. She felt vibrant and alive and was happier and more deeply satisfied than she had ever been in her entire life.

Chapter Nine

*T*he next morning, lost in thought, Katherine walked
through the main lobby and out of the front door.
With no specific plan in mind, she strolled down the
narrow, flower-lined path that led down the side of
the house past the swimming pool and the tennis
courts. In the distance to her left, she could see the
stables and to her right were the kitchen gardens and
outbuildings. She quickened her step and hurried
past. She didn't really want to meet anyone right now.
She felt she needed to be alone and absorb what had
happened to her the night before in Assam's suite. She
felt that in some strange way her life had been
changed and she wanted time to be alone and think.
Or maybe she shouldn't think at all, she told herself.
Maybe she should just give herself some quiet time
away from the hotel, away from Assam, away from
everybody and everything except the beautiful surroundings of this marvellous place. So much was
happening to her; so much was being stirred. Yet
perhaps this wasn't the time to analyse or try to

understand it all. Perhaps she should take a moment to just relax and enjoy herself and let things take care of themselves. She wished she could find a nice quiet spot in the woods where she could be alone and just commune with the beauty around her.

With this in mind, she was delighted when she chanced upon a hidden pathway just past the last outbuilding. It was partially concealed by some heavy underbrush and seemed to invite her into its cool dim shadows. She responded immediately, eager to get away from the hot sun and any prying eyes that might be monitoring her actions.

The moment she stepped through the underbrush on to the path, it was as if she had entered a magic world. It was quiet here and cool, with just the occasional chirping of birds to remind her that she wasn't completely alone. The woods were fragrant with the scent of pine needles and damp moss. She took a long deep breath and felt instantly soothed and calmed by the silence, the smell of the damp earth and the pale golden sunlight streaming down through the trees. Yes, this was exactly what she needed, she thought with an inward sigh. For some reason unbeknown to her, she was still not completely comfortable with her decision to let go and explore her sexual tastes. She was relaxing more each day and was definitely enjoying herself more and more and yet she still felt frightened by the emergence of the new Katherine. Sometimes, she felt overwhelmed and a little frightened at the intensity of her sexual feelings and the pent-up emotion that seemed to be stirred every time she had a sexual encounter. However, she knew she had come too far now to give into fear and turn back. She sensed she was nearing her goal, approaching some kind of resolution and she was more determined than ever to see this adventure through to some exciting and positive conclusion.

This was certainly the right milieu for her experiment, she thought. The place was completely private and the people she had met were definitely uninhibited. She was delighted that Phyllis had arranged for her to come here and that she had been given the chance to explore her sexuality with so much creative freedom. It seemed that here even her wildest dreams were coming true.

Oblivious to the passage of time, she continued walking through the woods deep in thought. When she came out of her reverie, she looked around her and realised she had come a very long way and was completely lost. She was totally disorientated and had no idea where she was or how to get back to the house. For a moment, she looked around in panic. She had not left any markers on the trees and she was so turned around she didn't know whether she was facing north or south. In the distance, she spotted a small clearing and walked quickly in that direction. Much to her delight, in less than a minute, she found herself in an enchanting little glade where a small woodland pool was nestled in a grove of towering pine trees.

There was no doubt about it, she thought to herself, this was definitely an enchanted place. She ran over to the pool and sat down on a big rock. The sun was streaming down through the branches of the huge pines that arched over the place like the vault of a cathedral. 'What a magnificent place!' she said. Without meaning to, she had spoken out loud and she heard her voice echo strangely in the soft warm air. For a moment, she just sat there basking in the quiet energy all around her. Then she took a deep breath and allowed herself to relax and absorb the beauty of the place. The rays of the sun filtered through the trees, dancing on the surface of the still water, while birds cheeped intermittently and unseen little animals scurried through the underbrush.

She took off her shoes and slipped her feet into the cool, emerald-green water. She closed her eyes and wiggled her toes; it felt delicious. She marvelled at the fact that somewhere, across the ocean, lawyers in her firm were running around screaming out orders to their secretaries, making long complicated phone calls and trying desperately to return their messages for the day as they engaged in an endless struggle to handle all the cases they had on the go. She could see them now with their tense bodies and harried expressions, running around stressed out of their minds. And here she was in this little paradise with no time constraints, no cares, and no one around for miles to bother her. It was bliss.

She had no idea how much time had elapsed since she had left the hotel or where she was or how she was going to find her way back. But, somehow, now that she was in this place, it didn't seem to matter. She felt relaxed and confident that later she would find her way home safe and sound. For now, she just wanted to sit here and soak her feet in the soothing green pool and do absolutely nothing. Katherine closed her eyes and gave herself over completely to the wonder of the place.

Suddenly, a crashing in the underbrush nearby startled her out of her reverie and she sprang to her feet. Who could it be? she thought, feeling a little spasm of fear catch in her throat. She shivered as she realised just how alone and unprotected she was in this isolated spot. Then, before her astonished eyes, a horse and rider broke into the clearing and stopped dead in front of her.

'So, here you are!' the man exclaimed with a sigh of relief. 'No one had seen you for a couple of hours and people were starting to get worried about you. You left the hotel without telling anyone where you were going and no one knew where to find you. They were afraid you might have got lost. It's a pretty big estate, you know, and there are lots of little paths with all kinds of twists and turns. A person could get lost and disorientated very quickly.'

'Oh, I'm sorry. I certainly didn't mean to worry anyone. But, listen, I'm fine so uh ... I'm afraid I don't know your name. I've seen you around the grounds but ...' she stammered slightly, smiling faintly at the tall red haired man she had seen working in the gardens around the estate.

'My name is Tom, miss. I'm the assistant gardener here,' he said with a friendly grin. 'Your friends thought we'd better try to find you just in case you had wandered off the main path and lost your bearings. So, Rob and I decided to set out on different paths and see if we could track you down.'

Katherine's mind raced back to the scene at breakfast her first morning at the hotel when she had been introduced to a gorgeous black man called Rob. She relaxed somewhat but still could not shake the uneasy feeling that she was all alone in the woods with a complete stranger.

'That's very kind of everyone to be so concerned, Tom. However, I think their worries were misplaced. I'm sure, in fact, I know I could have found my way back without any trouble. One thing I do need though is to know what time it is. I deliberately left without a watch this morning because I didn't want to be worried about the time. Now it seems that I've succeeded in worrying everyone else,' she added lightly, trying desperately to diffuse the feeling of rising tension in the air. 'That wasn't my intention of course and I'm sorry if I've upset anyone. But, as you can see, there was no cause for concern. I'm just fine. So, would you be kind enough to tell everyone I'm all right and that I'll be back later?'

'It's a beautiful spot, isn't it?' Tom remarked, ignoring her subtle attempts to get rid of him. 'I come here a lot when I need a break from my work. Sometimes, I even go for a little swim. The water is so clear and cool. You know, I think I just might take a dip right now. Would you like to join me?'

Katherine was annoyed at his intrusion but she couldn't think of a polite way to get rid of him. She smiled and shook her head. 'Thanks, but I don't think so, Tom. Actually, I really came here to be alone. But you go ahead.'

'You're not trying to get rid of me, are you?' Tom asked smoothly, his demeanour changing slightly.

'Oh, no, it's not that at all,' Katherine stammered, catching her breath at the subtle change in his manner. 'It's just that . . .'

'Come on, Katherine, you spend way too much time alone. You need to be with people, people who understand you and know what you need. I think a little company is exactly what you need right now. I can tell just by looking at you that you're feeling lonely. You know, Rob told me what you were up to at the breakfast table the other day. He said you were so turned on, you could hardly sit still.'

Katherine could hardly believe what she was hearing and quickly put on her shoes. She knew things were moving too quickly and she had to get out of

195

there fast. She ignored his reference to her aroused state at breakfast on the morning in question and, instead, responded to his other remarks. 'I don't know what you're talking about. I feel completely comfortable being alone,' she countered, taking a haughty tone which she hoped would put him in his place.

However, her manner only seemed to encourage him and, in one graceful move, he dismounted, tethered his horse to a tree and began walking towards her. When he was within touching distance, he stopped and ran his eyes hungrily up and down her body. Katherine shuddered when she saw the expression in his eyes and tried to walk past him but he was too fast for her and grabbed her by the wrist.

'You're wrong, Katherine. I think being alone right now would be the worst thing in the world for you. And why fantasise when you can have the real thing? And have it right here in this ideal spot? Beautiful, secluded, far from prying eyes. And no one knows where we are, so we won't be disturbed. We can do whatever we want for as long as we want.'

Katherine began to waver. She remembered how she had promised herself that she would explore every opportunity that was offered to her. And yet, today she had planned to spend some quiet time alone with her thoughts trying to assimilate her intense experiences of the past few days. After her encounters with Rolf and Jasmine in the cave and then her unbelievably wonderful night with Assam, she felt she needed some time to just be, to assess her situation and her feelings. And yet, as she stood there alone in the clearing with Tom, she knew she was not going to say no. She knew she was hungry to explore every kind of sexual adventure that came her way. And now here was another one staring her right in the face. She continued to hesitate a little longer, feeling somewhat shocked at her voracious sexual appetite. However, at that moment, she knew that the element of danger implicit in this situation was acting like an aphrodisiac on her. Already, she could feel her nipples pushing hard against the silky material of her bra.

Tom was becoming impatient. It was clear he was not going to wait forever while she tried to make up her mind. In a sudden move, he pulled her against him and pressed his groin against her tummy. His body was taut and muscular and the smell of his maleness mingled with the earthy scent of the woods all around her. It was intoxicating but she felt she must not give in. Not right away anyway. She wanted to prolong things, tease him a little, play out the game, feel her own inner resistance, and struggle against his advances. It was more exciting that way and she wanted to exert some control in the situation. Also, she wanted to make him work for what he wanted.

Katherine wriggled in his embrace but he was very strong. His arms pinned her against him and ran his hands firmly down her back and over her squirming buttocks. He placed one of his hands in the small of her back to keep her pressed her to him. Then he lowered his mouth and forced her lips open. He pushed his tongue past her teeth and began probing deep inside her mouth, licking the sensitive inner lining and using his mouth to suck and nudge her tongue until she finally responded and began snaking and twining her tongue around his. Her senses were reeling as he continued to ravage her mouth and run his hands up and down her body, exploring every curve, kneading her flesh, caressing every inch he could find. Her body quivered under his sexual explorations and she pressed hard against him and arched

197

her back. His body moulded itself against hers then he slid his right hand down the left side of her body and placed his hand behind her knee. With one deft move, he raised her left leg until it was on his right hip. Then he moved in closer to her and pressed himself against her so she could feel his male hardness against her soft yielding pussy.

Katherine pressed up against the hard bulge in his pants. Then she leant back a little way from him and ran her nails down the front of his chest. When she reached the 'V' of his open-necked shirt, she slipped her fingers inside and began pulling on his silky red chest hairs and raking her nails over his muscular torso.

Finally, Tom tired of these preliminaries and, in one quick move, picked her up and carried her across the small clearing to a clump of trees near the waterfall where he set her down. Katherine's breath was coming fast and her whole body was trembling in anticipation. She looked up at him and ran her tongue over her full lips.

'Rob was right. You are always hot for it, aren't you, Katherine?' Tom remarked, grinning broadly. 'Well, so am I. So I guess I'm the perfect man to put out that fire that's burning you up.'

He reached down to the ground, picked up some loose vines and tied her hands behind her back. Then he slipped the vines down around her waist and tied her to the tree. In a moment, he had secured each of her legs to the tree as well.

'I feel like I've been captured by Robin Hood,' she said, the laughter catching in her throat as the situation began to escalate a little beyond her expectations. What was she doing? she thought wildly. She didn't know this man at all and she was completely alone with him in this isolated spot.

Katherine swayed slightly. Every inch of her was responding to his closeness and his musky male smell. A mixture of intense sexual excitement and a sense of adventure washed over her and her stomach muscles contracted with anticipation as he began kneading her breasts. Currents of sexual desire raced directly to her clitoris as he tweaked and pulled her nipples. She closed her eyes and gave herself over to the delicious sensations that were coursing through her.

'I knew you would like this,' he whispered. He yanked her blouse out from the waistband of her skirt and pushed it up over her heaving breasts which were swollen and straining against the flimsy material of her lacy bra. Tom stood back for a moment and let his gaze wander down the entire length of her trembling body. Katherine tried to wriggle free as a pretence of attempted escape but it was no use. She was tied to the tree good and fast. She looked over at him. He was still devouring her with his eyes. A delicious shiver rippled through her body when she imagined what lay ahead. Then, deep within her, she felt that familiar hot energy beginning to build at the base of her spine and she knew everything was going to be all right. She could feel her own sexual power moving within her now and she knew that, very soon, it would burst into a burning need that would have to be satisfied. She squirmed beneath her bonds in eager anticipation. She didn't want Tom to stop. Just the contrary. She wanted him to quell the fire that was burning in the pit of her belly and she wanted him to do it now. Still, she didn't want to give in too soon. She still wanted to resist him a little bit. She liked the feeling of being restrained and then resisting. It provided such a delicious conflict and turned her on so much that, during her stay here, she found herself almost missing it when it wasn't part of her love-making. She rubbed her body against the rough bark of the trunk and moaned softly. She could almost picture what she looked like as she stood there half naked tied to the tree. She felt so aroused now, so excited by these unexpected circumstances, that she was afraid she would come too quickly and not enjoy to the full everything that was waiting in store for her.

She looked over at this wild red-headed man who had appeared so suddenly in the woods and disturbed her peaceful reverie. She shuddered in anticipation. She knew he was going to feed that deep sexual hunger that was gnawing at her. She knew he was going to do unspeakably wonderful things to her; exciting her and arousing her to a peak of ecstasy. She shivered violently. She could feel her nipples pucker into hard nubs as the familiar hot wetness began to gather between her legs. Suddenly, her knees gave way beneath her. Only the vines held her upright. She was so hot, so ready. She hungered for his touch now. At this moment, that was all she could think of. Tom stood back and observed her writhing against the tree. He was enjoying making her wait, knowing that by the second she would be getting wetter and wetter.

Finally, he reached out his hand and, with maddening slowness, let his fingers drift across her breasts which rose in delicious mounds above the top of her bra. Then he lowered his mouth to the hollow of her neck and began licking her flesh, nipping gently with his teeth here and there as he ran his mouth all the way down over her shoulders and into her deep cleavage. She writhed beneath his touch, still struggling against her constraints as wave after wave of electricity radiated over her skin and down into her throbbing pussy.

'I want to see those delicious breasts of yours,' he whispered in her ear.

Katherine gave a soft cry as he undid the front clasp of her bra and her heavy breasts were released from their silky confines. She was moaning softly now as she felt his hot hands on her flesh. Her nipples were hard, jutting. She arched her back and thrust herself forward. His fingers felt like flames as he teased her nipples and massaged her breasts. He flicked her raw tips and rolled them between his thumb and fore-finger, sending crazy little electric thrills racing down into her crotch. Her juices were trickling out of her now, soaking right through her knickers. She could feel the wetness as he pressed her against the tree. Rhythmically, she began grinding her pelvis and gyrating her hips. Her mouth opened in a silent scream as his hands moved from her breasts down her belly to her mound which was still imprisoned beneath the tight material of her skirt. She jerked her hips forward, inviting him to stroke and rub her quivering sex.

'You were made for good sex,' he murmured. 'You're so hot and so ready all the time, aren't you? Rob was right. I bet you would like me to slide my fingers way into your sweet pussy. You would like that, wouldn't you, Katherine? And you would like to feel my cock stoking that red hot furnace inside you, wouldn't you? Why don't you admit it? You would have a hell of a lot more fun if you did,' he added, as he reached down and pushed her skirt up around her waist.

Breathless with excitement, Katherine gasped at his words. Her senses were reeling and she moaned loudly as another gush of her juices oozed out of her and soaked her panties. She moaned and struggled against her restraints. She felt crazy, wild with passion. All resistance and reservations were gone. She wanted him to touch her, to play with her, to discover every part of her aching flesh. Her knees sagged and she felt she was going to faint with the pleasure of it all. She had given herself over to him completely and now she was totally under his spell. She was greedy for all that he had to offer. She wanted to feel his hands and fingers all over her, in her, thrilling her, taking her to higher and higher peaks of pleasure. The raging hot energy that was building between her legs and the insistent urgency of her tight, aching clitoris demanded satisfaction and release.

With slow deliberate movements, he trailed his big rough hands down over her belly, drawing lazy little circles on her trembling flesh until she could bear it no more. She ached to feel his hands between her legs, to have his fingers playing with her clit. Would he never get there? She sobbed inwardly as she tried to position her body to guide his hands where she wanted them to go. She let out a long low sigh as his hands finally slid down over her vulva and began massaging her through the flimsy material of her bikini panties. She pushed forward on to his hand, urging him to make more intimate intrusions into her most private place.

He responded immediately and, as she gyrated lasciviously beneath his touch, he slowly pulled her panties down over her quivering hips and let them fall in a little silken pool at her feet.

Her cries echoed softly in the glade as his hand finally slid down into her thick curly bush and his fingers began feathering back and forth along her dark crease. With his skilful fingers, he stroked and caressed her there until she was almost fainting with pent-up sexual need. With tantalising slowness, he drew his nails back and forth over her swollen labia, sending delicious sexual thrills rippling deep inside her, electrifying her clitoris until it was fully engorged and protruding out from between the wet lips of her sex. A wave of weakness rushed over her and she went limp. Her body was on fire, aflame with the desire he was creating deep within her. She moaned loudly. She couldn't believe she was allowing another stranger to arouse her so completely once again. And yet, if she were to be completely truthful with herself, that was part of the excitement. Allowing a stranger to take these most intimate of liberties was a big part of her sexual arousal. She loved having her breasts fondled and her pussy stroked by someone she hardly knew. She loved to be brought to a peak and then not to be permitted to fall over the edge. It was so exciting, so titillating to reach the point of orgasm and then be pulled back so that the passion could begin to mount again. It was delicious, intoxicating, but right now, she didn't know how much more she could take. She tried to spread her legs, inviting him to go deeper.

His response was instant. His fingers gently parted the pink lips of her swollen sex and slithered deep inside, sliding up and down the shaft of her clitoris then skimming over the hard aching little nub that was rigid with desire. As his expert fingers exerted more and more pressure on the fleshy bud the glade echoed with her moans of pleasure. Her head was thrown back in abandon, tossing from side to side as his hands continued to discover and plunder the very core of her desire.

She could hear herself crying out as the delicious torment went on and on but she didn't care. All she cared about was the pleasure his fiendish fingers were giving her. Just when she thought she was tipping over the edge, Tom withdrew his hand. She wailed out her protest but he ignored her cries and, in a flash, untied her arms and legs and laid her down on a soft bed of aromatic pine needles. Before she could say a word, he straddled her, parted her legs, unzipped his fly and took his penis in his hands. He began pumping himself, working himself up to the inevitable act as Katherine looked up at him in amazement. He whipped a condom out of his trouser pocket and eased it down over his cock. Then he leant over her, nudged her legs apart and inserted it only part way inside her pussy. Slowly, he began circling it round and round over her inner folds. When he stopped and hovered briefly at the opening to her vagina, Katherine lost all control.

'Do it, for God's sake, do it. I can't stand this any more,' she screamed, jerking her hips wildly and straining to impale herself on his rod which quivered so tantalisingly at the entrance to her pleasure. With a growl, Tom grabbed her hips with his big hands and held them. Then, in one long smooth move, he plunged deep into her as far as he could go. She gasped at the size of him and immediately began sliding back and forth, wild with the feel of him deep inside her at last. She moved with total abandon, giving herself to his pounding cock. She was insatiable; she wanted more and more. Her engorged clitoris was screaming for release, her vagina convulsing in wave after wave of mounting excitement. Over and over, he eased into her as her hips rose wildly to meet his every thrust. Matching his passion with her own lust, she urged him on, grinding rhythmically against him, fingering herself as she begged him to ride her harder and harder.

Finally, she reached the crest of a monumental wave and began to climax. Her orgasm ripped through her, overwhelming her entire being with the fire of her insatiable passion. She felt as if she were being consumed by flames which engulfed her body, licking and flickering over every part of her. Through her haze, she could hear Tom grunting out his own climax. Finally, spent and exhausted, they lay quietly together, the glade still echoing with their moans of ecstasy.

A few minutes elapsed as they recovered from their wild lovemaking. Katherine looked over at Tom who was lying beside her with his eyes closed. She let her eyes run over his magnificent body. His shirt was half unbuttoned and his flies were still wide open. Being a redhead, his skin was fair and slightly freckled and, through the opening of his shirt, she could see that his chest was covered with a thick mat of dark red wiry curls which thinned out into a narrow band at his midriff then disappeared into his waistband. Katherine saw the thick tangle of wiry red curls just above his penis and her mouth began to water. She wanted to taste his skin, run her tongue up and down that muscular torso and feel his semi-erect shaft grow and extend into its full magnificence in her mouth. But she wanted to do this on her terms. She moved over towards him and kissed him lightly on the cheek.

'Could you get me some water to drink? I'm dying of thirst,' she asked softly.

Tom smiled, got to his feet and walked over to where he had his horse tethered. He took a small drinking cup from his saddle bag then headed down towards the pool. Quickly, Katherine got to her feet and picked up some of the vines from the ground. When Tom returned carrying a cup full of fresh water from the pool, she drank greedily and then returned the cup to him.

'Thanks, Tom. Now, could you please put that down? I need all your attention.'

Tom put the cup down on the ground and, when he stood back up, Katherine was in front of him, pressing her body against him, rubbing her pussy against his penis and sticking her tongue deep inside his mouth. Her hands trembled as they fumbled with the buttons on his shirt. When his chest was fully exposed, she buried her face in the thick red mat on it. Slowly, she tasted him, running the tip of her tongue lazily up and down his chest, taking little nips at his nipples and pulling on the strands of his thick red chest hair. The taste and smell of him were intoxicating. Her senses were reeling. She wanted to savour more of him, all of him.

'Take your arms out of the sleeves,' she whispered.

He did as he was told and removed his arms from the sleeves. The shirt fell to the ground. Katherine stood there for a few moments running her eyes over his bare flesh. She was so excited she could hardly breathe. This was the first time she had had a chance to take a good look at the man who had just made passionate love to her. She stepped up to him and ran her hands over his shoulders then feathered them lightly down over his nipples and tangled her fingers in his chest hair. She gave his nipples a pinch and smiled as he groaned and tried to kiss her. But she held him off. She lowered her mouth to his flesh and began licking and lapping his skin. It was as smooth as silk under her tongue. The taste of him drove her wild. She began gently biting his skin and running her tongue and her fingers all over him. She felt crazy for him, greedy. She couldn't get enough of him. She released the button at the top of his trousers and they fell to the ground in a little heap around his feet. He wasn't wearing any underwear and his fully erect cock jutted proudly from his bush of thick red pubic curls. Katherine licked her lips and sighed. He was lithe and slender with well-toned muscles and lean hard thighs. His arms and legs were covered with reddish hair and the thick wiry curls at the base of his cock were just as profuse. She looked deep into his eyes then led him by the hand over to the tree. Then, quietly and methodically, she bound his arms, legs and torso to the tree with the vines that he had previously used to restrain her. Taken unawares, Tom was momentarily jolted out of his sensual haze but, when the full impact of what she was going to do dawned on him, he thrust his pelvis forward, his erect penis jutting towards her in a clear invitation.

She looked up and saw the lust in his eyes and she fell to her knees in front of him. He gasped as she closed her two hands around him and ran her fingers up and down the smooth velvety length of his penis. Over and over, she stroked and pulled on him until he was thrusting wildly in her hands. She was so excited, she thought she was going to come just by touching him but she controlled herself. She wanted to take him deep in her mouth and eat his gorgeous rod. She removed her fingers from his penis and opened her mouth wide. As she closed her lips around him, she almost gagged; he was huge. He began thrusting wildly. She relaxed and opened her mouth as widely as she could to accommodate him. He was long and hard and he filled her mouth completely.

'You taste so good, so good,' she groaned as she

sucked and pulled on him like a madwoman, stopping every once in a while to run her nails over the seamed underside until he was almost roaring with delight.

His hands were tangled in her hair and he was pumping hard now, pushing back against the tree for support. She knew he was very close to coming. She closed her lips more firmly around him, reached her hands down around the base of his penis and gave him one long hard squeeze. That was all he needed. As she continued to lick and lap the full length of him, she felt him surge against her tongue then pump and pump his hot seed into her mouth as he groaned her name over and over again.

Greedily, she drank him in and milked his surging cock until it was so sensitive, he couldn't bear even the silky touch of her mouth and begged her to stop.

With a reluctant sigh, she let him go. She was still hungry for more of him. In fact, she felt consumed with a deep sexual hunger that she had never felt in quite this way before. Maybe it was being outside in the woods – feeling at one with the forces of nature. Maybe it was the chemistry between them. Whatever it was, she felt she would never quell this hungry fire burning her up inside. She could still taste him on her tongue and her mouth still throbbed from the feel of his glorious cock. Her pussy ached and she wanted to feel his cock inside her again. She looked at him. His naked body was slumped against the tree and his eyes were closed. When he opened them, he looked straight at her and smiled. She loosened his bonds and they both collapsed on the soft carpet of pine needles.

'You are so good, so hot,' Tom moaned a couple of minutes later as he looked over at her body still quivering from the onslaught of their lust. 'Why in hell do you always wander around as if you have a poker up your behind? You really ought to let yourself go like this more often. It would do you a world of good, not to mention the lucky guy you might choose to do it with. You know, that gets me to thinking. Speaking of behinds, how would you like to go at it with two of us?' he drawled, his eyes sparkling with excitement.

Katherine could hardly speak. She was over-whelmed by the intensity of the experience they had both shared. For a moment, she did not understand what he was suggesting.

'Two?' she mumbled, her senses still awash in her ebbing passion.

'Rob said he would meet me here if he couldn't find you. And I just thought, well, what a chance for all of us to have a go. Sex with you is so good and so hot and I know you're hungry for more. Why not two of us at once? I have a feeling you might have wanted to do that for a long time but never had either the chance or the nerve.' He stopped talking mid sentence and looked over at an opening in the underbrush. 'Well, what do you know? Hey, Rob. We're over here. Come and see what we've been up to.'

Katherine sat up with a jolt. Sure enough, there was Rob walking across the clearing, leading a wonderful white Arabian stallion behind him. He stopped briefly to tether the horse to a tree then strolled over towards Tom and Katherine, who were lying sprawled on the ground.

Katherine could only imagine how she must look with her blouse pushed up over her bare breasts, their nipples boldly erect with residual passion and her skirt rucked up around her waist, her thick black bush in full view. She struggled to cover herself before Rob could see her state of undress but it was too late. He was standing there looking down at her, a big grin on his handsome black face.

'Well, well, what do we have here?' he said with a friendly smile as his eyes ran boldly over her breasts and down to her pussy. 'It seems I've been doing all the work and you two have been having all the fun. The whole time I was looking high and low for Katherine, you two were going at it hot and heavy.'

Katherine stammered out an incoherent reply but Tom laughed lustily and beckoned Rob to sit down and join them.

'Looks like I took the right path doesn't it, old man? I mean, I found Katherine very soon after we separated but I just couldn't bring myself to let you know, at least, not until we had some fun together.'

'Fun!' Katherine spluttered.

'Yeah, fun,' Tom countered. 'She's amazing, isn't she?' he continued, turning to smile at Rob. 'I mean, here we are, we've just been going at it like a couple of rabbits and she still wants to come on all uppity and ladylike and pretend it wasn't fun, as if just minutes ago we weren't having the hottest sex either of us has had in ages. You know, Katherine, it might just be time for you to take a reality check. Sex is fun and the sooner you can admit that to yourself, the more fun it will be.' Tom smiled and winked at her. 'I guess I'll just have to give you a refresher course to jog your memory. Or, better still. Maybe we both should do that. What about it, Rob?'

Katherine gasped as Rob's eyes lit up and he nodded eagerly.

'Hey, wait a minute. What are you . . .?'

Before she could get the words out, Tom eased her

skirt down over her hips, unfastened the zip and pulled it all the way off.

Suddenly, the situation had taken a completely different turn. Tom came up behind her, lifted her shoulders up off the ground, pulled off her blouse and her bra, and threw them in a little pile with her skirt at the base of the tree where, just minutes before, she had been moaning in ecstasy.

Katherine had no time to absorb what was going on. Rob had stripped his clothes off and Tom had lifted her up in his arms and was carrying her toward the pool. She moaned and closed her eyes; she knew what was coming. She could hardly believe that one of her wildest fantasies was going to come true again. Twice in two days as well! How lucky can you get? she thought, her mind racing now with images of the woman in the park she had envied so much. It seemed so long ago. Now, here she was, about to enjoy what she had longed for so desperately that night back home.

As he walked behind them, Rob grabbed his semi-erect cock and began massaging it quickly back and forth. 'The whole time I was looking for you, Katherine, you and Tom were making it. Well, you know what? I don't think that's fair,' he added with a playful grin on his face. 'The way I see it, it's my turn now. After all, I busted a gut looking for you. And now that I've found you, I want my reward. It's such perfect timing. I arrived at the perfect moment. I mean you're both so hot and ready, it's like you were just waiting for me to show up. So, what do you say, Tom? Shall we get on with it?'

Katherine moaned in anticipation and arched her naked body in Tom's arms as he continued carrying her across the clearing toward the pond. His arms were like iron and she was helpless in his grip. This was exactly the way she liked it.

'Let's do it in the water,' Tom yelled over his shoulder.

'Fine with me,' Rob replied as he grabbed his thick penis again and began pulling on it until it was fully erect.

Tom walked steadily over to the pond and waded into the water. Katherine shrieked at her first contact with the cool water but Tom paid no attention and continued lowering her into its dark green depths until she was standing on the hard sandy bottom with the water washing up over the tips of her breasts.

'You're going to love this, Katherine,' he crooned to her softly as he lifted her up and put her legs around his waist.

Katherine crossed her ankles behind him and pushed her sex against his member which felt big and hard against her belly. The water was soothing against her flesh which was still hot and feverish from their wild lovemaking. Soon, the exquisite sensation of Tom's hairy chest rubbing against her raw nipples and the feel of his huge cock rammed up against her stirred the embers of her passion again into a searing hot flame.

'Everything set?' Rob asked as he came up behind Katherine and slithered his arms around her waist.

'She's all ready, Rob. I'm getting her nice and hot just for you,' Tom said as he reached down under the water, parted Katherine's bum crack and began massaging the puckered rose of her anus.

Katherine moaned and pushed her behind against his exploring fingers.

'You're going to love it, Katherine. You were made for this. Just relax and go with it,' Rob murmured in her ear as he pushed his penis against her from the back. 'I know what you were thinking about that morning at the breakfast table. Did you think I didn't notice? You were just aching for a good man, two, if I'm not mistaken,' he added with an impish tone in his voice. 'Well, here we are. It looks like your fantasy is about to come true,' he panted. 'And we are just the boys to carry it off for you.'

Before she could even think of responding, Tom closed his mouth over hers and, as he slid his thick warm tongue past her teeth into her mouth, he slid his huge cock deep into her hot wet tunnel. Wild muffled little screams escaped her lips as he penetrated her over and over again. Slowly, the fire deep within her began to ignite. She could feel the walls of her vagina begin to quake as waves of sensation washed through her and the fleshy head of her clitoris reared up, tight and insistent.

Their movements roiled the water all around them as Tom speared relentlessly in and out of her, taking her to the same level of passion that was consuming him. Slowly, she started to match him thrust for thrust. In the heat of the moment, she had almost forgotten that Rob was standing close to her buttocks, ready to enter her from behind. She shuddered violently when she felt his long smooth finger on her bottom hole, massaging and gently probing it, matching perfectly the rhythm of Tom's relentless penis. She moaned loudly when his finger pressed her harder, pushing her to release and open up her puckered little anal opening.

Drunk with renewed passion, Katherine felt her anus open wide enough to accommodate her new lover. At that moment, Rob slowly inserted his swollen cock through the narrow opening and began matching Tom thrust for thrust.

Impaled on the two men, Katherine bucked wildly, her imagination on fire with images of depravity. Once again, she was experiencing the wild sensual abandon she had craved that night in the park. And, once again, it was exactly the way she had imagined it. She twisted and turned lasciviously on their cocks, wresting from their hardness every ounce of pleasure that she craved. As the two men plundered every inch of her two openings, the cool water that splashed up on her fell like drops of liquid ice on her fevered skin. Katherine felt mad with all the sensations crashing in on her. She arched her back and rode the two men like a wild woman. Her first introduction to this kind of sex had been just the night before with Assam and Kadir. But already today, she felt she had always known what to do and how to increase her pleasure. As Rob and Tom scythed in and out of her two openings with deep penetrating thrusts, Katherine matched their relentless rhythm, positioning herself time and time again in such a way that her swollen clit would be grazed and teased. She leant back and reached down to the root of Tom's penis. Slowly and firmly, she squeezed the base, pulling on his wet pubic curls, pushing herself along the length of him, milking him with her strong vaginal muscles. Then, leaning in toward him, she began to bite and nip at his neck and shoulders while she trailed her long nails down his back.

Groaning and panting behind her, Rob slid his hands around Katherine's waist and cupped her breasts which were bobbing in the roiling water. He held their heavy fullness in his hands while he flicked his thumbs over her puckered raw tips.

Katherine was awash in a sea of sensuality. She loved the feel of Rob's hands on her and thrust her breasts forward to meet his caress. She felt so complete, so full, with two cocks spearing her. She jerked her hips faster, riding the two men harder and harder as they continued scything back and forth. Slowly, she could feel the cresting wave of her oncoming orgasm. She was almost fainting with the pleasure that was washing over her. She could feel her climax building. Her vagina was contracting, her clitoris engorged. Her anus was so sensitised by the relentless thrusts of Rob's penis that it was quivering wildly at every penetration. She was panting and gasping for air. She knew she couldn't hold out against the onslaught of their passion any longer. Her vagina lurched, sending hot sexual thrills undulating through her body. Her clit reached the point where it quivered and melted into wild electric spasms and the rose of her anus opened and closed convulsively around Rob's penis.

When it all burst upon her, she came with such an overwhelming intensity that it sent her body into paroxysms of sensual delight. As she rode the wave, the once quiet little glade rang with her cries. She gave herself over completely to the onslaught and allowed her orgasm to sweep through every fibre of her being. As she climaxed, she spurred the two men on to reach their thunderous orgasms, too. As all three peaked, they bucked and rocked together, grunting out their pleasure in unison as the rippling water of the pond splashed all around them, cooling and soothing their feverish bodies.

When it was over, they managed to wade over to the edge of the pool where they threw themselves down on the grassy embankment. Panting and gasping with the intensity of their experience, they lay there for quite a while before anyone spoke.

Finally, Tom sat up and looked over at Katherine who was sprawled on the grass. Her breasts were swollen and her nipples were raw. Wet tendrils of her long black hair spread out on the grass around her head and her legs were parted wide to reveal the furry lips of her wet sex. He licked his lips at the sight but knew he could go no further today.

'It's time we got back or they'll have the local police out looking for us,' he murmured with a smile.

Katherine said nothing. She was still in a post-climactic haze. She got up and retrieved her clothing from near the tree, then got dressed. How on earth was she going to get home? she wondered anxiously. She had walked all the way here but there was no way she could walk back now, not after her wild love making. She was exhausted and she was sure she was miles from the hotel.

'You can ride home with me, Katherine,' Rob offered suddenly, as if reading her thoughts. 'You must be pretty tired after the workout we've all been through,' he added, a satisfied smile on his face.

Katherine was so relieved by his suggestion that she almost kissed him. But instead she just smiled her appreciation. Her body was still tingling and pulsing from his ravaging assault and she felt marvellous but, like with the stable lad, she didn't want to set up any kind of personal contact between them. The sex was great but anything beyond that was out of the question; at least for now.

Tom had dressed, mounted his horse and was waving farewell to them by the time she had her clothes on and was ready to go.

'Goodbye, Katherine,' he said quietly. 'If you

enjoyed that as much as I think you did, we can arrange to have another go whenever you feel like it. You're a beautiful woman. If you can relax and enjoy your true nature, the sky's the limit for you.'

He gave her a long searing look then ran his tongue over his lips and rubbed the bulge in his crotch. Then, with a wave of his hand, he urged his mount forward and disappeared into the underbrush.

Katherine was amazed how Tom's lusty gestures could inflame her again so quickly. She turned to Rob who was already on horseback. He reached down and helped her up in front of him. He had chosen to ride bareback that day and the feel of the horse's body was warm between her legs. He put his arms around her, took the reins in his hands and urged the horse forward.

Her body felt alive and vital; every inch of her was tingling. She loved the way she felt after good sex. And today, for the first time, the feeling of having been cheated, although still there, was not as strong as it had been on previous occasions. She was definitely making progress. For the first time in a long time, sex had not been totally spoiled by her reactions afterwards. A wave of happiness flooded through her. Then, to her surprise, she felt the tides of her passion begin to build again deep inside her. Maybe she could do some more exploring with Rob, she mused. He was such an exciting man. Sighing softly, she lay back against his muscular chest and began grinding her behind into his crotch. Rob knew immediately what she wanted and slipped his hand over her breasts. Slowly, he began rubbing them through the thin material of her blouse until her nipples were hard nubs and she was squirming in his arms. When Rob felt her nipples stiffen, he let go of the reins and slipped his other hand down inside her panties. She wriggled sensuously against him as he began stroking her pussy and feathering his fingers over her furry crease.

Rob knew his horse could find its own way back to the stable so both his hands were free to fondle and caress every part of her. And this is exactly what he proceeded to do. As they rode along the narrow woodland paths and later, out into the open fields, Katherine came in a series of short harsh orgasms. Rob's expert fingers teased her into climax after climax and, as she surged beneath his touch, the sounds of her agonised delight shattered the silence of the warm afternoon.

After a while, Katherine quietened in his arms and gave herself over to the rhythm of the horse's easy gait. They seemed to ride on forever. She hadn't realised she had walked so far. It was lucky the men had found her, she thought, wriggling sensuously against the horse's warm skin.

Suddenly, she was jolted out of her reverie. Rob was pointing at dark clouds on the horizon. Katherine looked up at the sky and, sure enough, there were storm clouds gathering and the wind was beginning to pick up. Almost immediately, thunder began to rumble around them. The atmosphere was electric. Instantly, she felt herself responding to the intensity of the moment. As the electricity of the pending storm built, so did her sexual excitement. There was a wildness rising up in her, a wildness that mirrored the fury of the wind and the crackling electrical energy of the pending storm. The atmosphere was charged and the tension was building. All her senses were responding. Her sex was throbbing. She pressed herself down hard against the horse's sweating back and wriggled back against Rob's chest. Instantly, she felt his hot breath on her neck .

'Storms really get to me,' he whispered in ear, flicking his tongue quickly over her sensitive ear lobes. 'What about you?'

Katherine's sex quivered and she wriggled against him, feeling the rising hardness of his member against the small of her back.

'Everything seems to get to me these days,' she replied, thrusting her buttocks back against him even harder.

Without a word, Rob slid one arm around her waist and whispered in her ear. 'Press down hard on the horse's back and let yourself move and slide over his skin in time to his rhythm. If you do this, your sweet little clit will be all hard and ready to go off like those lightening bolts over there.'

Katherine let him nudge her forward a little and she did what he suggested. Gradually, she allowed her hips to move back and forth in time with the horse's rhythm, the smooth, silky crotch of her white lace panties sliding back and forth over the animal's warm skin, slippery now with his warm sweat. The heat of the horse's skin, the smell of its sweat and her sliding motion had a devastating effect on her. She felt almost drunk with sensation. A low, animal-like sound rose up in the back of her throat as waves of sensation undulated through her sex. She felt wild and natural – and totally united with her environment.

Rob unbuttoned her blouse and massaged her breasts through the lacy material of her bra; first one then the other. Her nipples peaked instantly and she moved restlessly under his touch, little sighs of pleasure escaping her parted lips.

'Your breasts are delightful,' he whispered in her ear, as he palmed them more roughly now. 'I want you to take your bra off for me, Katherine. I want to run my hands over your naked breasts. I want to feel them all smooth and heavy in my hands. Come on, let me get my fingers on those big nipples of yours. I want to make them nice and hard. I can make you come just by playing with them. Let me play with them, Katherine. You won't be sorry. Oh, they're so sweet. Mmm, if only I could get my mouth around there. I'd suck on them like they were honey wine.'

Katherine moaned at his sexy talk and fumbled with the front clasp of her bra. Finally, she loosened it and her luscious breasts tumbled free.

With a groan, Rob removed his hand from the reins. 'Bud here can find his own way,' he said as he began massaging her swollen breasts with both hands.

The touch of Rob's hands on her breasts together with the rocking motion of the horse against her clit was almost too much for Katherine to bear. She felt overstimulated and knew that if she didn't get to have sex with Rob again soon, she would go crazy. She reached behind her and clawed at his flies. When her hands encountered the enormous bulge in his crotch, she stroked and squeezed it until she could feel it begin to pulse and strain against the tight confines of his riding pants. Rob sighed as her fingers played over him and he jerked his hips forward to meet her eager hands.

Caught up in his own passion now, Rob let the other rein go and slid his hands between her legs. Katherine let out a long low groan as his hand slid over the smooth material of her panties – which were now soaking wet with a mixture of her dew and the horse's sweat. Gasping with pleasure, she ground her pussy into his hand. Just when she thought she couldn't take any more, Rob stopped rubbing between her legs, reached up to the waistband of her panties and slowly slid his hand inside. Katherine thrust her hips forward in a spasm of pleasure as his fingers slipped down into her silky bush, pulling at her pussy hairs and grazing his sharp nails over her sensitive skin. Slowly, he trailed them across her plump labia then took his index finger and ran it back and forth along her crease.

'Oh, God, yes,' she moaned, as the sensation of his finger running back and forth over her furry cleft sent electric waves of sexual pleasure radiating deep into her crotch. Her clitoris reared up under his expert touch and she began rocking back and forth, using the rhythm of the horse's movement to stimulate herself even further.

'Oh God, this feels so good,' she gasped and reached her hands around her back and began pawing again at his crotch which was straining under the pressure of his enormous erection.

Rob thrust his pelvis forward while he continued to fondle her. He could feel her clitoris swollen to almost twice its normal size, protruding boldly now from between her retracted pussy lips.

Moaning incoherently, Katherine jerked and rocked under his touch, grinding her sex against his exploring fingers. She wanted to feel him, to touch him. She groped for the zip on his pants. 'Oh God,' she cried aloud, as she clawed frantically at his crotch, totally drunk now with passion. 'I want your cock. I want it now. I want to feel it in my hand, all long and hard and smooth.'

Finally, with some difficulty, her trembling hands dragged the zip open and his huge member sprang free into her eager hands. He was hot and he was hard. Keeping her hand stretched out behind her, she closed it around him and began sliding it up and down the full length of his cock. Frantically, she began pulling and squeezing until he roared out his pleasure.

'Do it, Katherine, do it, oh yeah,' Rob moaned, as all around them the rain began to fall.

The storm was getting more fierce and the wind was whipping Katherine's hair across her face and into her mouth. The clouds were dark purple and the sky was a watery shade of green. The air was getting colder by the minute but the fury of their passion kept them warm and they continued fondling and teasing each other as the thunder continued to resound ominously around them.

'We're not going to make it back in time before the storm breaks,' Rob yelled over another thundercrack, breathless from the way she was handling his penis. 'There's a little shack near here where bales of hay are stored. We can stay there until it's over.'

Katherine could only nod her head. She didn't care about anything now except her mounting desire. Rob urged his mount onward. They reached the shack just as the first drops of water began to fall around them. Rob jumped off the horse, pulled Katherine down, and the two of them ran inside, leading the horse behind them just as the rain came pouring down and lightening split the heavens.

Bud settled down nicely once they were inside and started munching on some fresh hay that was piled up in a corner.

Rob walked over to Katherine and looked her straight in the eye. His semi-erect penis was still protruding from his open pants. 'We're not going to let this storm get in our way, are we?' he asked, his eyes dark with passion.

Katherine gasped at the naked lust in his eyes but she was so aroused she couldn't say a word.

'I have a feeling you like doing it from behind,' he growled. 'So that's exactly what I'm going to do.'

Overwhelmed by her state of arousal, Katherine could only stare at him and nod. Breathless, she watched him remove some tackle from two hooks embedded in the far wall. He turned to face her. Katherine's breath was coming in short rapid gasps. She cried out sharply as he grabbed her, turned her toward the wall and quickly secured each hand with a heavy piece of rope to one of the hooks which were positioned slightly above her head. Then, standing behind her, he cupped her naked breasts in his huge hands. She let out a long low moan as he weighed their heaviness. Her knees sagged beneath her. She gasped aloud as his fingers trailed back and forth over her nipples, teasing and pinching them lightly until her cries of pleasure rose up over the noise of the storm raging outside.

When he knew her breasts were too raw to take any more, he got down on his hands and knees behind her and pushed her skirt up over her hips. Then he pulled down her panties and gently parted her bum crack. Katherine pulled against the ropes and her knees gave way beneath her as he slipped his fingers in her crack and started massaging her anus.

'Do you like that, Katherine?' he whispered. 'Do you like it when I play with you there? Do you like it when I touch your breasts? I bet you like sex a little rough too, don't you? Tell me how you like it, Katherine. Tell me how much you like it, how much you want it.'

'Oh, Jesus,' she said, as his words inflamed her even more and her juices started trickling down her legs. 'I do. I do want it. I want it all,' she wailed, as his fingers continued their relentless probing.

Rob stopped fingering her anus and turned his attention to her pussy. 'Ask me nicely,' he panted. 'Ask me nicely for my cock. I want to hear you say how much you want it.' He didn't wait for her to answer but instead pressed himself hard against her. Then, slowly, he inserted one finger between her furry cleft and slid it along the shaft of her clitoris until it found the fleshy head. Katherine moved sensuously against his finger and began to rock in time to his expert handling. The more she moved with him, the wilder she got, until she was practically sobbing for release.

'Do you want me, Katherine?' Rob whispered, ramming his member right up against her buttocks as his fingers continued to fondle her.

'Yes, yes, I want you. I want you. Fuck me, fuck me now. I want to feel your long hard cock inside me. Fuck me, you beautiful bastard,' she screamed at the top of her voice. 'Stick it up me. Ram it up as far as it can go. I can't stand this any more. Do it now.'

With a growl, Rob loosened her restraints and placed her face forward over a bail of hay. Using his knees, he parted her legs and mounted her from behind. Then, in one long sliding motion, he drove his cock deep into her vagina.

With a grunt of pleasure, Katherine thrust her behind up to meet him as he rode her like a mighty stallion, their wild, animal-like cries muted by the sounds of the crashing thunder.

In the flashing lightning, their bodies heaved and jerked against each other, rocking and bucking as they grunted out their pleasure. Katherine strained, reaching for her climax. Then she felt the walls of her vagina lurch and her clit explode into a wild searing orgasm which surged and rampaged through her with the same fury as the storm raging outside.

Rob stayed with her all the way, servicing every inch of her pussy until she collapsed sobbing with relief.

'I'm not done yet, Katherine,' he murmured softly. Racked by the force of her orgasm, Katherine could barely muster enough energy to pay attention to what he was saying. Suddenly, she felt herself being turned over onto her back and urged up on to her knees. As she moved, she became aware that her clothes were in complete disarray. Her blouse was ripped and gaping open, her bra was undone, and her breasts were bobbing free. Her skirt was clumped around her waist and her panties lay in a little heap by the wall. She looked up and saw Rob standing in front of her, his penis still erect, still glistening with her own dew.

'Suck me, Katherine. Suck me hard,' he muttered, his voice thick with passion.

Katherine gasped and opened her mouth but, before she could make a move, he pulled her to him and slid his penis into her open mouth.

'Suck my cock until it talks back to you,' he growled as he started sliding his ebony-coloured member in and out of her mouth.

Greedily, she began devouring him. Energised by the taste of him, she ran her tongue up and down and around the full length of him, nipping gently here and there, sliding it up and down his pulsing shaft. As she continued to lap and suck him, she used one hand to cup his big hairy balls and the other to exert pressure at the base of his cock which was jerking and pulsing in her mouth. She stopped sucking on him for a moment and looked him in the eyes.

'Oh, God, it's just like those liquorice sticks I used to suck when I was a child,' she said as she played with his cock. 'But they were really thin and wouldn't last very long. Not like you, Rob. You're so thick and long and hard. You're going to last forever, or at least as long as I want you to. Mmm, it's so good, so good. My nice long stick of liquorice candy.'

It was now Rob's turn to gasp at her raunchy talk. He gave a long drawn-out moan as she took him deep in her mouth one more time, giving him little nips on his sensitive tip. Then, as she sucked harder and harder on his thrusting penis, she slipped her hand between his legs and gently scratched his balls. He groaned loudly and jerked his hips forward, pushing his cock further into her mouth. When she slid her hand between his legs and rubbed that special place between his penis and his balls, he went wild and began pumping furiously, his fingers tangled in her hair as he crooned her name over and over again. She could feel him throbbing in her mouth. She knew he was ready to come. Keeping her lips firmly closed around him and one hand in that very special place, she used her other hand to cup and squeeze his balls then pinch them gently with her thumb and forefinger. With a growl, his body stiffened. Then he began to climax. Over and over he surged, coming in a series of long pulsing waves, spurting out his seed which she drank greedily, her hands still holding him until, moaning with delight, he fell back, spent, into the sweet-smelling straw.

An hour later, they were still lying side by side in the fragrant straw, having dozed in a blissful post-coital haze, listening to the gentle rain falling on the roof of the barn as the force of the storm died away and moved off into the distant hills. Katherine knew that soon they would have to start the ride home but, for now, all she wanted to do was savour the experience she had just had with Rob and revel in the feelings of vitality and well-being flooding through her body.

Chapter Ten

*I*t was a grey, rainy afternoon and Katherine felt like exploring. She knew there were many floors and rooms in the house that she had not seen yet and she was feeling adventurous. Most of the other guests had gone in to town for the day and she was looking forward to some time on her own. She felt energised and deeply moved by all her sexual experiences of the past few days but especially by her time with Assam. In fact, she felt like a completely different person. She felt like a woman more deeply in touch with her sexuality than she had ever been before. She thought back to the occasions on which she had allowed Assam and Daniel to use their little whips on her. That had made her so hot. At first, she had been shocked at her reaction, but later she had been able to accept this as just another facet of her new-found sexuality. She felt wonderful and ready for more adventures but she couldn't stop thinking about her time with Assam. There was something about her encounter with him that overshadowed everything else. She wondered if he felt the same way. He was a guest here too, she told herself. Maybe, he was looking for some changes in his life just like she was. Maybe, in each other, they had found someone who could give them the sexual satisfaction and emotional connection they were seeking in a partner. She tried not to dwell on these tempting possibilities. After all, he had given her no reason to believe he was serious about her. Also, she was still just learning about herself sexually and she wasn't ready yet to get involved with anyone no matter how wonderful they were. Some day maybe, she thought dreamily. Some day.

Katherine stepped out of her room into the hall and stole a glimpse of herself in the gilded mirror that hung over the dark mahogany table by her door. She looked radiant today, she noted, much to her satisfaction. Her low-cut white blouse and red dirndl skirt set off her dark hair and pale skin to perfection. She ran her hands over her breasts and tweaked her nipples which instantly rose into sharp peaks. Yes, she was feeling on top form today.

She turned away from the mirror and started down the hall. Despite the many and varied sexual encounters she had experienced recently, she still felt restless and vaguely agitated. Something was missing, but what? Deep in thought, she proceeded on her way, following the twists and turns of the narrow hallway.

Then, with no warning, she found herself in a very different part of the house. She looked around in confusion. How had she arrived here? Without any obvious transition, she seemed to have passed over some invisible boundary and entered a section of the house that had a different, almost sinister, atmosphere. She knew she had never been in this wing of the house before, and yet there was a familiar aura about it.

The decor was totally different. The thick plush carpets were blood red, the wallpaper a textured cream colour and the dim, almost topaz, coloured lights which were mounted in iron wall sconces cast an eerie glow over everything. As she made her way along the long narrow hall, it seemed to twist and curve back on itself until she was thoroughly lost. She felt uncomfortably disoriented. Shaking off an uneasy feeling, she told herself she could find her way back when necessary and continued on her way.

The hall was lined with a series of black doors, none of which would open when her curiosity got the better of her. Aside from the unusual decor, there didn't seem to be anything of interest here. Still eager for adventure, she decided to continue her exploration, the sound of her footsteps muted by the thick plush carpet beneath her feet. Something seemed to be pulling her forward and there was a growing sense of urgency inside her that had to be satisfied. She tried to shake a feeling of apprehension that had settled in the pit of her stomach. She picked up her pace and walked more quickly down the dimly-lit passageway.

After a few moments, she stopped dead in her tracks. Before her, loomed a huge, iron-studded oak door. Her feeling of apprehension increased. What should she do now? Should she try to go in? She hadn't had any luck with the other doors. Maybe she should just leave it alone and go back the way she came. However, to her amazement, she found she couldn't move. For some reason, she felt strangely drawn to whatever lay behind the door. There was something there waiting for her, something that she wanted to see. And she was going to see it no matter what. She grabbed the huge brass door knob and pushed. The door opened.

With a sense of relief and rising anticipation, Katherine stepped into the room. At first, it was difficult to see clearly because the room was so dimly lit and the thick, black velvet drapes at the windows were drawn against the gloom of the rainy day.

As her eyes adjusted to the gloom, she could see figures here and there but she couldn't make out exactly what they were doing. As she drew nearer, she could hear muffled groans and grunts. Intrigued, she kept going.

Moving as if in a dream, Katherine walked down the length of the narrow room, taking in every detail of her strange surroundings. The air was thick with the musky scent of the sandalwood incense. What was this place? she wondered. The room was hushed and dim and the decor unusual to say the least. Black velvet curtains kept out the daylight and a black plush rug, red textured wallpaper, black leather couches and red velvet chairs helped to muffle sound. She felt almost suffocated by the predominance of red in the room and the richness of textures. This sudden assault on her senses left her feeling dizzy and slightly claustrophobic.

The furniture was odd, too. Metal tables with strange gaping holes, black *chaises longues* with white fur rugs thrown over the back, chairs with hand and feet restraints, curious indentations in the walls here and there, leather swings, stirrups and chains hanging from the walls and an assortment of mysterious-looking instruments lying on shelves in a huge, walnut display cabinet.

Katherine could hardly breathe. Deep inside her, something familiar was stirring, something she couldn't quite put her finger on. Images of her encounter with Alan in the library flashed briefly before her eyes.

Before she could identify her feelings, she came upon a fantastic scene. A naked man was lying face down on a low metal table, his hands in leather cuffs which were chained to the floor. His feet were tied the same way. He was completely immobilised. There was a hole in the table just beneath his pelvis and, beneath that, lying on a mattress, a woman was sucking on his penis which protruded down through the opening straight into her mouth. He was moaning in ecstasy and struggling against his restraints but he couldn't move. This seemed to arouse him even more and he writhed in delight against the cold metal, his groans mingling with the grunts and sucking noises coming from the woman below him.

Katherine felt the urge to take his cock in her mouth and suck it until he was begging for mercy. She wanted to be the one who made him writhe and pant on the cold metal table. She took a step forward. The man turned his head. With a shock, she realised it was Johnny, the stable hand, the same man who had fucked her so thoroughly in the barn. Her pussy throbbed when she remembered. It seemed so long ago now. She had gone through so much since then; a lifetime of experience almost. She remembered the scene very clearly though. She blushed when she remembered how she had got down on all fours and presented herself to him like a hot little filly, how she had moaned and panted as he mounted and rode her like a stallion would his mare.

She realised he was looking at her from beneath hooded eyes that were dark with lust. His tongue snaked out between his thick sensual lips and began darting in and out. He wanted to lick her. He wanted her to join in, Katherine realised in amazement. A wave of dizziness swept over her. She could feel her juices ooze out into the crotch of her panties. Suddenly, her clothes felt too tight and her breath was coming in rapid little gasps. She almost walked over to him but, just then, the woman servicing him did something that made him groan with ecstasy. In a flash, he forgot all about Katherine and disappeared back into his world of sensual delights.

With a sigh, Katherine left him to his exquisite torture. When she had moved further down the long room, she came across another scenario which took her breath away.

A woman wearing only pantalettes and a tightly-laced boned corset was bent over a leather couch. Her hands were tied behind her back and her full breasts were tumbling out of the half cups touching the carpet. A man dressed in a lace and brocade ensemble was standing over her. In his hand, he held a set of leather thongs with little white balls attached to the tips. Katherine edged closer. She saw that the pantalettes had an open crotch and the man was lightly flicking the leather thongs over her exposed sex.

'Tell me how much you like it,' he commanded, flicking even harder.

Her answer was a high pitched cry that sent shivers skittering down Katherine's spine.

'Do you deserve more? Have you been a naughty girl?' he demanded.

'I don't deserve it, but I want it,' the woman gasped, rubbing her breasts against the rough surface of the carpet.

'You are right. You don't deserve it. And so, you shall not get any more,' he added softly.

'Oh, please,' she begged. 'Just a little bit. Please.'

'You must learn self-control. Only with the greatest self-discipline, can we learn the excruciating pleasure of pain.'

The woman fell silent and arched her back, wordlessly willing him to touch her in his very special way.

This time, however, he put aside the thongs, picked up a small black riding crop and inserted its tip between her buttocks.

'That is very good. You are learning, my dear,' he murmured softly, referring to her strangled silence. 'Now, for your next lesson,' he added.

He eased the crop even deeper inside her. Soon he was sliding it back and forth, twisting and turning it inside her anus. He reached down between her legs and began fingering her clitoris which was engorged and pushing out from between her silken lips.

'I can't do this,' she gasped, panting wildly,

'Oh, but you can. You know you always say that. And then, you discover that you *can* bear it, that you actually love it. And then you give in to it and you come over and over. You remember. Then, after it's all over, you always tell me how you can't live without it and you show me how grateful you are. Isn't that true, my dear?'

'Oh, yes, yes, it's all true,' she said, grinding her crotch against his skilful hands.

Katherine tore herself away and continued on her way through the dimly lit room, the woman's cries of agonised delight echoing behind her. She felt incredibly excited. The clinic was obviously geared to meeting every kind of sexual need. What other titillating sights lay in store for her? she wondered.

As she approached the far end of the room, she became aware of a woman sitting near the wall on a black wooden chair. She was wearing a red leather outfit, a sort of bustier that pushed her full breasts up until they were bulging over the top, revealing just a hint of her dark pink nipples. The bustier extended downwards towards her waist where it flared out over her hips to become a suspender belt that held up her sheer black stockings. In front, the bustier narrowed to a thin strip that ran down into her thick blonde bush then disappeared in between her legs. Her hair was long and blonde and she wore a red mask over her eyes. Her hands were bound behind her in a leather cuff which was attached to an iron ring in the wall behind her. Her ankles were manacled and anchored to the floor. Her legs were spread wide, exposing her moist sex which was intersected by the narrow red thong and glistened with her dew. Her head was thrown back, her mouth open, her eyes glittering through the slits of the mask. She writhed lasciviously against the constraints, jerking her hips and grinding the thong even deeper into her.

Katherine jumped nervously as another woman stepped out of the shadows. She too was wearing a mask. Hers was black with elaborate designs on it. She was naked except for a harness of black leather straps with silver studs which thrust her breasts up and outwards. The garter straps, a continuation of the leather harness, held up her sheer black stockings and contrasted dramatically with her milky white skin. On her wrists, she wore wide silver slave bracelets. She was very slim with short dark hair and there were clamps on her dark red nipples. When she sat down in the chair opposite Katherine and spread her legs, a glitter of gold could be seen shining in the dark tangle between her legs. In her hand, she carried a small silver riding crop.

Katherine's breasts tightened and her sex began to tingle as she stood rooted to the floor watching the scene unfolding before her. Both women were clearly aroused. Their breasts were swollen, their nipples tight little peaks, their eyes glazed with passion. The dark one walked over to the woman in the chair and slowly used the crop to trace the outline of her full sensual mouth. With deliberate movements, she dragged it down her neck, trailing it over her partner's breasts and her torso until it disappeared into her blonde bush.

Katherine shifted her weight uncomfortably, aware of the gathering tension between her legs.

The blonde woman moaned and wet her lips, thrusting her hips towards the leather crop as it snaked its way down her body. She gasped aloud when it dislodged the material over her voluptuous breasts. The darker woman smiled and dragged the crop across the tender flesh, just missing her swollen nipples. Her partner groaned and arched her back, begging for more. The other responded immediately and began circling and teasing the blonde's nipples with quick darting motions until they were elongated even further. The blonde woman threw her head back and spread her legs even wider. Katherine could see the narrow red leather thong between her legs. It was dark red now, soaked through with the woman's juices. The woman sighed deeply when her partner freed her from her restraints and led her to a nearby leather couch where she was told to lie across it face down.

Katherine tried to turn and leave but she couldn't. She was transfixed by the scene in front of her. She jumped with a start as the dark woman flicked the whip over her partner's creamy smooth buttocks. The sound of leather contacting with flesh echoed through the thick musty air. With each flick of the whip, the other woman groaned with pleasure, writhing and squirming as she hung over the leather couch. Her bare behind was rosy from the assault but raised in welcome as each stroke convulsed her body into spasms of tortured delight.

Katherine could almost hear her own heartbeat as little sparks of sexual energy ignited her passion. Each crack of the whip seemed to go right through her and she felt that she was the one being spanked.

The blonde woman was whimpering now as her partner turned her over on her back and began trailing the thongs of the whip lazily over the tender flesh of her inner thighs. In long deliberate strokes, she dragged the whip closer and closer to her swollen sex.

Katherine was so aroused she was trembling from head to toe. Her breasts were tight and swollen and the hard spears of her nipples chafed painfully against the confines of her bra. Her panties were drenched with her dew and there was a fiery heat between her legs. She slid one hand inside her bra and began rubbing her breasts.

'Fuck her, fuck her,' she heard herself saying at the top of her voice.

Horrified at her words, Katherine was even more surprised at the reaction of the two women. Instead of recoiling at her lewd words, they just looked over at her and smiled. Both were obviously enjoying her participation. It seemed to arouse them even more.

'Would you like to join in, dear?'

It was the dark one who spoke. Her voice was cool and inviting and strangely familiar.

Shocked at hearing a voice after the long silent spectacle, Katherine could only stand there paralysed, unable to put two words together. How could she have cried out like that? She didn't understand what was happening to her. Her encounter with Alan in the library flashed before her eyes. She had used the whip on him and had made him come. Then there had been the scene in the playroom with Alan and Karen where they had tied her down and done all those delicious things. And, of course, Assam had used that little satin whip on her and had driven her into a frenzy of sexual excitement. She had loved the feel of it on her breasts and the way her clit tightened in response. Just thinking about it made her wet. What was going on with her? She felt hotter than hell just thinking about all this. And now, here she was watching two women enjoying one another and she could hardly contain herself. She knew she had resolved to explore her sexual tastes but she never dreamed this would include whips, restraints and all manner of kinky paraphenalia.

Her train of thought came to an abrupt halt. Her thoughts were wild, erratic. She collapsed on a nearby leather *chaise longue* and closed her eyes. She could hear the moans of the two women as they continued their love making. When they finally reached their climax, their sighs and groans drove her wild. She slipped her hand inside her panties. She was so wet. She slid her finger into her moist pussy and began playing with her clit. It was hard and slippery and pulsed under her finger. She began stroking herself just the way she liked it. Oh, it felt so good, so good. If only . . .

'Hey, honey, what are you doing? Are you being a naughty girl? I think maybe someone should give you a good spanking for touching yourself like that.'

Katherine's eyes flew open. She recognised Jasmine's voice. The young blonde woman was standing beside the chair looking down at her. She was the one dressed all in red, wearing the red mask and the red leather bustier. Jasmine was the woman in the erotic tableau she had just witnessed, the one making all those incredible sounds that had turned her on so much. Katherine's thoughts were racing. She was stunned at this unexpected discovery. As she stared at Jasmine in wild disbelief, a man strolled over and joined them. It was Steve, the black man she had met at breakfast on her first day at the clinic. He was wearing a black leather jock strap and nothing else. In his hand, he held a small whip. Katherine's brain could hardly process everything that was happening. She let her eyes run down the length of his body. She couldn't keep from staring at the bulge between his legs. She looked over at Jasmine again, her eyes wide with surprise.

'That's right. It's me,' Jasmine whispered, smiling as she saw the realisation dawn in Katherine's eyes. She snuggled up to Steve as they both stood there looking down at her.

Katherine gasped at the naked lust she saw in their eyes. Then, before she could protest, she felt herself being lifted up and placed in a kneeling position in front of the *chaise longue*. Jasmine knelt on the other side and pulled her forward until she was bent over the *chaise longue*, her arms pinned in Jasmine's firm grip, her buttocks raised and waiting. When she felt her skirt being lifted up and her panties being pulled down, she gave a small sharp cry of protest but in her heart, she knew she didn't want them to stop. She was excited beyond her wildest dreams. Her body craved satisfaction, she couldn't deny it. She wanted this. She had wanted this for a long time. She had wanted to experience this and now she was being given that chance. She had to take it. Her body relaxed. She was not going to resist.

At the first flick of the whip on her bare bottom, she cried out sharply and tried to wriggle away but it was no use. She couldn't break Jasmine's hold on her. Her struggles only seemed to increase her excitement and she could feel her juices beginning to flow. She was more sexually excited than she had ever been in her entire life. Her clitoris was tight, swollen, and pulsing wildly between her legs. Her nipples were tight aching nubs. She longed to rub her pussy but she couldn't move. Her breath was coming in short harsh gasps and she was trembling from head to toe. She felt crazy. She didn't care now what she had to do to assuage this fire that was burning her up. She would do anything with anyone.

Katherine's senses were reeling. She was at a fever pitch of arousal. Each flick of the whip sent delicious tingles radiating directly to her clitoris. Ripples of a pain that quickly turned to pleasure skimmed over the surface of her skin then intensified into wild sexual thrills that added to the excruciating tension between her legs. The sensations were almost unbearable. She loved the feeling of the whip on her backside and the way it electrified her clit. She never wanted it to end. She wanted to stay here on the edge, savouring every ripple of pleasure that surged through her, that hot driving passion that seemed to be melting the cold hard core at the very centre of her being. As the strokes came harder and harder, she bucked and jerked her hips wildly as she strained to meet each nip and bite of the whip.

'Oh, God, yes, yes,' she sobbed, wailing out her pleasure. Every nerve in her body seemed electrified and exposed. Then, just when she thought she couldn't stand any more, a well-oiled finger slid into her rear cleavage and began gently stroking and probing the delicate rose of her anus. She groaned as Steve's thick, flexible finger probed this most sensitive and forbidden area of all. She heard herself begging him to stop but deep in her heart she knew she knew she didn't really him want to. Her passion had the upper hand now and any resistance she might have had was quickly dissolving. Her hips surged to welcome the finger that impaled her like a hot spear. She gasped in delight as it thrust and churned in and out of her arsehole, matching the tempo of the crisp flicks of the whip that kept landing squarely on her writhing bare bottom. Katherine was beyond all resistance now and she arched her buttocks up and back to meet Steve's invading finger.

'The whip makes you hot, doesn't it, Katherine?' he asked, groaning as his own lust surged within him. 'Well now, let's see if we can pay attention to that clitty of yours. From what I can see, it's just begging for attention.'

Instantly, Jasmine who had been enjoying the spectacle, released Katherine's hands and came around to the front of the *chaise longue*. She spread Katherine's legs a little wider then slid under her kneeling body and buried her head between her legs. She caught Katherine's bucking hips and pinned them in her strong hands. Then she stuck out her long tongue and slowly began to lick Katherine's swollen pussy.

Katherine groaned and rubbed her nipples against the soft velvet of the furniture. Jasmine's tongue was hot and smooth. She licked and jabbed, darting everywhere, lapping Katherine's clitoris with long deliberate strokes. Her mouth was sucking her, her teeth nipping gently, pulling at the soft fur that ringed her pink sex lips.

A strange animal-like sound rose up in Katherine's throat as Jasmine's tongue slid down to the entrance to her love passage. She gasped then ground her hips lasciviously as Jasmine shaped her tongue into a sharp arrow and used the tip to draw lazy little circles around the rim of her dark slit. She teased Katherine a little longer then, when her whimpers began to get louder, she pushed her tongue deep into her passage and began fluttering it in and out.

Katherine was wild now as both Jasmine and Steve continued their relentless ministrations. She bucked and jerked her hips back and forth, moaning and panting as Steve's long slick finger foraged deep in her anus and Jasmine licked and sucked every part of her throbbing sex. She felt drunk with their attentions. She ached for release but Steve and Jasmine were experts in pleasure and, still, they refused to let her ride the wave her body was craving. They knew there was more to feel before they let her go.

Jasmine stopped tonguing her slit and sucked Katherine's entire pussy into her mouth, closing her lips around her aching nub. Then Steve eased one more finger into her bottom hole and began probing and churning them in all directions.

At that point, Katherine lost all control and began bucking uncontrollably.

'Ooh, but aren't you a hot little thing!' Jasmine groaned, lifting her mouth from Katherine's swollen sex. 'I knew you would be like this. I knew you would love to be sucked this way. I bet you never dreamt how good it would feel to be whipped, licked and ass-fucked all at the same time. I guess you thought that was too naughty to even think about. Well, now you know, don't you? You know you're a naughty girl, just like me. We love being bad because it makes us so hot.'

'Yes, yes,' Katherine cried, aroused even further by Jasmine's raunchy talk.

Once again, Jasmine claimed Katherine's throbbing little nub as her own and began sucking fast and hard.

As Katherine's moans grew louder, Steve slipped off his jock strap. His erect cock, sheathed in black latex, sprang free. He looked down at Katherine's pouting sex just waiting for him. Then, with a groan, he mounted her from behind and slid easily into her.

Katherine caught her breath as he entered her. His cock was long and thick and filled her completely. He began to pump slowly then gradually quickened his pace. She placed her hands on the seat of the chair to support herself as she pushed her buttocks up to meet him, matching him thrust for thrust.

Jasmine got up and came around to the side of the *chaise longue*, climbed on to the seat and positioned herself between Katherine's outstretched arms. Then she wriggled up to the edge of the seat and pushed her pussy up against Katherine's mouth.

'Suck me, Katherine, suck me hard.'

With a groan, Katherine greedily ran her tongue over Jasmine's moist sex then pushed it past her crease and foraged in her pussy until she found the stiff peak of her clitoris. With a groan, she clamped her lips around the fleshy protuberance and began to suck and pull on it until the blonde woman's moans matched her own.

With Steve's massive cock pumping in and out of her and Jasmine's silky sex in her mouth, Katherine felt aroused to the point of madness. She was wild, ecstatic, moving in a frenzy of sexual delight. She ground her hips on Steve's driving cock, the muscles of her vagina clutching at him, milking him over and over. She could feel her orgasm building and she clenched down on him even harder. Then Steve slid his free hand between her legs and ran his index finger over her rigid bud. She cried out and pushed back against his penis, impaling herself as deeply as she could. As he began thrusting faster and faster, her hips bucked wildly to match his pace. Her whole body tensed as the walls of her vagina contracted and waves of agonising pleasure began washing through her.

'Oh, God, I'm coming. I'm coming,' she moaned and her hips strained to grab her pleasure.

Her climax blazed through her, seizing her in its searing grip. Her body arched and convulsed as she came, shaking and trembling with the force of her passion. Her mouth clamped down on Jasmine's pussy, sucking and pulling on it as her vagina clenched around Steve's cock and milked it again and again. Finally, panting and moaning, she fell forward on to the *chaise longue*, overwhelmed and trembling in the aftermath of her climax.

Hours later, Katherine opened her eyes. She was sprawled on the black velvet couch, her legs wide apart, her skirt flung way up over her waist. For a moment, she didn't know who or where she was. Then she remembered and shuddered as she re-experienced the waves of intense pleasure that had driven her almost mad with delight. For the second time in two days, she felt alive and vibrant. She was exhausted but revitalised. She knew that something deeply personal had happened to her. She had been moved and totally satisfied. Her last two experiences, plus the one with Assam and this one today had seemed to draw on something deep inside her, something that touched the very core of her sexuality. She sighed contentedly and covered herself with the white fur rug that lay over the back of the *chaise longue*. Then with a satisfied smile, she fell in a deep dreamless sleep.

Chapter Eleven

Katherine awoke with a start. For a moment, she didn't know where she was and what had happened to her. Then she remembered: the entire scenario of the previous afternoon came flooding back. She stretched voluptuously in her bed and sighed blissfully. Someone must have carried her back to her room yesterday, undressed her and put her to bed. And she had slept through the night. She sighed happily, grateful for the way people looked out for each other here. She looked at her clock. It was seven o'clock in the morning. She had an interview with Martha at ten. Plenty of time for a shower and some breakfast. She was absolutely ravenous.

Just then there was a knock at the door and Annie walked in with a breakfast tray and laid it across her lap.

'Good morning, sleepy head,' she said with a smile. You look like you've been having a really good time.

Katherine smiled at her and sat up in bed breathing

in the tantalising aroma of freshly-brewed coffee and home-made rolls.

'I'm so hungry I could eat a horse, Annie. And yes, I have been having a fine time.'

'You know, you really look great, Katherine. Your stay here has really done you the world of good. Your eyes are bright and you look so much more relaxed than the day you arrived. I hope you found what you were looking for.'

'I have, Annie. I really have. And today, I'm meeting with Martha to discuss everything I've experienced since I arrived. Oh, and by the way, Annie, I never did use the butterfly. Somehow, the right moment never seemed to arise.'

'Some people don't need that particular kind of help, Katherine. It's a great little device, though, and can really come in handy when you're stuck for other sources of stimulation, if you know what I mean,' she added with an impish grin. 'Keep it if you like. You never know when it might come in handy. Well, I've got to go. I'm running late.' Annie smiled warmly and blew Katherine a kiss as she hurried out the door.

Katherine dug into her breakfast with relish and, before long, had demolished two cups of coffee and three delicious breakfast rolls. When she got up out of bed, she was aware of a soreness in her buttocks. She smiled to herself as she padded naked into the bathroom for her shower.

It was 9.45am when she knocked on the door to Martha's office.

'Good morning,' Martha boomed in a warm friendly voice as she ushered Katherine into her office. 'And how are you feeling this beautiful morning?'

'I feel better then I have in years,' Katherine admitted with a smile. 'I have enjoyed every moment of my time here. I've done so many things and I feel so differently about myself and my sexuality that I don't know where to start.'

'Well, first of all, don't worry about knowing where to start,' Martha suggested with a smile. 'I already know everything you've been up to. I even know you decided against trying the butterfly. You see, I keep very close watch on my clients. I know you've been doing splendidly and have responded very positively to all the opportunities that have been offered to you. You seem to have taken my advice and maintained an open attitude. It shows.'

'Oh, yes, I feel like a totally different person,' she said.

'Well, our staff are really first rate, you know and – '

'Could you tell me,' Katherine interrupted hesitantly. 'Is Assam Aswabi a member of your staff too? Or is he a client like me?'

'Assam? Good heavens no. Assam is one of our oldest investors. He put money into the clinic right from the start. Part of the deal was he would have his own suite here and would have free run of the place for himself and his guests. He has nothing to do with the therapeutic side of things at all. Why do you ask?'

Katherine was stunned. Assam was one of the investors in the clinic as well as an honoured guest. That explained a lot; the special suite, his access to parts of the hotel others did not have, the fact that Jasmine had seen him here on so many different occasions. He wasn't one of the clients at all. What had she got herself into with him? Was he really serious about her or had he just seen her as some sexual neophyte that needed help? Some sex-starved, naive child-woman who had come here to work out some sordid little sexual problem? And he had decided to take pity on her and show her a good time. Was that all she had meant to him? Her cheeks burned when she remembered their time together, of how she had offered herself to him with complete abandon. She realised her insecurities were getting the better of her and tried to marshal her thoughts into some coherent order.

Martha's voice jolted her back to the present. 'Did Assam introduce himself to you, Katherine?'

'He did a heck of lot more than that,' she blurted out.

'Tell me what happened,' Martha said softly.

'Tell you?' Katherine stuttered in amazement.

'Yes. Look, Katherine, you have made great strides here all on your own. However, if you're really serious about getting to the bottom of things, you'll have to go that one step farther. I want you to talk about your experiences, go into detail, let yourself get aroused. And then answer any questions that might be asked of you without embarrassment. This will test your level of inhibition or lack of it and will tell me what kind of progress you have really made and how comfortable you are with yourself sexually. This is also your chance to try to find out once and for all why you always feel so cheated, thwarted almost, when it comes to sex. Take this one last risk and see where it leads. You might just be pleasantly surprised. What do you think? Can you try to answer my questions as honestly?'

'I'll try.'

'That's the spirit. Now, let's get right to it. Did he suck your breasts?'

'Uh, yes he did and uh . . .'

'Did you like it?'

'Oh, God, yes, it felt wonderful.'

Katherine was beginning to feel excited but she felt reluctant to reveal this fact in front of Martha.

'Did he lick your sex? Did he manipulate your clitoris with his tongue? Did you like that? How did that feel? What was it about his lovemaking that you liked best?'

Katherine was squirming in her chair as she tried to respond to Martha's probing questions.

'I loved everything about it. He licked my clit then he pushed his tongue deep inside me. Once, he even tied me down and sucked and licked my nipples until I thought I would come just from that. There was another man too. He licked my behind then stuck his finger inside me. Then he and Assam both screwed me, one from behind and the other from the front. I thought I was going to die, it was so wonderful.'

Katherine was wriggling on the chair now. The memory of their lovemaking was driving her crazy. Her breasts were straining against her bra and the crotch of her panties was soaking.

'You're doing just fine, Katherine. I can tell you are very aroused. Just the memory of that night with him is getting you very excited, isn't it?' Martha persisted.

'Yes, it is,' she gasped as she tightened her buttocks against the hardness of the chair.

'You've had many different sexual encounters, since you've been here, Katherine. Now, I would like you to tell me how you felt after they were over.'

'Well, at first, I'd feel really great. Then I'd start to have the feeling that I'd been cheated, that something just wasn't right, that I'd lost out on something. It's hard to put into words but I'd end up feeling really sad and even a little angry. This spoils sex for me. No matter how good the sex is, I always start to feel this way a little while after it's over. Before I came here, it was so bad I decided sex just wasn't worth the effort. The feeling got stronger and stronger until it was starting to feel like an ordeal rather than a pleasure. I even started to think the only way to handle this was to avoid sex altogether. Pretty soon, I was so uptight and unhappy that my love life started to be really boring and humdrum. It was as if I just turned off. I just didn't have the nerve to try to live out any of my fantasies. At least, I didn't until I came here. Anyway, my work started to suffer and when that happened, I knew I was in trouble.'

'You have been able to do more or less what you wanted here, haven't you, Katherine?' asked Martha.

'Yes, and it's been great. I've never had the freedom to explore my sexuality. I've discovered a lot about myself.'

'I'm sure you have. You have given yourself a freedom you have been missing for a long time. You know, I think that when you were just beginning your sex life, something thwarted you from truly exploring and experiencing your sexuality in a normal healthy way. I think whatever this was, it is still having an effect on you. It is making you feel that you can't have what is rightfully yours; a healthy, vigorous, multi-faceted sex life. What happened to spoil things for you, Katherine?'

Katherine took a long time to answer. She was not used to delving into the past. She was a person who was focused on the present and it went against the grain to look behind her instead of forward. However, as she sat in the warmth and security of Martha's office, memories of her mid to late teenage years flashed through her mind: the parties, the sports

251

events, the heavy necking in the car after her latest boyfriend took her home from a Saturday night film. It all been quite innocent. And then she had gone away to boarding school. She had missed all her friends and had to make new ones. It had been hard being away from home but then she had met Joe and of course . . . Joe! she thought excitedly. She had been so crazy about him and then . . .

'What is it, Katherine? Have you remembered something?' Martha's voice asked insistently.

Katherine sat silently for a moment, her brow furrowed, her body tense. 'I haven't thought about this for years. It's probably nothing. It's something that happened to me when I was at boarding school. I was madly in love with a boy named Joe. We used to go out all the time. My parents didn't like him because he was wild and different. They even told the head-mistress of the school to do everything she could to keep us apart but nothing could stop us. Joe and I were so nuts about each other we spent every free moment we had together. I was only seventeen at the time but I was deeply and passionately in love with him. I've never felt like this about anyone since, except maybe Assam . . .' her voice trailed off into silence.

'Try to stay focused on the past, Katherine,' Martha urged her gently. 'This is important.'

'Well, we were parked in his car one night outside the school. It was late. It was almost time for me to go in. We were necking and petting as usual. We had never made love before, just the usual teenage stuff. Somehow, this night was different. All of a sudden we couldn't stop ourselves. We started making wild passionate love in the car. He had my blouse open and was sucking on my breasts, his hands were all over me. Then he had my panties down and before I knew it, he was licking and sucking my pussy. He was moaning and panting and I was so turned on I could hardly breathe. I had opened his flies and was rubbing his cock. It was so big and smooth and I wanted him inside me. And then his tongue was on my clit sucking and pulling on it and I was groaning so loudly it's a wonder the whole school didn't hear me. Then, suddenly, the headmistress was there shining a torch down on us. The look in her eyes made my blood run cold. She looked at me as if I were a prostitute or something. She ran her eyes all over my body. I was lying there with my breasts bare, and my legs draped over Joe's shoulders. He had his head buried between my legs and his tongue half way up me. We must have been quite a sight.

Anyway, she looked at us for a long time and let her eyes run all over my body until I got a really sick feeling in my stomach. Then she called me a dirty slut and ordered me inside. I heard her telling Joe that, if he didn't get out of there fast, she was going to call the police. I can't tell you how horrible she made me feel. However, the worst thing was that she caught us just when I was on the point of having an orgasm, my first orgasm with my first love. I can't tell you how traumatic that was for me. I felt like I had been cheated out of what was rightfully mine. Before I knew it, I was in my room. I felt numb, ashamed and in agony. You know how intensely teenagers feel everything, but it was more than that for me; I was really devastated by the whole thing. I realise now I never really got over that whole incident. And I never really got over Joe. I never saw him again, you know. Those who had power over our lives had finally succeeded in separating us for good. Oh God, I feel so angry when I talk about this. I feel so sad too and cheated of all that could have been mine. I was cheated out of my first real sexual experience that night with a boy I loved. I was cheated out of my first orgasm. I lost Joe, my first love, and I lost the chance to explore with him all the facets of our sexual relationship. It might not sound like much to you but the more I talk about it, the more I realise it meant the world to me. I know now that the incident affected me much more deeply than I ever realised.'

Katherine's voice broke and she began to sob uncontrollably as years of pent-up sadness washed over her. Martha sat by quietly, letting her cry it out.

Finally, she stopped and fell back in the seat exhausted.

'People who had authority over you took away something that was very precious to you,' Martha said softly. 'They cheated you of what was rightfully yours, a full and exciting sexual life and continuing contact with the first man you deeply loved. These are not small issues. Your sadness and anger at the way you were treated have stayed with you until this present day. These feelings come from long ago, but, now that you have felt them, you will be able to enjoy your sex life here in the present with no more painful residue from the past.'

Martha stopped talking for a moment until she felt Katherine was ready to hear more. 'Now that you have acknowledged your sadness at your loss, I want you to watch something on the TV monitor.'

Feeling overwhelmed by the circumstances, Katherine could only nod and turn towards the monitor. The screen flickered briefly and then a scene appeared.

In a parked convertible, a young man and woman were locked in a passionate embrace. The man's head was buried between the girls legs. The girl's full breasts were naked and her nipples were hard little nubs.

Katherine gasped aloud. Her recognition was immediate. This was the scene she had seen on the monitor in her bedroom, the one that had been cut off so abruptly. She remembered how peculiar she had felt when that had happened and how, later, she and Alan and Karen had shared some pretty wild sex.

She looked again more closely at the screen. This was how she and Joe must have looked that night. Joe, her first love. She had wanted him so much. She remembered his touch, his mouth on her pussy, his hands on her breasts. Her sex quivered as the memories came flooding back.

Then the scene changed abruptly and an older woman came striding over to them. The two young people started violently and sat there befuddled in the light of her torch, as she berated the girl in a harsh unforgiving voice.

Katherine sat up in her chair with a jolt. That was just the way the headmistress had talked to her the night she had found her in the car with Joe. She remembered how her passion had drained out of her, leaving her cold and ashamed, bereft of Joe and cheated of the pleasure they could have shared. It had been the end of their relationship and sex had never been the same after that. Katherine thought she was going to start screaming as her anger and a mounting sexual tension began to escalate to a fever pitch.

'Is there anything you would like to say, Katherine?' Martha asked softly. 'You couldn't say or do anything that night. You were totally under her control. That miserable woman stole your pleasure right out from under you. She cheated you of the ecstasy that was rightfully yours. You can remedy all that now by just telling her exactly how you felt then and how you feel now. If you do, you can put the past behind you once and for all.'

Katherine's anger and the memory of her thwarted passion built until they fused into one burning energy that burst out of her in a stream of angry words that shattered the silence of Martha's office. In her mind, the headmistress was standing in front of her, denying her the right to have sex with her lover; she was demeaning her, wrenching her away from her beloved Joe.

'You can't do this to me anymore. I am in control now, not you. And you know what? I love sex. I love it when a man licks my pussy and sucks my clit. I love it when he fondles my breasts and pinches my nipples. It makes me hot. But you, you old witch, you can't have any of this so you try to take it away from those of us who can. Well, you can't take it away from me anymore. You're not going to cheat me of what is rightfully mine. I saw the look in your eyes when you saw Joe and me. You pretended to be disgusted but I know what you were feeling. You wanted it just as much as I did but you couldn't have it. So you didn't want me to have it either. And you took your frustration out on me. You punished me by taking away everything that what was rightfully mine. You cheated me. You cheated me out of the ecstasy that was waiting for me that night with Joe. You took Joe away from me and you took away any control I had over my own sexual choices. I have never forgiven you for that. Never.'

Katherine was writhing on the chair now as she continued to yell at the top of her lungs. She felt wonderful, free, well beyond the control of the horrid woman who had cheated and stolen from her everything she held dear so many years ago. She thought about Joe. She had loved him so much. She had grown up and moved on but, in her heart, she had remained frozen in time, still craving what could have been between them. Over and over throughout her life, she had judged all experiences in the light of what she had lost with Joe and had found them wanting. Ever since that night, she had been unable to enjoy a full sexual life because she was so sad and angry about what she had lost.

'Just watch, you bitch,' Katherine gasped, panting with passion and anger, as she slid her fingers down into her panties and began fingering her rigid clitoris. 'I am going to come right in front of you and you can't do a thing to stop me. Not now, not ever. You can't lay a finger on me. I am going to come just the way I wanted to come that night with Joe. I'm going to come right here and now. I feel so hot and so good,' she panted, as she slid two fingers into her slit, and began to thrust them in and out with quick jabbing strokes. 'You can't stop me any more because I am in control now. I'm the one who's going to decide when and with whom I have sex. Not you. You can't take my pleasure away from me anymore.'

The floodgates of her anger and her passion burst wide open and Katherine was transported into a realm where the past and the present merged into one. Her body was on fire. She was wildly aroused like she had been all those years ago with Joe. As she rubbed her breasts and stroked her clit she revelled in the delicious surges of sexual energy that flooded through her body and screamed out what she had wanted to say for a long, long time. At last, she was free to have her say. At last, after so many years, she was truly free to satisfy her sexual appetite without being haunted by the past. She was in control of her life and of her sexual pleasure now. No one else would ever play that role in her life again.

Katherine was writhing around like a madwoman. One hand was deep in her pussy, stroking and pulling on the fleshy nub of her engorged clit while the other squeezed and tweaked her nipples. Her hips pumped back and forth as the scathing words continued to pour out of her. Then, finally, her voice dropped and she collapsed on the chair, her legs wide apart, her pussy drenched with her juices.

'I'm coming. I'm coming,' she gasped.

Her eyes glazed over and she tensed from head to foot. She thrust her hips upward reaching for her pleasure and, as it seized her, a long animal-like wail rose up in her throat. As she cried and moaned, all the years of anger and disappointment and denial melted away and dissolved before the onslaught of her raging passion – so long held in check.

The orgasm seemed to go on forever; a combination of sexual release and emotional catharsis, wrenching her from head to toe, dragging cries and groans from deep within her body. Finally, after what seemed like an eternity, it began to subside and she collapsed back into the chair, trembling and quivering from head to toe.

Martha smiled quietly to herself. She knew she had another success on her hands. Katherine had made a astounding breakthrough and was now free from the hold of the past, free to go on to a better and more fulfilling life in every way. She got up from her desk and walked over to the woman slumped like a rag doll in the chair. She put her arms around her and rocked her until her sobs faded away and she was still.

* * *

'How did you know?' Katherine asked a few hours later when Martha visited her in her room. 'How did you know about Joe and me?'

'It was something Phyllis Manion said when she talked to me about your past. Apparently you mentioned to her something about a failed teenage relationship and an unfortunate run-in with your headmistress at boarding school. She said she had the impression that you had never got over that. I just took it from there.'

'This is all so amazing,' Katherine exclaimed. 'I can hardly believe what has happened. I feel as if I have been released from prison. You know, Martha, I feel really free for the first time in my life, and free to live my life the way I see fit. I also feel completely exhausted,' Katherine added with a tired little smile.

'It will take you a while to assimilate all this and to realise how much that one night has affected your life right up to the present,' Martha explained. 'You're been through a lot and you're tired but you're OK now and you're free to go home any time you want. You don't need what we offer here any more. You have broken through to the truth of your feelings and your sexual needs. The final test will be going back to your old environment and trying your wings. Now, you know, of course, that your sexuality will never be the same as that young girl's?'

Katherine nodded silently as the older woman continued talking.

'Sexually, your tastes are now a collage of what you wanted then plus all the ways you have found to express yourself since. You have discovered your true sexual identity and have come to the end of a very long and successful journey. I think you will have some choices to make down the road. From what you tell me, it looks like there might be a future for you and Assam at some point in the future. His wife died five years ago and he's been very lonely ever since. He's been trying to find someone for quite a while but he hasn't had much success. It's been hard for him because he is such a special man. He requires a very special woman, a strong intelligent woman, one who is sensual and passionate as well as sensitive; a woman who is able to freely express her own sexuality as well as meet his needs. It seems to me that, after you get your life in order, you might just be that woman, depending of course on how you feel about him.'

'I have never met a man who attracts me so powerfully or moves me so deeply,' Katherine admitted. 'I want to be with him more than anything. I also know I have to get used to the new me and experience myself differently in my own world before I can even think of getting involved in what I know will be a very intense and complicated relationship with Assam. I agree with you, Martha. I think something could work out for us.'

'This sounds very hopeful,' Martha replied warmly. 'I'm so happy we've been able to help you, Katherine. You know the change in you is really remarkable. You have really bloomed. I know you have fought hard for this change. You have been wise and you have been courageous. I wish you all the best and I hope that you can make things work with Assam and, if not with him, then with some man who will fill your sexual and emotional needs. Well, it looks like we've come to the end of a long road, Katherine. I assume you will be leaving soon. So, I will say my goodbyes now and wish you the best of luck.'

'Thank you, Martha. Thank you for everything,' Katherine murmured.

Then, feeling too overwhelmed to say anything further, she fell back in her chair and closed her eyes as Martha walked out of the room and shut the door quietly behind her.

The next day she was packed and ready to go. She was passing the library on her way to the lounge for her farewell party when someone reached out through the open doorway and pulled her inside. She was about to cry out when she looked up into Assam's cool blue eyes.

'Don't be afraid. It's only me. I wanted to speak to you but I couldn't say what I have to say at a party. I needed to talk to you privately. Here seemed the best place. I hope I didn't frighten you,' he added, an amused glint in his eyes.

Katherine sighed with relief and smiled up at him a little shyly. 'You always seem to do things in such a dramatic way,' she teased lightly. 'But that's one of the things I like about you.'

'Katherine, I have something I want to ask you.' He stopped for a moment and looked deep into her eyes as if searching for an answer before he had even asked the question. 'Would you consider coming to visit me now that your stay here is over?'

Katherine couldn't believe her ears. This was exactly what she had been hoping. She wanted to do this more than anything in the world. And yet, she knew it was too soon. She needed time to process and reflect on everything that had happened, time to try her wings in her own world first before she even attempted to function in his. Also, she had to make some very important changes in her life before she

261

could get involved with anyone else. She had changed drastically and needed time to get used to the person she was becoming. Also, she had to end her relationship with Paul. There was no way she could continue with him after the exciting sex she had experienced here. But how could she reject Assam's offer without hurting his feelings? She certainly didn't want to do that and she didn't want to jeopardise her chances with him in the future.

'Don't worry if you have to say no,' he murmured, reading her thoughts almost exactly. 'You have been going through some very intense experiences here and you will need time to absorb them. I know too that you might be somewhat reluctant to pack up and visit me in my country. After all, we've only known each other a short time and there's a lot we have to discover about each other. So, please, don't worry about hurting my feelings. I understand completely. I suppose I was just hoping against hope that you may wish to be with me immediately but I don't want to pressure you in any way. I want you with me, Katherine, if not now, then soon. I hope the next time we see each other, you will feel ready to pursue our relationship further.'

'Thank you so much for your invitation,' she whispered, hardly daring to believe her ears. 'I can't tell you how much it means to me. I do so want to come and visit you but, as you say, I really need time to process my experiences here. I also need to make some changes in my life at home before I start anything new. I do want to see you again so terribly. I hope you will not take this as a rejection because I certainly don't mean it that way.'

'I don't take it that way at all. In fact, I find your honesty refreshing. Please don't concern yourself,

Katherine. We'll see each other again when you're more settled and comfortable with your new life. We can decide how we want to proceed then. For now, I just want you to know that I take what happened between us seriously and I want to pursue a future together when the time is right. For now, I wish you a safe journey home and success in your new life. I must go now. I am going home tomorrow and I have a great deal to do before my flight. I will miss you and think of you often. I wish you only the best. I know some day we will be together again. *Au revoir* for now.'

Assam bowed and kissed her hand, lingered for a moment then turned quickly and left the library.

Katherine could hardly believe what had just happened. Assam wanted to establish a relationship with her. She realised they had known each other only a short time but she knew too that she felt more comfortable with him than with anyone she had ever met. He had connected with her in a way no one else ever had. Her body tingled from the nearness of him and already she was missing his touch. She wanted this man more than she had ever wanted anyone and she was determined to have him. However, that would have to come later. For now, she had to get her life in order.

She looked around the library. This was where she had her first encounter with Alan. That had been such a shattering experience for her and yet it had been just one step in her journey into the passion that was deep inside her; a passion that had never flowered but had lain forgotten and neglected deep in her soul. Well, thanks to her determination and the help of everyone at the clinic, she had rediscovered her true sexuality and now here she was ready to move on. It seemed

263

like years since she had first arrived, tense and over-worked, at this beautiful place. She had gone through so much in such a short time. She smiled and cast a nostalgic glance around the room. Then she opened the door and walked quickly down the hall towards the lounge.

It had been difficult saying goodbye to everyone on the the staff. They were such a marvellous group. The party had gone well and they had all wished her luck in the future. She appreciated their kindness but she didn't linger a moment longer than necessary. She hated long goodbyes. After about an hour, she thanked everyone and hurried outside to where the limousine was waiting to take her to the airport.

As the big car moved smoothly along the highway, Katherine's thoughts turned to the office. Thoughts of sweet revenge and sexual interludes danced in her mind as she remembered the smart young lawyers in the firm who had treated her badly and Phyllis's somewhat overbearing attitude. In fact, if she were completely honest with herself, she would have to face the fact that Phyllis was attracted to her. She would have to decide how to handle this in an appropriate fashion that benefited both of them.

Katherine smiled to herself as she felt her breasts tighten and her crotch start to throb. Oh, yes, there were all kinds of interesting adventures waiting for her back at the law firm and, with her new-found confidence, she knew she was just the woman to explore every one of them to the fullest.

Katherine lay back against the seat, poured herself a gin and let her mind conjure up the delicious little scenarios she was going to play out with some of her co-workers and perhaps even with a few of her friends. However, what she was really looking forward to was meeting interesting new men, men with whom she could explore her new-found sexual freedom. Paul would have to go, she decided. He was just too tame for her tastes now. Besides, she knew he would not like the self-assured and more aggressive person she had become. He would be better off without her and she without him. Oh, yes, her life was going to be very different. She was really looking forward to it. From now on, there would be moans of pleasure echoing down the corridors of power as she initiated young hot shot lawyers and repressed senior partners into more interesting ways to climb the corporate ladder. A dreamy look came into her eyes and she looked back at the clinic rapidly disappearing in the distance. Thank God she had come, she thought. She giggled at her unintentional *double entendre* and turned her thoughts once more to the future.

On a Friday night, some six months later, Katherine was at the office finishing up a few last-minute details on a long and difficult case. Everyone else had gone home early and she was all alone in the building. Even though she was now a partner in the firm, she still found herself tidying up loose ends and doing some of the odd jobs that were really the responsibility of her clerks. And yet, she was such a perfectionist, she always wanted to be involved in every aspect of the case. So, it wasn't unusual for her to be involved at such a basic level. However, the hours were gruelling and she knew if she didn't learn how to delegate work, she would burn out before her time.

She stopped working and thought back over the last few months. Life had gone pretty much as she had planned. She had shared some very exciting sexual interludes with some of the young men in the office; two of whom she had introduced to some of the more unusual erotic delights like the whip, restraints and even the occasional ice cube. Her breath came a little faster as she remembered. Also, she had confronted Phyllis with her suspicions. This had led to a brief but unsatisfying affair with the older woman. It had ended as soon as Katherine had realised her sexuality didn't really lie in that direction. However, it had been fun and very exciting while it lasted.

She had changed a lot in six months. She had got a lot out of her system and now she wanted something more. She had resolved a lot of issues and her life was much more satisfying than the day she had arrived anxious and stressed-out at the clinic. God, was it only six months ago? It seemed like an eternity. So much had happened. She had finally been made a partner in the firm and her career was going great guns. She had more work than she could handle and the money kept rolling in. Also, she had been able to orchestrate her social and sexual life on her own terms and was enjoying herself immensely.

The ring of the phone broke into her thoughts. It was her private line. Who could be calling her tonight? She only gave that number to a small coterie of very special friends and most of them were out of town this weekend. Intrigued, she picked up the receiver.

The instant she heard Assam's voice on the other end of the line, the scent of roses flooded her senses. She knew it was time. It was time to go to him. They spoke quietly for a few moments. She felt immediately connected to him, as if they had talked only yesterday. Then, after she agreed to meet him for a late supper that evening, she hung up the phone and looked out over the lights of the city. She was a successful lawyer and her life was firmly under control. She could have any kind of sexual experience she wanted and always on her own terms. She had made it in her world just as she had planned. And now, sensing that she was ready, he had come back to her.

She knew it was time to make room for him in her life. As she remembered the extraordinary sexual experiences they had shared, an intense heat suffused her body. He had introduced her to so many new and varied sexual delights. Now, however, after six months of experimenting with her new-found sexual freedom, she would be able to teach him a thing or two as well. She shivered slightly as she remembered the night he had introduced her to the delights of the whip. Perhaps now, she was ready to show him some of her 'thorns'. Her breasts tightened and her pussy tingled as she pictured the sensual relationship that lay ahead for them. Her breath began to come more quickly as she imagined all the possibilities. She couldn't wait to see him again. She got up from her desk, turned off the lights and walked out of the office.

As she waited impatiently for the lift, she considered the new vistas opening up for her. A mixture of the familiar and the unknown was calling her and she could feel herself responding with every fibre in her being. She was filled with a sense of urgency which was heightened by a familiar hint of danger that always added to her excitement whenever she thought of Assam.

The elevator doors opened. She walked inside and pushed the button for the main lobby. As the lift began its smooth silent descent, Katherine realised she was trembling. Her life was about to take a dramatic turn. It would never be the same again.

There would be many twists and turns along this new pathway. Who knew where they would lead? She took a deep breath. She welcomed the challenge. She was young and strong, eager to taste all that life had to offer.

The elevator stopped and the doors opened. She waited for a moment then stepped out into the lobby. With rising anticipation, she walked quickly out into the street and hailed a cab. When it screeched to a halt in front of her, she got in, shut the door and gave the driver directions to her favourite restaurant. Then she lay back against the seat. Her heart was beating wildly. Soon they would be together again. She shivered slightly as the cab lurched forward into the late evening traffic. She could hardly wait for the adventure to begin.

BLACK LACE NEW BOOKS

Published in October

THE BRACELET
Fredrica Alleyn

Kristina, a successful literary agent may appear to have it all, but her most intimate needs are not being met. She longs for a discreet sexual liaison where – for once – she can relinquish control. Then Kristina is introduced, by her friend Jacqueline, to an elite group devoted to bondage and experimental power games. Soon she is leading a double life – calling the shots at work, but privately wearing the bracelet of bondage.

ISBN 0 352 33110 0

RUNNERS AND RIDERS
Georgina Brown

When a valuable racehorse is stolen from her lover, top showjumper Penny Bennett agrees to infiltrate a syndicate suspected of the theft. As Penny jets between locations as varied and exotic as France, Sri Lanka and Kentucky in an attempt to solve the mystery, she discovers that the members of the syndicate have sophisticated sexual tastes, and are eager for her to participate in their imaginatively kinky fantasies.

ISBN 0 352 33117 8

Published in November

PASSION FLOWERS
Celia Parker

A revolutionary sex therapy clinic, on an idyllic Caribbean island is the mystery destination to which Katherine – a brilliant lawyer – is sent, by her boss, for a well-earned holiday. For the first time in her life, Katherine feels free to indulge in all manner of sybaritic pleasures. But will she be able to retain this sense of liberation when it's time to leave?

ISBN 0 352 33118 6

ODYSSEY
Katrina Vincenzi-Thyne

Historian Julia Symonds agrees to join the sexually sophisticated
Merise and Rupert in their quest for the lost treasures of Ancient Troy.
Having used her powers of seduction to extract the necessary information from the leader of a ruthless criminal fraternity, Julia soon
finds herself relishing the ensuing game of erotic deception – as well
as the hedonistic pleasures to which her new associates introduce her.

ISBN 0 352 33111 9

To be published in December

CONTINUUM
Portia Da Costa

When Joanna takes a well-earned break from work, she also takes her
first step into a new continuum of strange experiences. She discovers a
clandestine, decadent parallel world of bizarre coincidences, unusual
pleasures and erotic suffering. Can her working life ever be the same
again?

ISBN 0 352 33120 8

THE ACTRESS
Vivienne LaFay

1920. When Milly Belfort renounces the life of a bluestocking in favour
of more fleshly pleasures, her adventures in the Jazz Age take her from
the risqué fringes of the film industry to the erotic excesses of the
yachting set. When, however, she falls for a young man who knows
nothing of her past, she finds herself faced with a crisis and a very
difficult choice.

ISBN 0 352 33119 4

ÎLE DE PARADIS
Mercedes Kelly

Shipwrecked on a remote tropical island at the turn of the century, the
innocent and lovely Angeline comes to enjoy the eroticism of local
ways. Life is sweetly hedonistic until some of her friends and lovers
are captured by a depraved band of pirates and taken to the harem of
Jezebel – slave mistress of nearby Dragon Island. Angeline and her
handmaidens, however, are swift to join the rescue party.

ISBN 0 352 33121 6

If you would like a complete list of plot summaries of Black Lace titles,
please fill out the questionnaire overleaf or send a stamped addressed
envelope to:-

Black Lace. 332 Ladbroke Grove. London W10 5AH

BLACK LACE BACKLIST

All books are prices £4.99 unless another price is given.

- - - - - - ✂ - - - - - - - - - - - - - - - - - - -

Please send me the books I have ticked above.

Name   ....

Address   ....

            ....

            ....

         .... Post Code   ....

Send to: **Cash Sales, Black Lace Books, 332 Ladbroke Grove, London W10 5AH.**

Please enclose a cheque or postal order, made payable to **Virgin Publishing Ltd**, to the value of the books you have ordered plus postage and packing costs as follows:

  UK and BFPO – £1.00 for the first book, 50p for each subsequent book.

  Overseas (including Republic of Ireland) – £2.00 for the first book, £1.00 each subsequent book.

If you would prefer to pay by VISA or ACCESS/MASTERCARD, please write your card number and expiry date here:

....

Please allow up to 28 days for delivery.

Signature   ....

- - - - - - ✂ - - - - - - - - - - - - - - - - - - -

BLACK
lace

WE NEED YOUR HELP ...
to plan the future of women's erotic fiction –

– and no stamp required!

Yours are the only opinions that matter.

Black Lace is the first series of books devoted to erotic fiction by women for women.

We intend to keep providing the best-written, sexiest books you can buy. And we'd appreciate your help and valued opinion of the books so far. Tell us what you want to read.

THE BLACK LACE QUESTIONNAIRE

SECTION ONE: ABOUT YOU

1.1 Sex *(we presume you are female, but so as not to discriminate)*
Are you?
Male ☐
Female ☐

1.2 Age
under 21 ☐ 21–30 ☐
31–40 ☐ 41–50 ☐
51–60 ☐ over 60 ☐

1.3 At what age did you leave full-time education?
still in education ☐ 16 or younger ☐
17–19 ☐ 20 or older ☐

1.4 Occupation _____

1.5   Annual household income
       under £10,000   ☐   £10–£20,000   ☐
       £20–£30,000   ☐   £30–£40,000   ☐
       over £40,000   ☐

1.6   We are perfectly happy for you to remain anonymous;
       but if you would like to receive information on other
       publications available, please insert your name and
       address

       _____

       _____

       _____

       _____

SECTION TWO: ABOUT BUYING BLACK LACE BOOKS

2.1   How did you acquire this copy of *Passion Flowers*?
       I bought it myself   ☐   My partner bought it   ☐
       I borrowed/found it   ☐

2.2   How did you find out about Black Lace books?
       I saw them in a shop   ☐
       I saw them advertised in a magazine   ☐
       I saw the London Underground posters   ☐
       I read about them in _____
       Other _____

2.3   Please tick the following statements you agree with:
       I would be less embarrassed about buying Black
       Lace books if the cover pictures were less explicit ☐
       I think that in general the pictures on Black
       Lace books are about right   ☐
       I think Black Lace cover pictures should be as
       explicit as possible   ☐

2.4   Would you read a Black Lace book in a public place – on
       a train for instance?
       Yes   ☐   No   ☐

SECTION THREE: ABOUT THIS BLACK LACE BOOK

3.1 Do you think the sex content in this book is:
        Too much   ☐   About right   ☐
        Not enough   ☐

3.2 Do you think the writing style in this book is:
        Too unreal/escapist ☐   About right   ☐
        Too down to earth   ☐

3.3 Do you think the story in this book is:
        Too complicated   ☐   About right   ☐
        Too boring/simple   ☐

3.4 Do you think the cover of this book is:
        Too explicit   ☐   About right   ☐
        Not explicit enough ☐

Here's a space for any other comments:

SECTION FOUR: ABOUT OTHER BLACK LACE BOOKS

4.1 How many Black Lace books have you read?   ☐

4.2 If more than one, which one did you prefer?

4.3 Why?

SECTION FIVE: ABOUT YOUR IDEAL EROTIC NOVEL

We want to publish the books you want to read – so this is your chance to tell us exactly what your ideal erotic novel would be like.

5.1 Using a scale of 1 to 5 (1 = no interest at all, 5 = your ideal), please rate the following possible settings for an erotic novel:

Medieval/barbarian/sword 'n' sorcery ☐
Renaissance/Elizabethan/Restoration ☐
Victorian/Edwardian ☐
1920s & 1930s – the Jazz Age ☐
Present day ☐
Future/Science Fiction ☐

5.2 Using the same scale of 1 to 5, please rate the following themes you may find in an erotic novel:

Submissive male/dominant female ☐
Submissive female/dominant male ☐
Lesbianism ☐
Bondage/fetishism ☐
Romantic love ☐
Experimental sex e.g. anal/watersports/sex toys ☐
Gay male sex ☐
Group sex ☐

Using the same scale of 1 to 5, please rate the following styles in which an erotic novel could be written:

Realistic, down to earth, set in real life ☐
Escapist fantasy, but just about believable ☐
Completely unreal, impressionistic, dreamlike ☐

5.3 Would you prefer your ideal erotic novel to be written from the viewpoint of the main male characters or the main female characters?

Male ☐   Female ☐
Both ☐

5.4 What would your ideal Black Lace heroine be like? Tick as many as you like:

Dominant	☐	Glamorous	☐
Extroverted	☐	Contemporary	☐
Independent	☐	Bisexual	☐
Adventurous	☐	Naive	☐
Intellectual	☐	Introverted	☐
Professional	☐	Kinky	☐
Submissive	☐	Anything else?	☐
Ordinary	☐	_____ ☐	

5.5 What would your ideal male lead character be like? Again, tick as many as you like:

Rugged	☐		
Athletic	☐	Caring	☐
Sophisticated	☐	Cruel	☐
Retiring	☐	Debonair	☐
Outdoor-type	☐	Naive	☐
Executive-type	☐	Intellectual	☐
Ordinary	☐	Professional	☐
Kinky	☐	Romantic	☐
Hunky	☐		
Sexually dominant	☐	Anything else?	☐
Sexually submissive	☐	_____ ☐	

5.6 Is there one particular setting or subject matter that your ideal erotic novel would contain?

_____

SECTION SIX: LAST WORDS

6.1 What do you like best about Black Lace books?

_____

6.2 What do you most dislike about Black Lace books?

_____

6.3 In what way, if any, would you like to change Black Lace covers?

_____

6.4 Here's a space for any other comments:

_____
_____
_____
_____

Thank you for completing this questionnaire. Now tear it out of the book – carefully! – put it in an envelope and send it to:

Black Lace
FREEPOST
London
W10 5BR

No stamp is required if you are resident in the U.K.